BUTTERFLIES
& CHARACTERS

LIZ HSU

Butterflies & Characters. Copyright © 2021 by Liz Hsu.

Edited by Rachel Lynn Solomon. Cover by Sumo Design. Interior Book Design by Break Through Author.

Published by Li-Mei Publishing, 2886 12 Mile Road, P.O. Box 721414, Berkley, MI 48072-9998. For information, visit www.lizhsubooks.com. All rights reserved including the right to manufacture in any format, sell, or distribute copies of this book or portions of this book.

ISBN: 978-1-7365434-1-2

LI-MEI PUBLISHING

To my past students, who inspired this, and all young people living with chronic illnesses and autoimmune diseases. I'm with you. We deserve to love and be loved—and have love stories told about us.

To my husband—wo ai ni!

AUTHOR'S NOTE...

The romance and story are fictional. Liz has several diagnosed autoimmune diseases, including Systemic Lupus Erythematosus (SLE). The medical issues all reflect a modified medical experience of hers over the course of the last 20 years. All names of characters, medical professionals, and locations have been changed.

ONE

Rayanne

"Rayanne!" Jeffery drawled out my name like most people around here, giving it a true Southern twang. "So nice you could finally join us, honey!"

I stuck my head out the door of Ross's black four-door truck, my feet hitting the gravel with a cloud of dust. Nothing said summer quite like the familiar sands of Tybee Island just down the road from my house, even if nothing about the sun had seemed mundane recently. And this Sunday afternoon, if the parking lot was anything to go by, the beach would be packed.

I waved with a huge grin as I secured my beach bag, craning my neck to look at my hulking best friend and neighbor.

Ross threw his arm around my shoulders and hollered back, "My girl's been working. Shit, man. You knew that."

"All right, I know. But we missed you," Jeffery said as he tugged me away from my boyfriend and into his massive embrace. He'd always been bigger and taller than me. Now, as a linebacker, he was easily twice my weight.

"Ugh, you're sweaty, Jeff," I said, pushing away, but I secretly didn't mind.

He had such a cozy place in my heart, like a big brother. He was the one person I could depend on in my life. He might have blushed, making me feel a smidgeon of remorse. Usually, I was the self-conscious one, not him.

Then he tipped his ballcap, always the Southern gentleman, to my closest girlfriend and our classmate, Carolyn, as she slithered out of the back of the truck flipping her long, dirty-blond hair.

"Jeffery," she said without bothering to glance his way.

I sighed. While we ran in the same circles and both were my closest friends, they weren't friends with each other. Not at all.

Jeff had warned she was a fake flake when she befriended me days after Ross asked me out. She'd whined my best friend was an idiot before I told them both to shut it around me. Jeff was my oldest and most reliable friend, but Carolyn was one of my only girlfriends. As a kid I'd always liked bikes and playing tag more than dolls. And I'd used to be shy enough it could come off as stand-offish.

"All right, Ross, let's get the cooler," Jeffery said, shuffling up dust with his huge feet and drawing me from my pondering about why we couldn't all be friends.

With that, Carolyn and I turned back to the truck to unload while the boys and their friends hauled the heaviest items— sexism perks at their finest. I plucked at my three-quarter sleeve and adjusted my sunhat, making sure it was ready for the windy gusts the boardwalk would get nearer the waterfront.

Carolyn looked over and muttered something like, "Only you," under her breath.

Her words sent me stumbling slightly on the rough wood of the boardwalk. Lately my cheeks and biceps had been reddening so fast when I was outside. I'd been working at a brunch restaurant downtown and had missed a lot of the Savannah summer sun and almost all our friends' beach trips. And when I'd been running in the afternoons, I'd started wearing one of the "sun long sleeves" that I'd bought, along with a ballcap. My knees had been bothering me out of nowhere, too. I hadn't mentioned it to my mom or stepdad, Mark, yet. They both seemed to roll their eyes whenever I asked for anything.

"You like my hat?" I tried to joke, tilting my head in what I hoped was a diva-like way. I probably looked like an idiot, but Carolyn laughed.

"You can pull it off." Then she added, "like a Swedish model."

I managed a fake laugh instead of cringing. I was five-nine, and though I was skinny, just like my biological father, even if I could be, I'd never want to be a model—I didn't like too much attention on me. I didn't know why, but recently Carolyn had been teasing me more and more about my dad's heritage. It made me uncomfortable.

Everyone knew I was a big oops from my mom's one and only summer abroad. My dad was Swedish, and a few weeks of dating and a broken condom had led to me and her crushed dreams—or so I'd been told numerous times. He hadn't wanted me. She liked to remind me of that fact. And I looked just like him. I had his bright summer-sky blue eyes and almost white-blond hair, versus my mom's honey-hazel eyes and bottle-blond brunette roots. My three half-siblings—Gracie Mae, Mary Beth, and Matthew—all took after Mark with brown eyes and curly dark hair. I'd finally been able to call myself a blond, not the unusual platinum blond, last year for the first time in my life as my hair had naturally darkened a smidgen.

"Shoot!" I yelled as a gust caught my hat. I clutched my head frantically before securing it in my beach bag with a frown.

Sweat was dripping off us all by the time we hit the end of the sand dunes, and no one dared take off their flip-flops so far from the water in the South Georgia July heat. The sand was hotter than a firecracker.

Finally, we spotted what looked like half of the Tidemarsh High football team and cheerleading squad—Ross's regular crew, with me just by association. Sometimes I'd swear I'd been happier when it was just Jeff and me biking, singing Florida Georgia Line, and watching cheesy romances with his big sister. But where I hated attention, Ross loved it.

Rainbow shades of bikinis decorated bronzed girls who'd commandeered almost all the beach chairs while the guys tossed a ball back and forth. Almost everyone was as brown as a biscuit after weeks of tanning or working as lifeguards. Except me. I opened up my chair as Carolyn did the same on the opposite side of the group, after some nodded greetings. I settled in, getting my hat back out of my bag and staring at the gray Atlantic I'd barely seen this summer. Some boogie boarders claimed my attention, reminding me of summers past. I'd always loved the water. I sighed a little wistfully. Summer was already drawing to a close and I'd barely dipped my toes in the warm surf.

Ross's broad shoulders suddenly blocked my view. He gave me that cocky smile of his and knelt in front of me, sandy blond hair falling into his blue-gray eyes. He was the best-looking boy I'd ever met. Unfortunately, he knew it too.

"Are you going to take off your shirt or do you want me to?" he asked, leaning in and running a hand along the hem in a way that made me shiver with the mix of feelings he always gave me.

I shook my head at his flirting but handed him my hat and stripped to my coral bikini before stuffing my shirt in my bag. I prayed my arm wouldn't act up. Ross's eyes roved over me once as he dropped the hat back on my head and leaned in for a teasing, open-mouthed kiss. I returned it, not wanting to fight the day before I left for almost two weeks, even though I'd told him a time, or ten, how much I hated PDA.

"There's my pretty girl," he said with a grin as he stood and went back to the ball tossing, sending me one last heated look that promised he'd be back for more later.

I reapplied my 70 SPF, to everyone's amusement—they

used tanning cream or nothing at all. I blamed it on my fair coloring, even if I'd swear I used to turn a more pleasant golden, but the sun had been bothering me too much lately to ignore.

For me, today was this summer's last beach trip. Not that it mattered, since down here you could swim till October. Tomorrow I'd be flying to see my dad in Michigan before we continued on to Stockholm to stay with my grandparents. I'd never been one hundred percent comfortable with my dad, and my mom said he only brought me along for my grandparents' sake. Yet he always acted happy to see me, and Lord knew I loved seeing him.

I attempted to exhale my negative thoughts—I'd never had a bad time with Dad. I was already tired from my five o'clock wakeup for the breakfast gig I worked, so with my hat mostly covering my face, I gave in to the drowsiness and found myself nodding off to the girls' chatter, the rhythmic slap of the waves on the shore, and the cries of gulls overhead.

Sun blasted down on me as my hat was suddenly removed. I forced my eyes open to look up into Ross's blue-gray ones.

"Want to run?" His question took me a moment to process—I must have fallen asleep.

I smothered a yawn, nodding as he plopped down beside me, scattering sand across my legs. I toweled off my feet and reached for my sneakers. I did both cross-country and track, and running had always been calming to me—my safe place. Jeffery used to joke that one day, I'd run away.

Mom hadn't always been nice to me. I'd grown up hearing her stress about how I'd ruined her life. Even Jeffery had heard it. Heck, our whole dagnab island had probably heard it. I lost count of how many "bless her hearts" I'd heard directed toward Mom, or me. I'd even started kindergarten at age four, though my birthday wasn't until October forth, just so she could get rid of me a little early. I still wasn't sure how she'd convinced the school to enroll me, but my mom always got what she wanted. Well, except my dad marrying her. That was probably why she was always bitter when she looked at me: I really did look like him.

But running was great. I didn't have to ask for any sports fees, which I knew she'd give me H-E-double-hockey-sticks for, unlike my three half-siblings. Mark would buy anything they wanted. They were his kids. I wasn't. Mom spent her money on her hair, her nails, and her clothing. She worked just enough in Mark's dental office for that. Mark paid for everything else. It was a big reason I wanted to be a well-paid architect when I grew up. I didn't want to depend on a husband like she did. Plus, I loved drawing maybe as much as running.

Ross laced up as I secured my hat in the bag and threw my hair in a ponytail. As the starting running back and a lacrosse midfielder, Ross was an avid runner too. In fact, we'd met on the track after school, me a shy sophomore on cross-country and him a cool, flirty junior playing football on the field I circled. I'd always been a late bloomer, younger than my classmates, and Jeff had been kind of my best and only friend. Ross and Jeff were teammates, so we'd all started chatting after practice. That led to eating lunch together and flirting in the halls. Last winter, he'd surprised me by asking me out, and we'd been dating ever since.

I yawned once more as Ross stretched, giving me an up-close view of his golden toned abs and spectacular body. I still couldn't really believe the "It" incoming senior was my boyfriend. Rich parents, starting running back, stunning looks, and college recruiters watching him with the prospect of a Division I full ride—Ross seemed to have it all. And for whatever reason, he'd wanted "all" to include me.

As if feeling my gaze on him, he glanced down and gave me his typical lazy grin. That look sent fire and ice coursing through me. Fire, because like most almost-sixteen-year-olds, I was full of raging hormones and maybe wouldn't mind that gorgeous body all over me, but ice because I was petrified of the recent escalations in our intimacy. I'd been called a mistake my entire life. I wasn't ready to take the next step, and all that might entail.

Ross pulled me to him as I stood, and kissed me while his hand slid to the edge of my bikini bottom, guiding our hips closer together. My boyfriend was publicly groping me. Anger and embarrassment flushed through me even before I heard our friends hoot.

"Don't you dare," I said, pushing his chest.

He sighed and whispered in my ear, "One day, Rayanne. One day. You don't know what the sight of you in that tiny bikini does to me." He nibbled my ear, his breath fanning hot on my neck. "It makes me want to do more than look, beautiful." He drew back and gave me a slow once-over. "Let's get a move on."

My jaw clenched as we fell into a run along the beach. I didn't want to have sex, though I knew Ross wasn't a virgin. We'd fought about this since junior prom in April, when we'd been dating for several months. It seemed, at least for him, our handsy time was reaching its limit, and he wanted more than I was willing to give. I wasn't sure I was ready to let him go, but I didn't want to keep fighting with him, either. Something had to give. I just hadn't decided what—my virginity or Ross.

By the time we'd run almost three miles to the south side of Tybee Island, my knees were hurting again, but I pushed through. I didn't know what I was doing wrong that they'd been getting so swollen recently, but I didn't like it. When we made it back, we took our sweaty butts into the warm Atlantic.

Ross swam nearer as we bobbed in the surf. "I'll miss you, Rayanne," he said, pulling my back flush against his chest and rubbing a hand along my stomach. His stubble and lips tickled my neck.

"It's just ten days. You know I only get to see my grandparents twice a year." I hoped this would reassure him. "You have football conditioning. You won't even have time to miss me." He sucked hard on my neck, and I smacked his hand on my waist. "No hickeys!" My mom had flipped when he'd left them before.

He nipped softly once more. "Then give me something to remember you by," he said as he kissed my neck more gently.

"Ross," I said warningly, inching forward. "I don't want to keep having this fight. Condoms aren't that effective. When I'm ready, I can go to the Planned Parenthood clinic and start the pill, but I'm not ready yet, okay? I looked it up and I don't need parental permission, but I can't use my insurance, so I've been saving up."

"If the condom breaks, take Plan B. That's what Stacy did when we didn't have a condom that one time. Come on, Rayanne, I'll make you feel so good, I promise. Everyone's done it." He nibbled at my neck again as he caressed my stomach under the dark water and didn't let me pull away. I could feel the hard evidence of just how much he wanted me pressed against me.

Anger shot through me even as my body responded to his. I didn't want to hear about what his ex or everyone else was doing. The thought of sex terrified me. I pushed away hard enough for him to let go and said, "Then date *them*."

I fought the surf on my swim back to shore and stalked toward Jeff. It felt like Ross was right—everyone, even Jeffery, had had sex. We'd been dating six months. Maybe there was something wrong with me. I'd ask Jeffery. He'd keep it between us and tell me the truth.

"Jeff, I have to go watch the sermon from this morning. Can you give me a lift?" Since I worked Sunday mornings, I compromised and watched the church sermon from home. Mom and Mark were very religious. I believed in God, too, but their preacher was so angry and convinced we were all going to hell. I liked Jeffery's church better, and Fellowship of Christian Athletes, FCA. I could never tell Mom, but I hated watching her church's sermons. Sometimes they even gave me nightmares.

He arched an eyebrow but jumped right up. "Sure thing, honey."

A wet, warm body hit my back as a hand slid around my waist again. "Sit down, Jeffery. I got Rayanne, but can you take Carolyn? I want some alone time with my girl before she heads off to Michigan, Sweden, and everywhere else."

I'm sure he does. I'd felt that in the water. I stepped forward, removing his hand even as he threaded our fingers. "Ross, I'll see you when you get me tonight." Then I glanced at Jeffery. "Let's go."

Jeffery hesitated, clearly aware he was in an awkward spot, but his loyalty to me over his teammate won out. "Sure thing. Momma needed some ice anyhow. Ready?"

Ross squeezed my hand almost too tightly, but he managed to say smoothly, "What time?"

"Eight." I leaned up and kissed his cheek, not wanting to cause a scene. As I did, I whispered extra softly, "Think about what I said. *I'm not ready.*"

He turned his face and kissed me hard, thrusting his tongue into my mouth almost like a promise. He broke the kiss as quickly as it started. I met his eyes and we fought a silent battle. I didn't think anyone had ever told Golden Boy Ross Gutterson *no*.

"Carolyn?" I broke our stare-off, scanning the beach for her.

"Y'all go on. Jake will take me and Ava," she said from a few chairs away, without looking up from her magazine. Some friend. Ava, waved bye though, which I reciprocated.

With that, I bent to collect my stuff. Jeffery had that clench to his jaw he got whenever Ross was publicly handsy, but remained silent as we walked up the boardwalk. As soon as we sat in his car, he rolled down the windows. Dust from the gravel lot quickly clogged my throat but did little to cool the hotbox his beater Honda had become in the scorching Southern sun. We sweated it out in the temporary sauna as the car slowly rolled toward the road.

Finally, when we hit the highway, I asked Jeffery, "Is it

wrong that I don't want to have sex?" The car jerked slightly to the right. Jeffery sighed and didn't answer immediately. Embarrassed heat rushed through me, but I trusted him not to repeat this. "Am I neurotic because of my, my—" It came out in a frantic whisper. "You can tell me. Ross and I have been dating since—"

He mumbled something under his breath that burned my ears before turning down the Florida Georgia Line song he'd been singing along to. "Goodness, Rayanne, no. Honey, no. It's wrong if he's pressuring you." His Southern twang grew stronger with the emotion in his voice.

A nervous, awkward, "Mm, huh," bubbled out of me, and he reached his hand out. I threaded my fingers through his giant ones. "But you had sex with Mackenzie, and you didn't even date this long."

"Ray Ray, when you're ready, that's when you have sex— no matter what anyone says. Mackenzie wanted to have sex, honey. You don't. There's a big difference."

I sighed before saying in a stronger voice, "I told him if it was so important, he should find someone else. I'm actually really glad I'm seeing Dad tomorrow. I need to get outta here."

"You got 'em reasons to be nervous," he said. "Just wait till you want to. Ya hear, okay?"

"Jeff, what would I'd do without you?"

"Take the bus to school."

I laughed so hard I snorted.

"I've always been there for you, honey, and I always will be here. You're my best friend too. Bonnie and Clyde, remember?"

I leaned over and kissed his familiar cheek and squeezed his hand once more before letting go. More than anyone else in my life, Jeffery had always known what I needed to hear. He'd been there as a kid to catch fireflies with me, then save me a seat on the bus, and now drive me to school. He was right: he'd always been there.

"*Promise me* you won't do anything you regret, Ray Ray.

Don't let him pressure you or I'll have to kick his ass. Honey, I don't have grades like you or sports like him. I don't need a suspension, but if he pressures you, so help me God..." His hand was now white on the steering wheel. He was dead serious.

I chuckled. "Thanks, big guy, but I can fight my own battles. If he does something I don't like, well, he's almost eighteen and I'm fifteen—this is Georgia, and that's against the law in more ways than one."

His grip loosened a little on the wheel like I'd hoped. "All right, jailbait," he said with a laugh. "I'm scared now."

And with that, I turned the radio back up and sang along with him.

"Thanks, Jeff," I said when we got to my place. "See you tonight."

Relief washed over me as I got out of the car. He knew I'd always been told I was an accident, mistake, problem. An unwanted pregnancy. I needed to hear I wasn't being irrational about not wanting to have sex after dating someone for six months—half a year. He made me see the truth: consent isn't forced.

"Rayanne! Where have you been?" my mom shrieked when she saw me. "You are barely going to have time to watch the sermon, because I won't let you pack and watch it at the same time. You need to listen with your whole heart to the Lord."

"Momma," I said, the word rolling out like it did only when she really stressed me out. "I'll have time. It's only six thirty. I just need a quick rinse. Plus, I'm packed."

I left my sandy stuff at the door and hurried to the shared bath. The mirror revealed the sunburn and the start of that annoying rash I'd been getting on my face. I whimpered in the shower as agony laced my knees and hands. My fingers were so swollen it was painful and difficult to pop open the tops of my bath products. After I showered, I took some ibuprofen, praying for a miracle, and hurried into a sundress so I could watch the sermon before the party. My fumbling fingers could barely manage my hair into a French braid as I dressed. I was relieved I'd already packed. I was starting to get a nagging feeling this swelling wasn't a normal running problem. Why the heck did my *fingers* hurt?

I was still half-afraid a fiery inferno would consume me when Ross showed up barely five minutes after the sermon ended, all sugary politeness in a collared shirt for my mom's benefit. His dad was one of the most important developers in the area, and I knew Mom bragged to her friends that I was dating his son. I'd finally done something right in her book.

"Rayanne," he said quietly when we were alone in the truck. He coughed and seemed to struggle with his next words. "Sorry I was too handsy at the beach."

It wasn't quite what I'd wanted to hear, so I said simply, "Actions speak louder than words." I hated to be like Mom and Granny Young, quoting biblical verses at him, but I didn't want to continue our cyclical fights and apologies, either.

He nodded, but things still felt tense when we arrived at the party. Luckily, it was outdoors near the dimly lit tidal marsh in someone's backyard, so no one mentioned the rash on my face, or maybe my makeup hid it well.

Not much time had passed before I begged Ross to take me home. Exhaustion weighed me down. His eyes lit up, as though that was code for some one-on-one time. It was our last night of summer together, but my whole body hurt, and I just wanted my bed.

"So what do you really want to do?" he whispered when we got to the truck. His hand slid up and down my waist as he leaned over to kiss my neck.

I pushed him back, barely holding in a moan as my swollen fingers hit his hard chest. "Stop. I feel bad. Please, take me home." My voice sounded whiny, even to me.

"Are you serious?"

"I'm sorry," I said as he shook his head and grumbled,

putting us into reverse.

When he pulled up to my house—after his nonstop complaining —I left him for the next ten days with a short kiss and sour feelings. Lately, we'd fought more than we'd had fun. The worst was I was too tired to really care. I nearly crawled up the front steps, which was raised above the ground because of tidal flooding, then grumbled up the second story to my bedroom. I barely managed to change and wash my face before I collapsed into bed.

A groan escaped me as the alarm clock wailed. Pain tore through me, my whole body feeling like it had been badly bruised.

When I looked in the mirror, I saw a scaly raised rash covering my nose and cheeks. I flew down the stairs yelling, "Momma!"

"Stop yelling, Rayanne." She turned from the coffeepot to look at me. "What in the Sam Hill happened to your face? Sweet Jesus in heaven, I don't have time for this." She rolled her eyes heavenward.

Oh, no. I needed cream or medicine. Or something. "Can you please take me by Dr. Brown's before I go? Please, Momma." Then I appealed to her vanity. "It's so ugly."

Mom sighed. Everything I asked seemed to annoy her. "Well, don't just stand here yakking. Go on, get dressed. And don't take your sweet time neither. You have a flight to catch, young lady."

I raced back up the stairs, wincing as I did, and started coughing, feeling like I couldn't catch my breath. I hunched over, struggling for air as I threw toiletries in my bag, brushed my hair, and got dressed as quickly as possible. The whole time, my swollen fingers throbbed.

In thirty minutes, I was sitting on the exam table and Dr. Brown was telling us not to worry, that it was just a sunburn on my face and arm. He wasn't concerned about my hands or knees at all. With an irritated huff from my mom, we left the doctor's office.

"Well, I'll be, Rayanne," Mom said in the car. "Try not to such a drama queen for Nils. Let's get a move on."

Mom was so annoyed that I didn't dare mention I was hungry from not eating breakfast. Each breath I drew seemed harder than the last, and I couldn't stop coughing.

"If you are smoking, Rayanne, you better quit. If I catch you, I'll tan your behind from here to Tennessee, so help me Lord."

"I've never smoked, Mom—I promise. I'm a runner. I don't know why I'm coughing."

She muttered something under her breath that sounded like *Lord give me patience* but didn't respond. When we approached the terminal, I looked at my face once more in the mirror. The pattern of the rash on my nose and cheeks looked almost like an ugly butterfly. I tucked my ballcap down again and wished the day was over.

"Bless your heart, honey, but I still can't believe you went to the beach without sunscreen," Mom chided. "You know you deserve this."

"I told you *and* Dr. Brown I wore a hat and sunscreen," I said as I slammed the mirror back up.

"Hush up, now. Don't be ornery no more. Oh, how you are trying me this morning. You don't get a sunburn like that if you wear sunscreen, sugar plum. Your momma wasn't born yesterday. And don't forget to say your prayers while you're with those liberal atheists. You don't want to burn for eternity like he will." Mom could never talk about me staying with Dad without mentioning at least once he was an atheist and going to hell.

I nodded and waved goodbye, knowing that arguing that Dad wasn't damned was worthless. I didn't ever dare tell Mom, but I always looked forward to visiting Dad, even if it was awkward between us sometimes, neither knowing what to say. Plus, Stockholm and Dad's parents were so different from Granny and Grampa Young. So urbane.

And Charles was there. He'd always been my Michigan friend, even if it was only because his mom, my dad's best friend, made him be. He sent me a video of a robot a few months ago, and I'd been dying to see it in person. I still could only half-believe he'd built it. He was wicked smart.

As I grabbed my purse, backpack, and duffel bag, everything seemed to hurt again, and I briefly wondered if I had a fever. I struggled to breathe as I huffed to the check-in and tried not to cough for fear they wouldn't let me board. Mom would kill me if she had to come back and get me. It was a relief when I made it through, and I slipped into a sweater in the frigid terminal, where I could finally sit down.

I didn't know what was happening to my body or what I was going to do about the Ross situation. But as exhaustion took over, I was just glad to be getting out of town when I had this rash and grateful for some time to think.

TWO

Charles

Numbers scrolled by on the screen as I tried to figure out why the program hadn't gone live. I'd been at it all morning. I'd found and corrected two numerals. Still, the program glitched in the middle and failed again, even after extensive redoing and testing.

My phone buzzed for the second time, which forced me to answer it. "Hi, Ma."

She spoke rapidly in Mandarin, my first language. "Professor Ericson and I haven't finished planning the economics sections."

Professor Ericson and my ma were both economics professors at the University of Michigan and talked almost daily. They couldn't plan anything, whether it was adjusting the courses for next semester or prepping their next research project, without running it by each other first.

"Okay," I said into the prolonged silence, needing to get back to my internship.

"He's going to Sweden the day after tomorrow."

I knew that, too. We were having dinner with his daughter,

Ray, tonight. Professor Ericson wasn't just a colleague. He was my parents' closest friend.

"We need you to get Ray from the airport," Ma continued. So that was why she'd called.

"I have band practice," I said with a huff. We were going to play for two hours before dinner with Ray and Professor Ericson. I'd already confirmed with the guys.

She was silent for a moment.

It wasn't that I didn't like Ray—I did. *That* was the problem. I couldn't remember a time I hadn't had a crush on her. I'd been distracted with her looming arrival all weekend. She was that blond-haired, sporadic friend who never quite left my mind. I was only a grade above her, and we'd always had a strange kinship. Aside from being forced together, we were both the youngest in our grades. Ever since I could remember, we'd hung out when she came into town. From Legos to sledding, we always did something.

Sledding. I nearly groaned. Thoughts of her had plagued me for weeks after that, even after she'd gone back home. That was the worst thing about Ray: she always, inevitably, left. It was torture. *She* was torture.

"Do you have Ray's number?" Ma asked after a drawn-out pause.

She hadn't even acknowledged the band as a feasible excuse. I sighed before answering, "Yes."

"Good. Her flight lands at six. Then take her to Chengdu Taste. We will all have dinner." She hung up the phone. Ma had spoken.

I groaned as I texted James, Knox, and Kevin on our group chat. *Tiger mom attacks. Sorry, no practice tonight.* Out of all of them, likely only Kevin, who was Korean, would actually understand that. Knox's mom wasn't very strict and James was eighteen.

I refocused on my computer and attempted to get through the day at my programming internship without more surprises.

Just find the flaw, I repeated to myself over and over. For weeks it had seemed like the most intriguing thing in the world, and yet it didn't speed up my heart anywhere near as much as Ray Ericson.

She wasn't even here, but all I saw was that adorable blond I had to pick up in a few hours. All I heard was that tinkling laugh and wry humor. All I smelled was that intoxicating jasmine scent. Ray Freaking Ericson. I was perpetually getting over a crush on her. I'd focused on school, completely fine until we were forced together—again and again. It would help if she were conceited, but she wasn't. She was so genuinely nice and fun every time I saw her.

Before I left to pick her up, I sent her a message. I couldn't help but chuckle at our last message chain from a few weeks ago. I'd sent her a picture of a restaurant with a sign that said *Asian Fusion*. Ray had said, *Two-thirds of the planet. What a mix.*

My phone beeped as I drove, but I didn't check it until I stopped at a red light off the highway.

Ray: *Thanks, we landed early. I flew Delta. I'm waiting for my bag.*

I cursed softly when I saw she'd sent it ten minutes ago. I called her on my Bluetooth, and she picked up with a soft, drawn out Southern, "Hi."

"Hi, Ray. Um, did you get your bag yet?"

"I just did."

My hands started sweating at the sound of her melodious voice. I didn't know why this girl made me so nervous. She'd just look up at me with those big, blue eyes, so focused on what I was saying—like I was interesting as a person, not just the smart kid in class. And she had such dry humor once you got her going. I loved back-and-forthing with her. Maybe all girls made me nervous; I was the geeky never-had-a-girlfriend guy. But Rayanne Ericson did something special to me and always had.

"Okay, I'm pulling up soon. I have an old olive Forester. You know—"

She laughed softly, cutting me off. "I remember your car. You drove it when we went sledding this winter—golly, that was fun. I'm wearing a blue baseball cap and have my teal duffel. Station three?"

"Sure," I said as the call clicked off. Sparklers were going off in my stomach like it was damn Lunar New Year. I found myself wistfully hoping she'd hug me, even as I cursed myself for that thought. She always wore something jasmine-scented, which smelled mind-numbingly wonderful. Literally mind numbing. Occasionally that scent made me say something so weird I'd replay it for days or even weeks after in mortification.

A few minutes later, I thought I saw her ballcap and bright blond hair as I pulled around. I braced myself for how'd she'd bounce in her seat, unable to conceal her excitement about, well, everything. I smiled. She'd always talk so Southern when she first arrived, then her accent would mellow out.

She waved and walked to the trunk, which I popped open. Should I have gotten out and done that? Shit. I tapped a piano beat on the wheel to calm down. I didn't get people from the airport often. More like never.

"Thanks for getting me," she said, slipping in the passenger seat with her face tilted downward, shadowed by her hat.

Huh? Subdued, not bouncy. Surprise, surprise. She didn't look up. There was so teasing embrace; worse, she'd barely acknowledged me.

"I didn't have a choice," I joked, trying to make her laugh. I could always count on Ray to laugh at my jokes. I wasn't particularly funny. She was just a happy, easy-to-please person.

She didn't laugh. Crap. I tapped a faster beat, trying to think of something else to say. Or just drive. I should just drive. But then she glanced up.

"What happened to your face?" I asked. It just slipped out.

She flinched. She actually flinched.

Crap. Crap. Crap.

If she was red-cheeked before, she was red-faced now. She turned to the window.

Jeez, I was a jerk. *Just drive and shut up.* I felt red-faced myself as I tried to merge with traffic.

She spoke so quietly I barely heard her. "Sunburn?" She said it like she wasn't sure.

I coughed awkwardly, wishing I could turn back time. "Um, well, I hope it gets better."

Now my hands were so sweaty I needed to turn up the AC so I could grip the wheel. We fell into an uncomfortable silence over the blasting air.

Ray broke the quiet as I merged onto I-94. "Those videos of your robot were really cool. I can't believe you built that." I could hear the smile in her voice. "So have you finally decided to go Blue? Has U of M won you over like your parents joked?"

Wow, she really had paid attention. I did my best not to drop my mouth, but was stunned by her comment. I never thought she noticed me or knew what I did when she wasn't around. "It was better than I thought. But nothing compared to Caltech. That's number one by far."

Her laughter chimed through the car. "I *so* would not mind visiting you in LA. What else have you been up to? Winning piano awards?"

I cleared my throat, not wanting to say something that could sink this ride again. "I have an international piano contest in a month. It'll be one of the last things on my college applications, so I really want to place first. Plus, I have a programming internship." I shrugged. "It's cool, but"—I laughed humorlessly—"like always, busy, busy. You didn't do any camps or internships, right?"

She laughed, but it sounded strained. "Pleeeease, Charles. I worked all summer. Camp sounds so much better than the breakfast shift. 'How do you want your eggs? And how do *you* want your eggs?'" She lowered her voice. "I wish I could have done a drawing or architecture class. Savannah College of Art and Design—you know, SCAD—offers tons, but no freaking way. My mom would never pay for a program like that. You're lucky."

I was silent. I did not want to put my foot in my mouth. Not again. Between her and my ma's offhand comments, I didn't think her mom was the greatest. Plus, the few times she'd called Professor Ericson when I was there, he looked like he'd eaten an entire lemon.

Crap, it was awkward not to say anything. "Yeah, the camp was fascinating. And expensive. Sorry you had to work instead. I was disappointed to go to the one here at U of M, not the one at Caltech, but that was even pricier. I can show you the robot if you want. Even here, the labs were state of the art. I can only imagine how awesome they'll be at Caltech."

She smiled and I caught it out of my periphery. Despite her rash, she was still stunning. "Please! I've been curious about it. It's amazing you built it."

"What can I say, I am pretty amazing," I joked, hoping she'd laugh at my quips like usual.

She chuckled again and I loosened my hands slightly on the wheel. I hadn't made her hate me. Then she tilted her head, and I caught a whiff of jasmine. "So, what are the economists into these days?"

I couldn't miss the catch in her voice. I'd always gotten the feeling she'd do anything to impress her dad—to prove she wasn't her mom. She had always looked at him like he he'd hung the moon. He tried to be diplomatic, but got this set to his jaw whenever someone mentioned her mom that couldn't quite hide his disdain. And I'd heard him talk to her on the phone like talking to a child who didn't understand adult logic. But he'd never spoken to Ray that way, at least not in my presence.

I thought back to Ma's rambling. "They're working on a new course on multinational corporations' versus microeconomies' impact on international economies. They both seem rather fixated on it."

She grilled me intensely, leaning in, and I told her everything
I could remember about their latest projects, scrambling to
remember snippets I'd heard. I was surprised by her curiosity.

"So," she said with a dry laugh, "do you think Dad will be
impressed I got into AP Art?"

I found a parking spot in front of our families' favorite
Szechuan restaurant and pondered how best to respond. She'd
always liked drawing as a kid, so I wasn't too surprised. Plus,
she wanted to be an architect. "No, I don't, but my parents think
it's stupid I'm in a band, so…"

I'd mentioned it before in the few texts we'd exchanged,
but I'd never gotten the nerve to send Ray any songs. She didn't
say anything. Not as exciting as football or robots, I guessed.
I risked a glance. She stared, transfixed, at her reflection in the
pull-down mirror. As far as scaly, raised bright-red rashes went,
I wouldn't want it on my face either. Then she closed her eyes
and her shoulders sagged.

"It—" I started to say.

"Don't." She cut me off with a harsh voice. "It *does* look
that bad. Thanks for the ride, but let's just get inside. Eventually
this day will be over."

She was being a little hard on herself, but it did look terrible,
so I kept my mouth shut. I tried to tell myself her comment had
nothing to do with me, but that was worse. I'd thought about her
all day—all week! Clearly, that was just me.

Ray was almost gasping for breath as we walked inside.

"Hey, are you still running?"

She nodded with a frown and coughed like she had when
she'd gotten into the car. "I ran six miles yesterday. Today I
feel like I can barely walk without getting breathless. Maybe
I'm getting sick?" She sounded worried as she mumbled, "My
whole body hurts."

I held the door for her. Something wasn't adding up. I
briefly wondered if she'd done drugs or something, but she'd

never struck me as the type.

Our parents hadn't arrived yet. The hostess recognized me and spoke rapidly in Mandarin. I got us a table for five with a lazy Susan. When we were with friends, my parents had no shame in ordering dishes. Ray fiddled with her ballcap, which partially hid her rash. I'd never seen her wear a cap inside, but she left it on with a fire in her eyes that dared anyone to tell her to take it off.

Ray leaned down to read the menu. I glanced up to see our parents had miraculously arrived at the same time.

I heard the slightly British-English clipped accent of her dad, who had studied more British-English than American as a kid. "Wonders never cease. Ray wearing a hat to the table."

His sarcasm halted as Ray looked up. Moisture gathered in her vibrant blue eyes, which matched her father's more piercing ones.

"Hej, hej, Pappa," she said softly as she stood and hugged him.

He began questioning her in rapid Swedish, something he'd almost never done in my presence. Like I did with my parents, she spoke with her dad in his native tongue. Her replies were short and soft. When she sat down, he touched her knee and held her hand gently. His usually stern face turned even more serious.

Finally, Professor Ericson relayed her symptoms to my baba, including shortness of breath. She did seem to be panting slightly. Baba was an MD/Ph.D. in pathology who spent more time with cells than people. He never responded without a carefully thought-out answer, unless it was about school or piano. Then it was *all A's* and *you will play*.

It took him a long minute to reply. "You are leaving for Stockholm the day after tomorrow?" Baba asked pensively.

"Yeah," rolled off her dad's tongue, sounding much more Swedish than usual.

"Let me make a phone call." Baba rose from the table,

and I heard, "Suzanne, hello, this is Jing Wong, Director of Pathology. I have a friend…"

The rest of his conversation was lost as he stepped away. Did her rash and shortness of breath have something to do with each other? And her whole body hurt too. It wasn't adding up.

My ma, the other Dr. Wong, gave Ray a gentle hug. She reconfirmed Ray's favorites, many of which were the same as ours: gān biān sì jì dòu, mápó dòufǔ, and dòu miáo. Ma ordered enough to feed twenty by the time Baba returned to the table. He wrote something down and handed it to Professor Ericson.

"Dr. Murray has fit Ray in tomorrow at eight-thirty. She works in the department of rheumatology and that's her clinic's address. She wants to see Ray and do a few blood tests."

Rheumatology, huh. I'd never even heard of that.

Ray fidgeted with her hat. Turned pink again. Then said, "Thank you, Dr. Wong, but I went to my doctor this morning, and he said it was just a sunburn."

Baba gave Ray a cutting look. "Did he do any tests?"

"No, sir," she said with a shake of her head. Her hands moved restlessly on the table. "He said it was nothing."

"How could he know? He didn't test for anything." He'd clearly already decided her physician was inept.

Ray's eyes flashed in astonishment at my normally fairly silent baba's outburst. He patted her hand awkwardly, not really one to show affection. That was weird. Then scary. Baba wasn't the comforting type.

"Just let Dr. Murray check you out, then. University of Michigan is ranked eleventh in the country in rheumatology. I hope your doctor was right."

After that, the conversation fortunately became less strained, and our parents asked us about the classes we were scheduled to take in the fall. Ray was in more APs than just art, which didn't surprise me. No one as witty as Ray wasn't smart. Of course, I had all APs except Orchestra. The average GPA at Caltech was a 4.22; I needed all As in APs just to be considered. Our parents told us about the various courses they would be teaching, as plate after plate filled the table. Unless you looked directly at Ray, you could almost forget everything she'd mentioned earlier.

Ray asked a few questions about the microeconomics class, then sent me a warm smile that left me tingling as her dad launched into a passionate discourse.

As the leftovers were bundled and divided with my family's typical efficiency, Baba craftily handed his credit card to the waitress.

"Paid," she said with a shake of her head.

All eyes rounded on Professor Ericson, who must have paid the bill when he snuck to the bathroom. Squawking ensued from my parents—they couldn't believe someone had beaten them to the check.

Ma said loudly, at least once, "I'll never take you out again if I can't pay next time!"

Ray and I exchanged a smile, barely containing our laughter. Her shy grin made my heart flip. Fighting over the check remained a time-honored tradition between our families.

When we got to my car, I couldn't help but notice how swollen her hands were. Something pinched a little in me as I loaded her bags into her dad's car. She was okay, right?

She leaned in for a hug once my hands were free and her scent, the one I'd been dreaming about, finally engulfed me. "Thanks for the ride, and it's really good to see you again."

I hugged her back, but it was hard to think with her warm, toned body pressed against mine. "No problem. Hey, um, good luck tomorrow. If everything is okay, maybe you can meet my band before you go and see the robot." The words stumbled out as I grasped for an excuse to see her again.

"That'd be nice. Thanks again," she said as she walked away.

As I got into my car, I hoped her doctor back home was right—that it was just a bad sunburn. But the pinch in my chest tightened as I thought of that cough and those panting breaths.

No matter how much I hoped, somehow I didn't think Ray had just a sunburn.

...
THREE

Ray

For the second day in a row my alarm blared, and my first thought was agony. Why did my body hurt so much? Would I find out today, or would this doctor think I was hysterical too?

I turned to take in the bright Michigan morning and tried to cheer my thoughts. I drew comfort from my soft, baby blue duvet that matched today's cloudless sky. Dad made sure that when he bought this condo, I had my own room and twin bed. I had storage boxes on rollers under the bed, and the closet held the coats, old boots, and such I needed to stay warm here and in Sweden in the winter. This room also served as his office, and huge bookcases lined the far wall. Still, he'd tried to make it special for me.

Even after all the hurtful things my mom had said to me over the years, he was still my dad. Sometimes, despite living with my mom, I secretly felt more kinship with him. It was nice being in a city with open-minded people. And I wanted him to love me so much that I'd even studied Swedish and read the world news to impress him when we talked. We usually spoke a few times a week, and even if it was stiff sometimes,

I looked forward to it. My writing wasn't perfect, but we'd
spoken in Swedish together for years now, so I was certainly
fluent. I bought a few books a year in Swedish, not English, so
I wouldn't forget how to read it.

I stretched with a slight whimper and forced my stiff joints
out of bed. It was hard to sustain cheeriness with the pain I
felt. I fought to breathe, and I mildly panicked before reminding
myself I was going to the doctor.

The bathroom mirror revealed flaky red skin still covering
half my face and a huge chunk of my arm. I was glad Ross
couldn't see me now, not that the jerk had done more than
respond to my arrival text with a few short messages back and
forth. I moped my way to the glossy, modern kitchen for coffee,
the house so quiet that my breathing sounded louder that usual.

"Morning, Ray," Dad said as he poured himself a cup of
coffee over his gorgeous speckled-granite countertop. Maybe
because he was my dad, but I'd always thought he was strikingly
handsome. I got my height and leanness from him—he was six-
four. With his still mainly blond hair, he looked more twenty-
eight than thirty-eight.

"Morning," I said back, trying to stay brave. I couldn't tell
whether I was more anxious that they'd find something wrong
or that they wouldn't. If they didn't, I was a hypochondriac. If
they did—well, I tried not to think about *that*.

"Do you feel any better?" he asked, a note of hope in his
voice.

I looked down, feeling guilt churning inside my gut. "I feel
worse."

But Dad wasn't like Mom, who'd blame me for being sick.
He simply sighed into his cup and said, "Let's get ready and see
this Dr. Suzanne Murray."

And we did. Less than an hour later, I was sitting in her
office filling out a medical history on an iPad. My dad kept
casting me worried looks from the corners of his eyes. I'd been
coughing a lot and was struggling to suck in air. We'd had to

stop twice on the way from the parking lot to the rheumatology office. I'd never even heard of rheumatology before yesterday. I'd googled last night and learned they mainly treated "autoimmune diseases," or your body attacking itself. Weird. But I'd been so exhausted, I crawled in bed after minimal reading. Now I wished I'd investigated a little more.

"Ms. Ericson?" We stood as a nurse introduced himself as Tony and motioned us down the hall and then into a room.

Tony had barely asked me to get up on the table and told me I had a fever when a petite brunette in a long white coat entered, followed by a twentyish man.

"Rayanne?" the woman asked.

"Yes, ma'am, but you can call me Ray," I said. Rayanne never sounded right without a Southern twang.

"I'm Dr. Murray." She pointed to the man in the white coat. "This is my fellow, Dr. Ezra. Normally, he'd see you himself—well, normally, since you're fifteen, I might not see you at all, but I received a call about you last night." I shifted, embarrassed that I'd messed with her schedule, and that slight movement sent pain searing through me. "You must be Dr. Wong's friend?"

"Yes, ma'am." I shifted nervously again, unable to hide the wince on my face.

She motioned Dr. Ezra closer, and they asked me a series of questions about my family's medical history while taking my blood pressure and listening to my heart.

Then Dr. Murray said, "Ray, we are going to do a rheumatology exam on you. Have you ever had one?"

"No, ma'am," I said with a shake of my head. Jeez Louise, I'd already ripped the exam paper around my shorts to shreds.

She smiled, her amber eyes bright like a hawk's. Watchful. Observant. It was strangely soothing. "We need to feel and test your joints. I just warn you because it's a little more invasive than some physical exams. Are you and your father okay with Dr. Ezra helping me?"

Before my dad could answer, I felt my cheeks heat. "If it's not under what I'm wearing, that's all right."

She looked to my dad, whose face was pinched, but he nodded.

First, the doctors gently took my hands, which had turned bright white in the cold clinic. With one doctor on each side, they bent my tender fingers and flipped my hands over before exchanging a look.

"Do your hands turn white like this often?" Dr. Ezra asked after a nod from Dr. Murray.

"Yes, sir. In the summer, when I fill the ice tray or swim too long." I barely resisted the urge to pull my hand out of his to fidget. "Or if I get nervous. I'm nervous now. And cold." I was rambling. Dad had told me to wear shorts so they could see my knees. "In the winter, it gets worse, but not too bad. Savannah's not too cold. It just started about a year ago."

Dr. Ezra gave me a half smile and dropped my hand before clicking away on his iPad.

"Ray," Dr. Murray said, pulling my attention back to her. "How long have your hands been swollen, and is this the first time this has happened?"

"It started Sunday night. I went to the beach with some friends." I glanced down. "Lately the sun has been bothering me. I run a lot, but recently I've needed to wear long sleeves and a hat and tons of sunscreen." I pointed to my face, which neither had acknowledged. "I've gotten this several times, but never this bad. It's on my arm too. It started Sunday afternoon, and on Monday it got worse. My mom took me to my pediatrician, who said it was just a sunburn. Dr. Wong saw it last night at dinner and called you."

Dr. Murray held my eyes before scanning me again. "Please take off your sweatshirt."

I stripped to my tank top, and she ran a gloved finger over my puckered bicep rash.

"You can put it back on. I'm going to take off your shoes,"

she said, and she did after swapping gloves. Dr. Ezra observed stoically as she rotated my ankles, exchanging a glance with him over my white toes. When Dr. Murray reached my legs to bend my knees, I couldn't resist a small whimper of pain. "Ray, on a scale of one to ten, how bad is your knee pain?"

"Five," I said hesitantly. I didn't really feel like I was dying, which was probably a ten, but my knee was in agony. More than any other part of me, which was saying a lot.

"And anything else going on?"

This time Dad answered. "She has progressive dyspnea."

Both doctors turned to stare at him a moment, but I hadn't understood what he'd said.

"Yes, she was tachycardic," Dr. Murray said. "I'd like to admit Ray to the hospital and do some tests on her. I have a strong suspicion, but I don't want to say anything until the tests come back. However, I'm worried her condition is progressing, and I'd like to monitor her overnight as we wait for the test results."

"Of course," Dad said after the briefest halt. "Tell me what to do and we'll get it started."

At his words, a chill slithered through my belly stronger than I'd ever felt before. I hiccupped a little, worrying I might vomit. I stared down at my bright white toes. I'd never been admitted to a hospital.

"Dr. Ezra and I will do your workup and order some tests," Dr. Murray said. "We will see you both this afternoon and have more information for you then. Tony will be in in a few minutes with the details."

With a nod, they left. I felt myself gasping for breath and coughing violently as the cold blue door shut. Admitted? Tachycardia and Dyspnea? What was going on?

Dad stood and wrapped an arm around me, kissing me gently on the forehead. "You're going to be okay, sweetheart. I'll make sure they take good care of you." I turned my face into his chest, realizing I was crying as tears soaked the fabric of his shirt. "I'm going to call your mom."

I heard her pick up after two rings. "Nils," she said in a slightly aggressive voice. His arm tightened on me. I knew they'd had sex at least once, but it was hard to imagine. I'd never met two people more oil and vinegar than them.

"Chrissy." He was clearly trying to remain calm, but his voice had a pinch it didn't have a moment ago. "Ray's sick."

Her sigh made me flinch as I remembered how annoyed she'd been with taking me to the doctor yesterday. "Nils, she has a sunburn. I took her to the doctor, and he wasn't worried. I need to go to my manicure soon; I can't talk long."

Dad's hand on my shoulder tightened again. Now it seemed he no longer cared about keeping the strain out of his voice. "It *isn't* a sunburn. She's being admitted to the hospital. They haven't told us what it is, but they want to monitor her until her test results come back."

"That's ridiculous. She was just running on the beach two days ago. Mark and I don't want to pay an out-of-network hospital charge for a healthy kid. Dr. Brown's been practicing for thirty years and wasn't worried at all."

"Chrissy." He dragged her name out in exasperation, his voice turning to ice. "*She is being admitted to the hospital.*"

"If it turns out nothing is wrong, you're paying the bill," Mom responded in her normal flippant voice, like she's convinced my whole goal in life was to annoy her. Like I made the condom break to ruin her life.

Dad let go of me and began pacing more violently than I'd ever seen someone pace. "For fuck's sake, Chrissy, did you hear a goddamned word I just said? *Our daughter is getting admitted to the hospital.* I'll have her text you later. I can't have this conversation right now."

As he hung up, she kept talking. While I couldn't make out what she was saying, I was sure it had to do with not cussing or taking the Lord's name in vain.

Dad's expression was hard, his cheeks red. When he

noticed me staring at him, his face softened. "I'm sorry I cussed in front of you, sweetie."

He offered me a tissue from the box in the room before handing me my shoes and socks. I wiped my face. The shock of Dad cussing at Mom, something no one I knew would dare to do, had startled the tears right out of me. I was done crying.

I had one shoe on when Tony entered.

"Hi, Ray, we are going to get some blood drawn, and a transport person will take you down to get admitted and then to get a chest X-ray. Once you're done with that, they will take you to a room. Ready?"

I nodded, and Dad and I followed him out. I watched in surreal fascination as he drew about ten vials of blood and put one in a nearby machine while I sat waiting for a wheelchair to take me to the admission desk. I wondered what all they were testing for. I'd never realized how much blood talked.

As we waited, Dr. Ezra walked by and Tony said casually, "Stat platelets are at forty thousand." It must have been important, but I didn't know what normal platelets were.

"I'll let Dr. Murray know," he said, right as a young woman came with a wheelchair for me. I tried to protest, but everyone insisted.

The trip to admissions, chest X-ray, and then my hospital room seemed to go quickly, or maybe I was spacy because I was in shock. I was certainly friggin' tired. Before I knew it, Dad and I were sitting in the hospital room, and as much as I hated to admit it, I barely had the energy to move. I wanted to look up some questions and terms, but I couldn't muster the strength to lift my head off the pillow, and it hurt just thinking of typing on my phone. I must have fallen asleep, because I was jolted awake by Dr. Murray saying my name.

After giving me a moment to collect myself, she started again. "Ray, we are still waiting on some of your tests that take a few days, but from the test we have gotten back, we can confidently diagnose you with systemic lupus erythematosus, or lupus, SLE for short. It's an autoimmune disease and not something contagious. Have you ever heard of that?"

Suddenly, I was wide awake as I shook my head. I was slightly embarrassed by the relief pouring through me. I wasn't a neurotic mess. I wasn't a hypochondriac. Something *was* wrong.

"The American College of Rheumatology requires four out of eleven symptoms to be diagnosed. Ray, you have eight currently."

She handed me a sheet with eight numbers circled titled, *1997 Update of the 1982 American College of Rheumatology Revised Criteria for Classification of Systemic Lupus Erythematosus.*

She pointed at to the numbers as she spoke. "The rash on your face is called a malar rash, or sometimes the butterfly rash, and the one on your arm is called a discoid rash. Your platelets are far below normal, and your ANA test is strongly positive. You have positive antiphospholipid antibodies present, as well as a strongly positive anti-dsDNA antibody test. You show clear arthritis in several joints, another SLE marker. The whiteness in your hands and toes indicated you have Raynaud's, present in about a third of SLE patients. None of this would have made me admit you, except maybe the platelets, but I would have started to treat you immediately. However, your shortness of breath gave us all pause. You have fluid around your heart called pericarditis."

She paused for a minute, clearly realizing she might have overwhelmed me. I clutched the paper in my hand. I'd research on my own because I didn't understand most of what she'd been saying. I was sure my eyes were glazing over. I only really understood heart and arthritis, which I thought I was way too young to have problems with.

She handed me another packet of papers. "I'm going to let you read a little about lupus, but in the simplest terms, your body is confused, and your cells are attacking your body. Sun can trigger it. We've started you on three lupus medications. Your body, your immune system specifically, is attacking your own joints, skin, and, unfortunately, also your heart. We need to stop that immediately. One is a strong IV steroid to reduce the inflammation, especially around your heart. We will monitor your heart closely for a little bit. If that works, you can go home in a few days, and if it doesn't, we'll need to drain the fluid surgically."

"Will Ray have lupus forever?" Dad asked, reminding me he was there.

The doctor's amber eyes held us both for a moment before she nodded. "Yes. Currently, there is no cure. Lupus is a chronic and lifelong disease."

"Am I dying?" I heard the fear in my words. While I was relieved my symptoms had a name, I was also scared. *Forever.* How long would that be?

"No." She patted my shoulder ever so gently, as if aware my whole body hurt. "But your body is attacking itself. It shouldn't. You'll be on immune suppressants and steroids to turn off your immune system, but it doesn't have an on-and-off switch. It could take days or weeks, but right now the fluid is just around your heart and you are not showing signs of heart failure. It's good we caught it when we did. Lupus is a disease that flares. You are having a flare. If it goes inactive, you can go weeks, months, even years with no symptoms. But you'll be on medication for the rest of your life."

"A lot of people—doctors—have been by," Dad said with concern in his voice.

"Yes. The University of Michigan is a teaching hospital, so you might see medical students, residents, and fellows. But I will also be monitoring your case with Dr. Ezra. We're going to take good care of you," she said to me. "Do you have any other questions?"

I shook my head no.

"Why don't you read a little and we can talk in the

morning?"

"Yes, ma'am. Thank you, Dr. Murray."

I began devouring the packets as Dad asked about getting some paperwork together to try to cancel our flight to Sweden tomorrow. I tried to process term after term, having a hard time taking it in. I knew Dad wouldn't want to talk to Mom again, so I texted her, *I have lupus and pericarditis. Go to* www.lupus.org *for more information,* using the website recommended by one of the packets.

The room had gone silent. My dad was rubbing his neck and gazing at me with an expression that made me anxious.

"You can go home for a little bit and work on the flights. I'll be fine here. When you come back, can you bring my phone charger? Oh, and my Kindle." I was surprised my voice sounded so calm when I felt like I'd been caught in a riptide. But I couldn't read these all night. I needed something to tune out this room and the fear bubbling inside me.

He stood up and kissed my temple again. "Sure, sweetheart. I'll be back soon. Your phone is okay on battery now?"

I nodded.

"Call me if you need anything. I'll be gone an hour, maybe two, and I'll bring stuff to spend the night."

"You don't have to sleep here. I don't want to inconvenience you. I'll—"

Dad held a hand out to me, but his shoulders sagged. "Ray, I know your mom fills your head with whatever she says, and I'll admit, I let her. You live with her and she's your mom, but sweetheart, your words hurt me and—" His eyes drifted to the corner of the room and then returned to me with resolve. "I want to be clear: I *never* told your mom to have an abortion. The morning after, I asked her to take Plan B, but she didn't. When she said she was pregnant, I asked what she was going to do. She was nineteen, and it was her body." He took my hand. "Just like what happens to *your* body should be your decision."

He dropped my hand and his shoulders hunched more.

"She asked me to marry her when she found out about you. But sweetheart, even for you, I couldn't. As soon as I finished my Ph.D., I moved to America to be closer to you. I know she says I didn't support you when you were a baby, and she's right. I was a graduate student in London. I lived in a basement. I had *nothing*." He was pacing with renewed agitation now. "But your Farfar and Mormor sent her money, and I've paid them back. I'm not American, Ray. I couldn't just move here. It took years to finish my degree, get a job, and get the visa paperwork sorted. Years when I could only see you on Skype. I'm a U.S. permanent resident for *you*. I will be here tonight." A tear rolled down his cheek, and he pulled me close. "You are my daughter, and I love you." He pulled me to him.

"She said you never wanted me. She said you wanted an abortion. I didn't know," I whispered against his chest. I'd always wanted to believe, no matter what my mom said, that my father loved me. But her stories about him had been so harsh. After letting him hold me for several minutes, I pulled away and asked, "Why didn't you ever tell me?"

His cheeks pinkened. "Like I said, she's your mom, and I didn't want you to hate her, either. You were too young to understand before."

I took pity on him as relief and love filled me. "Thank you for telling me," I said quietly.

Dad just nodded. "Are you sure it's okay to leave you for a little while? I could just stay…"

"It's okay. I'd actually like to be alone to make a few phone calls." That was the truth.

He made sure they knew I was in the room by myself, and I had the nurse call button. Then he left after the nurse gave me some medications. Alone in the dreary, colorless hospital room, I decided to call Ross.

"Hey, Rayanne, I'm about to go back on the field. What's up?" He sounded a little uneasy. I glanced at the clock—I should have realized he was at football.

I didn't know where to begin, but I tried. "I'm in the hospital."

"Shit, are you all right?" True concern filled his voice as it softened the way it usually did just for me.

"Yes, well, no—I don't know," I stuttered out. "They said I have lupus, and something's wrong with my heart."

"What the hell is that?" His voice dropped to an anxious whisper. "Am I going to get it? Do I need to go to the doctor?"

"No," I said quickly, trying to alleviate his panic. "No, it's not contagious."

"God, girl, you just about gave me a heart attack." Annoyance ran through me at the relief in his voice. No, I didn't want him to be sick, but he sounded like he cared more about himself than me. I waited in silence for him to ask me what was going on. Some romantic part of me imagined him asking to fly out here. Finally, he said, "Well, I need to get back on the field. I'll call you later?"

"Bye."

Did he care at all? After that, I didn't think I could stomach another call, so I texted Carolyn and Jeffery the same message. *Hey, just wanted to let you know…I'm ok, but I'm in the hospital. I have lupus and pericarditis. Dr. said this is a good website* www.lupus.org . *My battery is low. <3*

I reviewed the papers on lupus and searched about it on the Lupus Foundation of America's website.

Forever. This frightening, painful disease was my new forever.

...
FOUR

Charles

I yawned my way into the kitchen and poured myself a big cup of coffee. My programming internship was cool, but it was annoying getting up early every weekday. Like it wasn't even really summer. Taking my first sip of coffee, I opened the fridge to decide what to eat, blinking in surprise at the copious amounts of tea eggs inside. There must have been two dozen still in the marinade. *Weird.* Normally we only made that many for New Year's.

With a shrug, I closed the door and yelled, "Ma! Are the tea eggs ready?"

Ma came busting into the kitchen. "Those are for Professor Ericson, not you," she fired back in Mandarin, swiping the container and placing it on the counter next to the sink.

I frowned and took another sip of coffee. "Ma, they can't take eggs to Sweden."

She opened her purse, pulled out a ten-dollar bill, and hurried back to the eggs with little Tupperwares. "Have breakfast on me today," she said, holding out the money. "Ray is in the hospital. Dr. Ericson doesn't need to worry about food. I'll take him the tea eggs and our leftovers from the noodle house."

I left the bill flopping in her hand. That was why she hadn't texted me back? "Why is Ray in the hospital?"

She pushed the ten at me and I finally took it. "She is having a heart problem."

Remembering her labored breathing, I started to sweat. "Is she going to be all right?"

She paused her egg peeling, frowned, and said, "Call your baba, he's the doctor. But don't forget you have work."

I nodded and called my father for a brief update on Ray. He said she had been diagnosed with lupus, an autoimmune disease she'd have for the rest of her life. The named seemed hauntingly familiar, but I knew nothing about it and couldn't figure out where I'd heard it. Baba said he'd email me some articles from UpToDate. I knew what I'd be doing over my lunch break.

I squeezed the phone after we hung up. Poor Ray. She didn't even have any friends here. I couldn't imagine how scared and alone she must be feeling. I had to see her.

When I went back to the kitchen, Ma was still peeling the eggs and putting them in Tupperware. "Can we go see her when I finish work?"

She stopped, looking momentarily surprised, then smiled. "Jia Jia," she said, using my short Chinese name affectionately, "we can go."

I felt uneasy the rest of the day. I was able to get the program live, but it didn't hold the joy it would have the day before. At lunch, I didn't have much time to skim through what Baba sent, but from what I read, lupus was more serious than I thought. I found myself counting the minutes until I could go see Ray. I remembered how happy she'd been when we went sledding over winter break and how infectious her laugh had been as she'd twirled, catching snowflakes. She'd looked beautiful and so alive. That had been the last time I'd seen her before last night.

Hours later, Ma and I searched for her room through the long, twisting corridors of the hospital. Carts squeaked by, machines beeped, and rumbling evening news channels created a disharmonious cacophony as we searched. Some families we passed had vacant eyes and others tear-stained cheeks.

"Code Blue Four North one-one-one," blared overhead twice, and feet thundered down the previously desolate corridors. We scuttled past a rapidly filling room as I heard a girl's voice demand firmly, "Who's keeping time?"

Followed by a male's deep, "Timing starting now."

We kept striding past the now-vacated nurses' station and around a bend. Her room sat far and oblivious to the unfolding emergency. It felt wrong to be visiting Ray in here where people were critically ill and dying. I tightened my grip on the stuffed animal we'd purchased for her.

Her room was silent, save the beeping of a heart monitor. She had her nose buried in her Kindle, her dad nearby with his laptop open. Despite the setting and the clamor of someone coding down the hallway, in the quiet of this room, the two seemed relaxed.

"Hi, Ray," I said softly.

She closed her Kindle and looked up. The rash on her face was still vibrant today. "Charles," she said, like she couldn't believe I was here. Then she looked at my ma. "Dr. Wong, thank you for coming to see me, and for the tea eggs." Her eyes darted around the room; the comfort from moments before seemed gone.

My ma smiled and approached the bed. "How are you feeling?"

"Not too bad. I'm actually just a little tired." She tried to grin, but I could tell it was forced. When she really smiled, her eyes lit up. A real Ray smile made your breath catch.

"We brought you a friend." I held out the stuffed husky dog.

She reached out and snuggled it like a little girl. Something about it tugged my heart, reminding me she was just a fifteen-year-old in a hospital bed—younger than me, even.

"I remembered you saying how much you liked dog sledding with your dad," I whispered into the quiet of the room.

She squeezed the husky before looking up with bright eyes on the verge of tears. "Thank you."

My cheeks warmed at how happy she was, and her dad must have heard emotion in her voice because he took control of the conversation.

After about an hour, during which we learned she'd be there a few more days, Ray yawned, and we said our goodnights.

"See you tomorrow," I said, wanting her to know she wouldn't be alone with just her dad the next day.

Her smile summoned something warm but sad inside my chest. I couldn't imagine being sick this far from one's friends. She looked so fragile and alone, and I could only leave knowing I'd be back tomorrow and that her doctors were taking good care of her.

When we got home, I felt heavyhearted in a way I shouldn't have for an acquaintance I saw a few times a year. Was it because she was even younger than me, or was it seeing her in the hospital that bothered me so much?

I picked up my electric guitar and strummed through our most recent songs, but I wasn't in the mood for their peppy rhythms. After a few minutes of deliberation, I switched to Pink Floyd and thumped out "Comfortably Numb" with its long guitar solo, before I turned off the amplifier and traded my electric guitar for the acoustic, which always sounded better when I felt moody. Continuing with Pink Floyd's "Wish You Were Here," I hummed the lyrics.

As the chords drew to a melancholy end, my eyes shut too. I felt haunted, even now, by the sadness penetrating Ray's eyes. Almost of their own accord, my fingers switched to "Behind Blue Eyes" by The Who.

After that, I decided to call it quits for the night. I felt something close to moisture in my eyes but couldn't force myself to play anything happier.

···
FIVE

Ray

I sat wiggling my freezing toes in Dr. Murray's office for the second time in a week. Finally, on Saturday, five days after being admitted, I was able to simply rest at the condo instead of being medically monitored at the hospital. Most of it had been lonely and boring, but at least Charles had visited me after work every day. He'd even sent me an e-gift card so I could buy more books on my Kindle as I lay in bed.

The fluid around my heart had finally started to reabsorb, but I had a lot of follow-ups and monitoring scheduled and was supposed to take it easy. Steroids for a few months, one lupus medication forever, and an immunosuppressant for months to indefinitely. I was still so tired. A fatigue unlike anything I'd ever experienced, except for the last two weeks. Eighty-five percent of lupus patients, apparently, complained about fatigue, so maybe this was just the new normal. And all the pills; I was on so many friggin' pills.

This was my last check-up before I'd go home to Savannah on Wednesday, the day after tomorrow. Clearly, we'd missed our trip to Stockholm. Dad had managed to get a refund from the airlines, so I felt a little less guilty, but still terrible he couldn't go home this summer because of me.

I wasn't sure if I'd be going home to Georgia on Wednesday at all, or be able to travel alone with how I felt, but I was supposed to start junior year on August 1st—Thursday. I wasn't up to starting school. There was still fluid around my heart, and the walk to the doctor's office from the car had been brutal. Island High was a huge school, and the mere thought of all that walking had me sinking deeper onto the exam table.

I hadn't mentioned it to Dad, but I was terrified to go back home. Savannah wasn't a small town, but Grandpapa, my great grandad, had to go to Jacksonville for his Prostate Cancer treatment, because they hadn't liked the options in Savannah. I'd seen the awards lining the hallways—the University of Michigan was a top center for rheumatology. I knew how much Mom hated taking me to do anything. If I ended up needing to go to a big city—Jacksonville, two hours away—I'd never hear the end of it. I'd need chest X-rays for a while, frequent rheumatology visits, and apparently biannual eye exams. I plucked at the disposable paper strip under me, trying not to rip it to shreds. All of that, even if it was at one of Savannah hospitals, would be a decent drive from our island home. I couldn't imagine if I ended up needing to do *all that* in Jacksonville. Mom would skin me alive.

My stepdad, Mark, was a dentist, and Mom worked part-time for him. I'd heard them complain about our insurance before, when my half-sister Mary Beth had to see an allergist. I dreaded the day my hospital bills came in. I hoped Mom wouldn't be too hard on me when I went home—I couldn't help any of this, but I knew it'd be a big burden.

The door opened. "How are you feeling, Ray?" Dr. Ezra asked as he, a resident, and a medical student who'd seen me in the hospital all crowded into the exam room.

"I'm feeling fine, thank you."

"Fine" wasn't a medical term, so he continued what I'd

come to realize was a routine rheumatology exam. "Do you have any joint pain today?"

"No," I answered truthfully. Between the NSAIDs and steroids, the inflammation in my joints wasn't too bad right now.

"And how is the dyspnea? How many stops did you make on the trip from the car to the office?"

The paper under me ripped audibly as my nerves got the better of me. "We stopped four times," I said with a shrug. "It's better than last week."

He quizzed the medical student about how long the pericarditis could take to resolve in lupus. The student didn't know, but the female resident answered it would be a few more weeks.

Dr. Ezra tested every joint and felt over my internal organs for inflammation. After we discussed my chart, which included more quizzing of the medical student and resident, he talked to Dad and me about my follow-up. Then we waited for Dr. Murray.

"Ray," Dad said softly when they left. "Sweetheart." He paused again and scratched his neck. I hadn't noticed until recently that it was something he did when he got nervous. We'd never had this much one-on-one time; usually, we visited my grandparents, aunts and uncles, and cousins when we were together. "School starts a month later here, and the healthcare is really great." He blurted it out, not sounding at all like the refined professor I knew.

Then he sighed and started again, more slowly this time. "What I'm hinting at is I'd like you to live with me, at least for a semester. Your school starts on August first, and the local high school here starts September fifth. You could use a little more time to take it easy, and I can get you switched to my insurance. I work for the university, so we'll have better healthcare options for you, and these doctors," he gestured to the door, "they know your case."

Eerily, the door started opening, but then stopped as I heard the student ask Dr. Murray a question. I'd gotten to know Dad better during this visit, but so much remained a mystery. For example, he'd been dating his girlfriend for five years, and I'd never even met her except a rare hello on video chats.

"Um, can I let you know tomorrow?"

I was still exhausted to the point where I could barely think. My face had finally lost its rash and my joints weren't aching, but I was still bone-weary and short of breath. Dr. Ezra had said my disease was still "active." It would be nice to have a few more weeks off, but what about my life back home? I had a guilty, fleeting thought of my friends and Ross, but I was annoyed that he'd barely called me in the hospital. Sure, we were more an in-person couple and rarely talked on the phone, even back home, but that had hurt.

"Sure thing." Dad took my hand. "We'll get everything scheduled like you'll stay, but I can cancel if it feels like too much. I just want what's best for you, Ray. I think this and a little rest would be best for you."

My eyes gathered dangerous moisture as I squeezed his hand back. The only good thing about this experience was Dad. Having him come out and say that Mom had basically been lying to me my whole life was hard. Right now I was as angry as a hive of hornets at her; just thinking about her made me practically buzz.

Things had always been a little strained with Dad. I'd believed he'd preferred an abortion and barely tolerated me. I'd thought he never truly wanted me in his life. Yet here he was, asking me to live with him. It wasn't what I'd been taught. He wasn't who I thought he was.

I squeezed his hand again and dropped it. It would be nice to spend more time with him, but I wanted to sleep on it. My whole life was in Savannah, along with all my friends and half-siblings. Even if they were pests sometimes, they were my blood too.

So I just nodded before Dr. Murray entered, confirming everything Dr. Ezra had said and telling us she'd see me next week.

We stopped by the front desk to make a follow-up chest X-ray and rheumatology appointment for next week, but Dad whispered to me in Swedish that we could cancel if needed.

He dropped me off at home so he could run some errands, and I headed into my bedroom, feeling lost. I rummaged through my stuff to find my sketchbook, rubber eraser, pencils, and vine charcoal sticks. I sprawled out on my belly on the wood floor with them. Finally, my fingers felt normal enough to hold a pencil. If I couldn't run yet, at least I could do this. I slipped on my headphones and turned on some alternative folk music as I flipped through a magazine until I found a perfume advertisement I wanted to draw, and started sketching.

This was my release. As the white page became smears of gray and black, the moody tempos and questions in my mind swirled like a kaleidoscope until there was nothing left but pressing and smudging. It felt cathartic to draw instead of thinking about what the heck was happening in my life.

My phone ringing startled me, Jeffery's photo appearing onscreen and interrupting the music. "Hello," I said, a little husky after having been silent for hours.

"Rayanne!" Jeffery's cheerful voice boomed. He didn't give me a second to respond before asking, "How was the doctor?"

I breathed in and looked down at my mournful sketch. My version of the ad didn't look sultry, just sad. *Jeffery.* Until recently, I thought some of my new girlfriends or Ross might have become closer to me than my childhood playmate, but no. He'd been loyal and steadfast—like he always had been—as I'd been in the hospital, unlike everyone else. He'd liked me long before Carolyn and the popular girls did. None of them had even known who I was before Ross had shown an interest in me.

"Dad asked me to live with him," I whispered, almost like it wasn't real. "School here starts September fifth, so I'll have a whole month to recover, and my doctors are here. He said I could stay a semester or however long I wanted." I paused, looking at my charcoal-covered fingers. I hoped I hadn't touched anything it wouldn't come out of. When I drew, a passion awoke in me, and I couldn't contain the urge to smudge and smear life onto the page.

Jeffery was silent for an uncomfortable beat. "I wish you would. Ray Ray, when you texted me those websites, it was scary. Dr. Brown said you were fine. I will miss you more than you can imagine, but it's just one semester. It'll be over before you know it. And whenever someone mentions your dad, you look like someone emerging from the desert and Dr. Ericson is water. When my dad used to fix your bike, you'd get this look in your eyes and, well, honey, I've been to your house enough to know Mark is not your dad. I think this would be healthy for you, and not just because of your lupus."

Jeff's dad had honestly been more of a dad to me than Mark ever was. "I know. I'll get to know my own dad." With a deep breath, I told him, "Jeff, my mom lied to me. I'm so furious, so maybe it'll be good not to see her. My grandparents sent her money. He couldn't get a visa to move to America before he finished his degree—"

"What?! You aren't pulling my leg, are you?" He sounded almost as angry as I was. "Why would she do that?"

"I don't know," I choked out. "I'm sure Ross will dump me when I tell him I'm not coming back next month. I don't even think I want to be with him anymore. I've been thinking about our conversation. Thanks again for talking to me after the beach. I don't know if I can be with someone who doesn't respect my choices." Dad's words from the hospital came back to me: *It was her body. Just like what happens to your body should be your decision.* I didn't want to have to keep saying no; Ross should just wait till I said otherwise.

"Ray," he said hesitantly in a way I associated with bad news. "I thought you guys already broke up?"

"Why do you say that?" I knelt and gripped my knee, then frowned as my smudged hands left black bruise-like spots. When he didn't answer immediately, I was forced to say, "Jeffery Lee Willis, you'd better tell me, or I'll come down there and so help me!"

He laughed. "Okay, okay. Carolyn's just been really flirty. Ross hasn't done anything, not that I've seen. But the way she was acting, I thought maybe—"

"Carolyn?"

He cleared his throat. "You know how I feel about that two-faced bitch."

"H-E-double-hockey-sticks! You're joshing me, right?" My leg pinched painfully, and I heard the pop of my charcoal pencil breaking. Holy guacamole, those were expensive.

"I always told you what kind of girl I thought she was. But I don't think they've actually done anything."

"Not yet," I grit out. "She knew I was in the hospital." I rolled the broken ends of the pencil back and forth. Back and forth. I barely had any girlfriends, since I'd been a tomboy when I was little and only had Jeff. Then I was shy. But I'd hoped Carolyn genuinely cared about me, in her own way. Sure she hadn't been the greatest, but she'd helped teach me how to style my hair and even given me her old straightener. Evidently, I was wrong.

"Is it such a bad thing, if you're going to stay up there?"

I didn't respond. Ross and Carolyn made me so furious I thought about using some real curse words, not my made-up ones. Instead, I just rolled the pencil, trying to calm down.

"Look, Ray Ray, I know the guy is what every girl wants to look at, I'm comfortable enough with myself to say that. But honey, he didn't treat you like you deserve. Even before you said what you did, I could see that."

"I need to go. My dad's calling," I said quickly before my

anger faded into tears.

I'd thought my relationship with Ross was special. He had always told me how pretty I was. When we went out, he never flirted with anyone else. Ever. I didn't think it was quite love, but it'd been nice, whatever it was. Worse, despite Jeffery's warnings, I'd thought Carolyn was my friend. I was going to be sick for the rest of my life.

Suddenly, it was all just too much. I struggled to suck in a breath.

"Honey, don't lie to me." Jeffery's voice was soft but steady. "We can talk later. Go draw it out. Heck, honey, even cry it out. But don't make your decision based on him. Get better and get to know your dad, then come back for the second half of senior year with me. It'll be like old times, Bonnie and Clyde-style."

Despite everything, he made me laugh. "Thanks, Jeff. And thanks for being honest with me. Please always be real with me. Don't take this the wrong way, but lying in the hospital makes me want to say it: I love you. You are more than a friend— you're my family." I looked at the ceiling so I wouldn't cry. "You've been there for me when everyone else I thought was my friend hasn't."

"Aw, Ray Ray, honey, I love you too. Get better so I can see you and squeeze the shit out of you." He couldn't resist trying to lighten the mood, but I heard the tension in his voice.

I laughed like he wanted me to and said, "Byyyyyyye," before hanging up.

I looked down at my melancholy figure drawing with haunted eyes, flopped down on my belly again, and continued shading. My moody mix started up again. I decided I'd probably listen to the two guys I considered family above all else—Dad and Jeff—but I just wanted to pour my frustration, loneliness, and sadness into this paper for a little longer.

SIX

Charles

For what felt like the hundredth time, I reread my message asking Ray to watch my band play tomorrow before she went home. She hadn't responded, but I couldn't blame her. Annoyed at myself, I closed it and read through some more of the medical journals Baba had sent me. I thought I was fairly intelligent, but the articles were confusing and complex. I'd been too busy and overwhelmed to have read too far. But I had twenty more minutes left of my lunch break, so I reopened one.

I became so lost in it that I had to pull myself away from my phone to go back to work. SLE was a top ten killer of women aged fifteen to twenty-four. Ray had been released from the hospital, so she couldn't be dying—yet. Beads of sweat dampened my shirt and made it cling to my back. Suddenly the phone was slippery in my perspiring hands. I didn't want Ray to have this, especially not forever.

When I walked into the house that afternoon, Ma was in the kitchen making tea. "Is Ray doing okay?" I asked. "She never texted me back."

Ma pursed her lips and poured a second cup of tea from the

water boiler. She motioned for me to sit down. "Ray is doing fine, but Professor Ericson wants her to stay in Michigan. She's considering it, so maybe that's why she hasn't written you back."

She's considering it! My stomach rolled at the thought of Ray living here.

"It's a lot to move like that. She has to leave her mom, stepdad, and siblings." She had a faraway look in her eyes, and I wondered if she was remembering her move from Taipei or stories of my grandparents'' expatriation from China in the 1950s. "She has to leave her friends and school. I think she will stay, because it's the smart thing and she's a smart girl, but..." She shrugged and left it unsaid. *It's hard.*

After finishing my tea, I went to my room and called Ray. The bedroom was suddenly too hot, my shirt sweaty again as the phone rang a second time.

"Hi," I said when she answered.

"Hi, um, sorry I didn't text you back about tomorrow. I think I'd like to meet your band, but I, well, I'm sorry I didn't write that." She sounded fumbling and awkward—shy like she used to be—not at all like the cool, gorgeous girl she'd seemed to have become.

I felt my throat tighten with nerves, even as I was relieved she was interested. "Great, but that's not why I was calling. My band sometimes plays at this restaurant-bar downtown. Sometimes we hangout, grab dinner, and listen to hear other musicians. Well, tonight is standup comedy. I was going to go with my friend, Knox, but I thought maybe you could use something to laugh about."

"A comedy show?" she asked.

"Yep." I felt a grin spread across my face. I plucked at my damp shirt, glad I hadn't showered yet, because I would've needed to do it again.

"Tonight?"

"It starts at eight. It's actually close to your dad's condo.

I can get you soon, and we can grab dinner. Or I can meet you at seven fifteen and walk over there together, so we can walk extra slow."

"I already ate, but I'd like to go. Let me ask my dad and I'll text you."

"Cool, keep me posted." I tried to say it nonchalantly, even though my belly flipped as I clicked off the phone.

A thrill raced through me when I got her text. *See you at 7:15! I've never seen a comedian before—thanks for the invite.*

I rushed to shower and then stood for several moments in front of the mirror in jeans, wondering what shirt to wear and how to style my hair. Genetically, I was pretty lean and thankfully tall—taller than her, at least, but I didn't look like her boyfriend. I'd seen photos she'd shared with me. He had that blond hair, washboard abs, and basically everything I wasn't look. I'd die of embarrassment before I admitted it, but I modeled my hair after Lang Lang. He was kind of my piano idol. I wondered if I should wear it shaggy like it was, or gel it up. In the end, I left it and put on a gray button-down with rolled-up sleeves.

I was a bundle of nerves, so I sat down at the piano and played Liszt's "La Campanella" from the *Grandes Etudes de Paganini*, then Ben Bernie's "Sweet Georgia Brown," both of which I would perform competitively in a few weeks. I practiced until it was time to leave. The rhythm of the piano and the songs I'd been practicing for months helped me calm down.

Despite the piano soothing my nerves, I blasted the AC on the way to Ray's. I had Dr. Ericson buzz me into his guest parking and texted Ray. *Coming down or do you want me to come up?*

A *dunk dunk dunk* on my window had me jumping, and I turned to see her laughing and pulling her hand back. Her smile and laughter, looking like, well, like Ray, loosened something that had been coiled tight inside me. I hurried out of the car and saw her in her tiny shorts, a loose sweater, and flats. Something ignited in my chest.

Her rash had faded. She appeared healthy—maybe a little too thin from her recent hospital stay, but still fairly normal, even if her collarbones stood out in sharp relief over the neckline of her sweater.

Conversation was a little halting as we walked to the Bob's Bar and Bistro. I didn't want to ask about moving here. When I was stressed I didn't enjoy discussing what bothered me. Tonight was for distractions, for making her laugh. We found a high-top after waving to the owner. Ray chatted with the waiter in her talkative Southern way. We'd barely ordered two pops and some pretzels with cheese dip when Knox sidled up to us.

"Yo," he said, sliding into a chair.

"Knox, this is one of my oldest friends, Ray. Ray, Knox. He's going to be a senior at Rosalind High, too. He's also the drummer in our band."

I forced myself not to tell him to back off as his eyes widened at her sweet Southern "hi," which seemed to draw on for days.

He raised a quick eyebrow at me—or I thought he did, it was hard to tell with his thick mop of brown curls—and replied, "Hi."

"So, what's the name of the band after all?" Ray asked, making me realize I'd just been saying "the band." She perched eagerly at the edge of her seat, foot tapping.

"The Snowblowers," Knox said.

"Is that something dirty?" a pink-cheeked Ray asked in a hushed voice.

I snorted on my pop and Knox chuckled. "No, just stupid. Ray, do you know what a snowblower is?" She shook her head and Knox asked in disbelief, "How can you live in Michigan and not know that?"

"Her dad lives in a condo," I said before turning back to Ray. "It's like a lawnmower for snow. You use it to get the snow off driveways and sidewalks. Some people don't like doing it, so they paid, and still pay, us to do it. It's how we saved up enough for the instruments. We thought the name fit—the Snowblowers."

I smiled at the O her lips made, and Knox took over the conversation, all excited about this new set he'd been working on. Out of all of us, he was the only one without a summer job or camp. After a few minutes of talking about the drum solo he wanted to add to a song, he asked Ray, "Do you go to Rosalind? I think I would have remembered seeing you."

"Maybe," Ray teased back. "It's a big school. I'll be a junior this year." I couldn't help the speeding of my pulse. She must have looked it up: it *was* a big school.

"So you do go there?" he pressed as he leaned in, his messy mop flopping into his eyes.

Her lips curved up as she cast a quick glance at me before saying softly, "I might."

My stomach fluttered as I nodded at her so she'd know I heard her. She hadn't decided, but she might actually go to school here. Having a crush on Ray in Savannah was annoying, but having a crush on her here—that might be worse. She drew me to her like a neodymium magnet, but someone like her would never date someone like me. And I was way too busy for a girlfriend anyway. The band was my one fun outlet. Even if I stood a chance with a girl like Ray, I wasn't sure I would be much of a boyfriend, between studying, piano, band, and robotics club. But I could dream, I guess.

The lights dimmed and the owner came up and joked the easily offended should leave—typical comedy. As the sets started, they weren't Comedy Central, but Ray's laugh and the genuine smiles she threw my way might have made it the best show I'd ever seen. When she slipped off to the bathroom, Knox leaned in and whispered, "Dude, she looks like a model. How are you even friends with her?

"Our parents are friends," I admitted with great reluctance.

He laughed and turned back to the show. "Should have

guessed."

I bristled but said nothing. Clearly, it was obvious even to my best friend that a girl like Ray would have never chosen to be friends with me.

"Why haven't you introduced us before? Wait. Wait, I remember. Doesn't she live in Savannah?"

"Yeah, she does. She splits her time between her parents' houses, but she might be switching schools. That's her story though, so don't ask."

"Cool, I got it." He zippered his lips, like the jokester he was and we fell silent, expect Knox tapping out a drum sound on the table.

I felt as much as saw Ray slide back beside me. I heard her panting louder than she should, and forced myself to try to relax and watch the show. It didn't matter how we'd become friends or what Knox thought. Ray needed a friend here, now. She was going through a lot. As her laugh tinkled like chiming bells, I promised myself, *I'll be her friend.* Somehow, I'd make time with her so she didn't have to deal with everything—with lupus, with moving, with starting a new school—alone.

We said our goodbyes to Knox around ten. Ray looked the happiest I'd seen her since we went sledding last Christmas. We strode home, and I was extra conscientious to keep the pace slow. I didn't want to strain her heart.

"Charles, I really appreciate you asking me to this," she said. "It was sweet. I needed a laugh."

"Hey, I had fun too. I know you've had the worst two weeks, maybe of your life, and you have a lot of things to think about. But I want you to know, if you move here, I'd be your friend. I know I don't have the same social circle you used to have, but you wouldn't be alone. Knox is a weirdo, but he's a great guy—loyal to the end."

She looked completely brittle—fragile—a moment. My stomach fell. I wanted her to feel happy, not worse. I was trying to think of what to say when she grabbed my hand and said, "That means a lot. Good gracious, it means a lot. " She dropped it quickly, and we kept walking. "It makes sense to move here. I'm not as smart as you, but I still want to get into a good architecture program. Ugh, can you imagine missing the first whole week of school, if I go back there?" She wrinkled her nose.

"You're smart. But, yeah, it'd be tough for anyone to start the year behind."

She nodded vigorously. "Yes. I want to think on it because these *have* been the worst two weeks of my life. While I have my whole life back home, it means a lot, you trying to make me laugh and reminding me I'm not alone. It means a lot you visited me in the hospital. I liked the dog, too. I needed something to hold on to in there."

"We're friends, right?" I said, trying to keep it casual. The sight of her vulnerability did something terrible to my insides. She'd always seemed so independent and brave.

"Yes, friends."

I nudged her shoulder with mine. "What are friends for?"

"I hope I can be as good a friend to you as you've been to me," she whispered.

Suddenly, we were at the condo. I didn't know how to respond. But it was already late, considering a few days ago she'd been in the hospital. "Do you need me to walk you up?"

"No, the door's just there and then an elevator. Hey, thanks again. I'll see you tomorrow evening. What time did you say you could get me?"

I froze for a moment, my insides doing a happy dance— she wanted to listen to the band!—and tried to sound casual. "Six thirty?"

"Cool. I get to see the robot?"

I laughed. "Yep. It's there."

She opened the door, her back to me as she said, "I'll answer Knox's question tomorrow about Rosalind High."

I nodded, even though she couldn't see me. "Night."

"Later, gator." With a flash of a grin over her shoulder, she was gone.

I shook my head at both how much fun I'd had tonight and how much I couldn't wait for her answer tomorrow. A little worry also had me cranking the AC in my car. If she stayed, I couldn't let her distract me. First quarter grades were the last thing all my early application schools would see.

Caltech—Los Angeles—had always been my dream.

···
SEVEN

Ray

G*o faster*, I willed my legs. The haze of humidity, the glow of the street lamps, and the swinging of Spanish Moss from the lumbering oaks in the menacing ghost tour area had me glancing over my shoulder, peering into the dark night. My feet pounded, radiating pain to my knees, on the winding cobblestones underfoot. Something stalked me, if I could just move faster—

"Chrissy, please!" My eyes flew open, at the sound of a loud voice. Shallow breaths filled the room. Perspiration covered my body. "Ugh," I groaned as I pulled off my sweat-soaked sheets in disgust and headed to see what the fuss was with my mom. One of my medications could cause vivid dreams. That nightmare was just, well, disturbing.

"I think we both know this is best for her," Dad was saying, pacing back and forth in the kitchen. "If she'd stayed there, who knows what would have happened? She needs more time to recover. I'm not spoiling her; she's been really sick."

I walked slowly in front of him so he knew I could hear, grabbed a cup, and poured some coffee. I couldn't hear what

Mom was saying, but judging by the jaw-clenching and pacing from Dad, it was something nasty.

After I'd downed half the cup, I had the fortitude to say, "Dad, please put her on speaker."

"Are you sure?" he asked in Swedish. "She's in a mood." I nodded, and he switched back to English. "Chrissy, your daughter wants to talk to you. I'm putting you on speakerphone."

"Hi, Mom," I said hesitantly.

"Hi, baby girl. How are you feeling?" Her voice dripped with fake sweetness like it normally did when we were in public.

"I want to stay here." I risked a quick glance at Dad. "At least for a semester, or maybe a year, if it'll mess up getting into college to switch midyear."

"Rayanne, I just don't know if your dad is capable of handling you. He never wanted children. This might be too much for him, and I don't want you to get hurt." She said it so gently I almost wanted to believe her.

"I can handle Ray," Dad said firmly. "I want her to stay. You've been complaining about the bills. I can get her insurance covered. Ray wants to stay."

I nodded at Dad. "Mom, I want this."

It was nerve-racking, but it was the right thing for so many reasons. Junior year was important on my transcripts and I didn't feel capable of starting school yet. I dreaded thinking about starting behind. I knew I was mostly to blame for Mom having 'just' an associate's degree, at least that's what she always said to me. I wanted to be an architect, and that took good grades and lot's of school. Jeff had agreed I should stay. And at least I'd have Charles; I wouldn't be all alone. Plus, I liked my doctors here.

My heart raced again, but I repeated firmly, "I want to stay in Michigan."

Mom and Dad agreed to call their lawyers and work out the details of a consent order and custodial parent swap if this was really what I wanted. I assured them it was. Then I left them to talk as I went to shower away my weird dream. Holy guacamole, I loved not fighting over the shower and bathroom with three other people. Having my own bathroom for the first time in my life was amazing. Guests could use it, but we hadn't had any, so it felt like my own. I was sure Dad's girlfriend, who lived in Chicago, would eventually visit, but it hadn't happened yet. Anyhoo, she'd probably use his.

When I came out, Dad had food ready for me: some toast with Swedish caviar paste, a few pieces of sliced cheese, and a glass of water. Maybe because I'd grown up with Swedish food, but pickled herring and fish eggs had always seemed like the perfect breakfast to me. Or cheese. I loved the hard white cheese Mormor and Dad always had. Surströmming you could only find at my grandparents'—Americans hated the smell—but Kalles Kaviar or Prästost we could buy at Ikea, and Dad always kept some in the fridge.

"Miraculously, I've gotten an emergency appointment with the lawyer," Dad said as I ate. "Someone canceled last night. Do you want to come or stay here?"

I chewed for a moment. "I'd like to stay and let my friends know."

He kissed my head. "I'll be back soon."

I called Jeffery as soon as I finished eating. He was supportive, just like before. He ended the call with, "Honey, you call me. Night or day, you call."

"We'll talk soon, big guy. Keep some air in my bike for me, ya hear?"

My heart buzzed like a cicada swarm as I imagined not having Jeff right next door, like he had been my whole like. I washed and dried the breakfast dishes by hand as I worked up the nerve to call Ross. After tidying the already clean kitchen, I found his contact and took a deep breath.

"Hi," I said tentatively when Ross picked up. I fidgeted with the hem of my cut-off shorts as I waited for him to respond. These cut-offs had become ridiculously frayed with all my nervous picking over the last few weeks.

"Hey, pretty girl, are you ready to come home tomorrow? I can't wait to see you and show you all the ways I missed you."

I jerked a thread out of my shorts and twirled it between my fingers. "I'm staying in Michigan."

He was quiet a moment. "You're going to miss the first week of school? Are you still sick?" His voice was tinged with worry, and I was glad. I didn't want to think I'd dated a monster for almost seven months.

"Ross, I'm *staying* in Michigan—living here." I breathed in deeply. "My dad and I talked about it, and it would be better for me to do at least one semester here."

"When did you decide this?" His voice had an edge to it.

"This morning."

"And you didn't want to talk to me about it?" He sounded shocked or disappointed—I couldn't tell which.

"The phone goes two ways, you know?" I said, maybe a little too harshly, then counted to ten for patience. "This is what's best for me. I'm going to have this disease for the rest of my life. I need to learn how to manage it. We thought it would be a good idea to let me start school a month later, like theirs do, and stay with my medical team."

The silence on the other end was brutally tense. Finally, he said in a flat, maybe pained voice, "Well, I guess this is the end of us, then."

Even though part of me was relieved, especially because I knew a breakup had been looming, his callousness hurt. Like the fountain of tears I'd been lately, I felt a few trail down my cheeks. "Yeah, I guess so," I said.

In a nicer tone, he said, "Rayanne, I hope you get better. I *will* miss you. You really are one of a kind." Now he sounded wistful.

"Thanks, Ross. Anyway, I gotta go call a few other people and let them know. And work—I need to quit officially." And just because I was feeling a little petty, I added, "I'm sure

Carolyn will want to know you're officially single now."

That got a chuckle from him. "I'm not the best boyfriend and I didn't call enough when you were in the hospital, but I didn't cheat on you," he said seriously. "I saw Jeffery giving me the stink-eye and I want to clear the air before he *forgets* to block for me and I get my ribs crushed in at the next football game. But Carolyn, that girl's not your friend."

I stiffened. It made me burn more than a bag of Takis that Carolyn would do something like Jeffery said she had. And I trusted Jeffery. I should have trusted Jeffery when he warned me about her the first time.

"I'm not the best, but I'm not the worst, either," Ross said. "Even I wouldn't cheat on a girlfriend in the hospital. Karma, pretty girl. I did like our time together. God, who else do you think I would go months without sex for? No one, that's for damn sure. But I can't do Michigan, not even for a jaw-dropper like you. Get better, ya hear?"

I wiped my cheek. "You're still a dog, just not a mongrel. Good luck this year."

His voice turned serious again. "I *do* hope you get better."

"Bye, Ross." Stupid as I was, more tears slipped out. He'd been my first boyfriend, after all.

"Bye, Rayanne," he whispered and the phone clicked off.

I looked around my tiny bedroom in the downtown condo and realized this wasn't just the guest room. Now it was *my* room. I got my sketching supplies back out and poured my emotions onto the page for hours, crafting a self-portrait of running at the beach. This would be the only way I'd be running in the sun for a while.

I drew until Dad came home with a late lunch. He looked at my puffy eyes and opened his arms. I was happy to sink into them, realizing how much I was starting to miss all the hugging from my little sisters and Jeff.

"Chrissy will be going to the lawyer tomorrow, and they'll submit something early next week to change the custody," he said, still holding me close. "Make sure you let her know anything else you want from home and I can pay for it to be shipped. Week after next we can go to Rosalind Franklin High School and get you enrolled in classes."

"Thanks, Dad." I hugged him tighter for a minute, then stepped away.

He scratched his neck. "And before my school starts up, I'll move my office out here and we can buy you a desk and whatever else you need to make it feel more like home in there."

We both glanced around the tiny condo. It would be tight, but he could make space somewhere in the living room, or even in his bedroom.

"Thank you," I said. "I like seeing your books. You can leave the ones you won't use this semester."

He nodded. "Thank you."

"I'm going to watch Charles's band practice tonight at his place."

"Yeah?" Dad said with a growing grin. When he smiled, it warmed up his whole face. "Charles is a fantastic kid. I'm glad you'll have some friends here when you start the school year."

I nodded mutely, but smiled. Charles had known me for years and always been kind. I trusted he'd help me settle in. There was something steady and comforting about him. I just hoped his friends were as nice.

"But still, take it easy, okay?"

I assured him I would. It wasn't like I had too much around here to do—just think about the changes in my life.

"Maybe we could do something too?" he said. "They have an architecture Brown Bag tomorrow morning. It'll be, um, professors and graduate students talking about their research projects. One of the students in my Economics of Urban Planning course mentioned it. I'd like to go and, if you'd like, we could both go."

"You'd take me?" Not only would it be something to do, but Dad was *inviting me*.

He blushed like my question embarrassed him. "Of course. Maybe it'd be boring for you, but it'll be about architecture."

"I'd love to go," I assured him, and gestured to the takeout he'd brought. "Now about this phở . I'm starving."

I opened the door to Charles's Forester that evening, trying to fake a bravery I didn't feel. "I'm staying," I announced.

Charles gave me his familiar lopsided grin with one dimple showing, and a little tension eased out of me. "That's great," he said as he backed up the car. "What did everyone say back home?"

I fiddled with the seatbelt strap. "Mom and Dad worked it out, or I guess their lawyers are going to. My best friend was glad because he wants me to be healthy and, well, my boyfriend said okay, but he wouldn't be my boyfriend anymore."

He cleared his throat. "Sorry to hear that."

I tried to brush it off. "No worries. It'da been tricky to stay together here anyhoo. And honestly, the writing's been on the wall a few weeks, but I hadn't taken the plunge yet…" I let my voice trail off. A part of me was even relieved. Ever since prom, I'd asked myself more often why I was even with Ross.

Kaleo's "Automobile" came on the stereo, and rather than continue the inquisition, I said, "Can I turn it up? I like this song." And I was done with the conversation.

Charles chuckled and turned it up. "Me too. We saw them in Grand Rapids last spring. They're amazing in concert."

We rode in comfortable silence except for the radio until we reached his place, where the worry I'd make the wrong friends, like Carolyn, or even to some extent Ross, surged again. I'd hated starting high school. What if these people didn't like me? Charles was, like, a genius. What if all his friends were too, and thought I was ignorant or country? I winced as my shorts frayed a little shorter before I jerked my hand away from the hemline. Oh, heck. At this rate I'd need another pair by the end of the week. I closed my eyes, suddenly afraid to get out of the car.

When I opened them, Charles gave me a small smile of encouragement, and we exited the car together. His light gray, two story Dutch Colonial house was almost as familiar to me as Dad's condo. His mom was super friendly, if overwhelmingly concerned about my health. I had to reassure her four times at the shoe rack I didn't need anything before she went back into her office.

I gestured toward his huge grand piano in the living room. "Will you play me your competition songs?"

Charles looked stunned by my request, but he nodded and sat down. "This is Liszt's 'La Campanella' from the *Grandes Etudes de Paganini*." Then he rolled his wrists and took a deep breath before his hands came alive.

I watched him, transfixed, as his agile fingers flew across the keys. As I observed the passion and complete concentration with which he played, it hit me that Charles was beautiful. He didn't look like a Calvin Klein model, like Ross had, but he'd matured into his tall, lanky frame and angular cheekbones even since last January, and his skin was a vibrant gold. His shaggy black haircut suited him. His hands and the sound they were making mesmerized me—I'd never seen or heard anything like it.

Unbidden heat coursed through me as I imagined what those dexterous fingers would feel like, playing across me, sliding across my skin. Would they hold that much skill and passion? I hoped I wasn't blushing. This was Charles, my only friend here, and yet suddenly I couldn't un-see it: *Charles was handsome.*

When he finally finished and looked up at me, I hoped he couldn't read my thoughts. Heat still sizzled through me. Despite my best intentions, I twisted the hem of my shorts again.

"That was the most incredible thing I've ever seen or heard," I whispered, still half-transfixed. "I hope you win."

It was his turn to blush. When he glanced down, he looked more like himself—the Charles I'd built Legos and snowmen with. Yet now, I couldn't un-see him as anything but attractive as he looked back up at me with his keen, almond-shaped eyes. He was striking in a way no one from my small island in South Georgia was, or at least no one I'd been friends with.

"It still needs work," he said modestly.

"Are you going to introduce us or what?" someone asked, breaking our stare-off. I turned to see a short, black haired guy standing there holding a guitar case littered with decals. He wasn't smiling. Nor did he look friendly.

Behind him walked in Knox and a guy so stinking cute with wicked hipster black-rimmed glasses, close-shaved hair, and wearing a fitted charcoal shirt that just showed so much yum. Two adorable dimples popped when he flashed a blinding smile at me that contrasted even more beautifully with the backdrop of his ebony complexion.

"Yeah. Basement?" Charles asked scrambling out of the piano bench.

Oops. I hoped he didn't see me checking out his friend, but goodness me.

Knox bumped my shoulder and said, "Hi, Ray," as we got to the staircase.

"Hiya, Knox."

As soon as we reached the basement, Knox indicated to the guy with the guitar case decorated with decals in what I assumed was Korean, judging by the South Korean Flag one. "Kevin the bass guitarist."

"Hi. Ray," I said with a wave.

He just grunted.

"And James is the vocalist," Knox said not missing a beat. "He's even cooler, which was already cooler than these robot nerds—"

"—Knox," Kevin interrupted.

"Sorry, sorry," he said throwing his hands up in mock surrender. "Robots are awesome. Anyway, James is even cooler than he used to be being a Freshman at Michigan now."

"Nice to meet you Ray," James said with a firm handshake. His large, warm hand dwarfed mine. My skin suddenly seemed even more pale in his grasp, and was a stark reminder of my time this summer avoiding the sun and my new lupus diagnosis.

Knox pointed to Charles, "You know our lead guitarist-slash-occasional keyboardist. And school prodigy." He pointed to himself. "And yours truly on the drums. Now you have met The Snowblowers. Be ready to be awed by our awesomeness."

"Honored," I said with a laugh grateful Knox broke up my nerves of meeting new people with his strange humor.

The guys set up their equipment, which took time because Knox moved the drums back and forth between his house and Charles's. I took out my sketchbook and drew until they were ready to play.

No one from back home played an instrument and I certainly never had. It was kind of amazing to watch the coordination and practice it took to make one song work. They had a rock vibe, and Kevin and Knox anchored the band perfectly. James had a stunning deep voice that rocked the vocals. And Charles, and his deft hands, created the most melodious sounds.

I couldn't forget the look on Charles's face as he'd played the piano for me earlier. I found myself recreating it on a page of my sketchbook as I listened to their practice. As I smudged those intense eyes, a hum of heat rolled through me and I glanced up to see those eyes on me, laced with concern. I gave him a half-grin, suddenly shyer around Charles than I'd ever felt. Self-consciously, even though he was too far away to see what I was sketching, I flipped the page and started drawing a large Georgia O'Keefe-style flower. I'd finish the Charles drawing later, when I was alone.

I eventually fell into a comfortable, cozy rhythm, drawing and listening to them practice. Maybe living here wouldn't be too bad.

EIGHT

Charles

"I'm going upstairs for a pop," said Kevin, interrupting my—hopefully discreet— checking out of Ray, who'd joined us again for band practice. "Anyone else want one?"

A chorus of 'no's went around the basement, and Ray stood and stretched. Her long legs were sculpted. Despite a few weeks indoors they still held some glow from having lived in Savannah and wearing shorts, at least for running, most of the year.

"Emory is my top school, you know?" Knox was saying. We'd been talking about college.

"Why Emory?" Ray asked.

Knox pushed his thick hair away from his eyes. "They have a good pre-med program. And maybe I'm tired of snowblowing. Atlanta is cool as shit." When Ray didn't immediately respond, Knox pressed, "Don't you think so, Ray?"

Her cheeks pinkened. "Atlanta seems nice. It's so much bigger than Savannah or Ann Arbor. But…" She shrugged. "I don't know it that well. Michigan and Tech have always been my top choices because they have great architecture programs.

That's Georgia Tech—sorry, we all call it just Tech back home. It's in downtown Atlanta."

She'd referenced Michigan and Georgia's most difficult-to-get-into state schools. It didn't surprise me, given how smart she was. I wondered whether her dad would pay her tuition, like mine certainly would. She'd never mentioned private colleges like the rest of us.

"I applied to Tech, too. They have a good robotics program. I've dreamed of Caltech forever, but I could stomach Tech or Michigan." I stood, indicating by touching my thumb to my cheek that she had a smudge from her charcoal pencil.

She blushed and rubbed her cheek. Her top school was my backup school. My own cheeks heated. Crap, that sounded rude. I hoped she hadn't thought so.

She looked down and mumbled, "I mean, they aren't Caltech or anything, but I'd still be delighted just to get into one of those. Even Georgia." She pulled on the threads of her shorts, just peeking out the bottom of the sweatshirt she'd put on when she entered the chilly basement. She looked bottomless and it was damn distracting. She pivoted back to Knox. "Why Atlanta?"

"My grandparents live there. In Toco Hills, near Emory, so I've been a lot." He brushed his hair back again and teased, "A lot of people like me down there. You know Atlantians nickname their Krogers down there? Where my grandparents live is Kosher Kroger. You should see what Toco Hills looks like on Saturday morning—people walking everywhere."

Ray looked posed to ask more, but before she could, James said in his rumbling voice, "My sister wants to go to school in Atlanta too."

At the mention of James's little sister, Knox flushed and dropped his sticks before hastily picking them up.

Ray's phone rang. "Hej, hej," she said, then immediately hung up. "My dinner date has arrived. *And* he always pays for my meals, what a gentleman," Ray joked, but I knew her smile well enough to know she loved the extra time with her dad. "Charles, you're getting me again after work tomorrow?"

"Yep," I said with a wave.

"Bye," Ray purred in her Southern drawl.

With damp palms, I watched her retreating figure. It was Sunday afternoon, just five days after Ray had agreed to stay. She'd been to most of our practices, which we'd had almost daily in summer. She'd always been laid-back nice, so I shouldn't have been surprised by how well she'd settled in with the guys despite how nervous and shy she was sometimes. Well, most of the guys.

"What's up with you two?" Knox said, interrupting my pining. "You're not dating, are you?"

I laughed. I couldn't help it. The idea of just about the prettiest girl I'd ever seen dating me, Charles the Geek: competitive pianist and Robotics Club nerd. It was comical.

When I was finally able to control my laughter, I said, "Have you guys not seen her?"

"Oh, we've seen her, all right," James said. "That girl is walking jailbait. It's unbelievable she's fifteen." He was eighteen and the only one of us who was going to be a college freshman next year. Luckily for us, he was going Blue.

"No, we're not dating."

"Does that mean—?" Knox started.

"No," I said firmly. "She just broke up with her boyfriend and is dealing with some personal things that are not my business to share. So yes, it would bother me if you tried to date her."

"What kind of things?" Kevin asked, coming downstairs and catching the tail end of the conversation.

I shook my head and picked up the acoustic guitar. Out of everyone, he'd warmed to Ray the least. Her business was really hers.

"Oh, no way!" James practically shouted, glancing down at his phone. "We got invited to play Thursday night in Detroit!"

"Seriously?" Knox exclaimed, and after James gave us

more details, we unanimously agreed to play.

"You should invite Ray, Charles," Knox said. Then he laughed. "Ray Charles. Whoa, I just got that."

Thursday rolled around, and I was sweating on my way to pick up Ray in the humid August heat. The storm earlier hadn't helped the mugginess in the air. Tonight, my seventeenth birthday—lucky Chinese 8/8—would be the first time the Snowblowers played in Detroit. And Ray had wanted to go—like, *really* wanted to go. I still couldn't believe it. I was glad the guys had goaded me into inviting her.

I turned onto her street, unable to stop grinning even as I wiped my brow. I was sad she'd gotten sick, had lupus, but was so glad she was living here. She was a breath of fresh air in my boring life. Just thinking of her made me happy in a way it shouldn't have—the way her lips curved up or her brow furrowed over her sketchbook. Her hair wasn't as uniquely white-blond as it once was, but she still had an almost untouchable, ethereal beauty to her.

She was waiting near the curb, her tall, slender form immediately catching my eye. I grimaced—I was five minutes late. Rather than her usual oversize long-sleeved shirts or sweaters and shorts, she was wearing skinny jeans and a black tank top, and it took a lot of willpower not to stare at her chest. Crap, where had she been hiding those? She wasn't large chested, but she was skinny enough that what she had stood out.

I inched forward in my seat, trying to get a slight breeze on my back as she entered the car. She was going to kill me tonight.

She turned to me and held out a little cupcake. "Happy birthday!" she said with the brightest smile.

I felt myself blushing. "Thanks, you didn't have to."

"I wanted to!" she said. "You've been a really good friend. I can't believe I get to see you play in a bar. That is just so cool." She bounced around, shaking the cupcake precariously. She must have thought the same thing because she thrust it toward me and said, "Here, eat up!"

I awkwardly took a bite, and she started giggling. I raised an eyebrow at her, but she just leaned over and wiped the tip of my nose with a fingertip before seeming to think better of it and used the napkin she had. Heat rushed through me at her innocent touch, and I felt super self-conscious suddenly stuffing my face.

I took a sip of water from the bottle in the cupholder. "Sorry, I should have offered you some."

Her laughter chimed through the car again. "I bought Dad and myself one too, so no worries." She reached down and handed me a thin box. "And I got you this."

"Thanks."

I cranked the AC to combat my intensifying nervous sweats before I opened it. I wasn't used to gifts. My parents had given me a red envelope with cash this morning, and I'd get another one on Lunar New Year, but this? This was different.

Inside the box were advanced jazz piano music sheets. I looked over at her, surprised at her thoughtfulness since I told her I wanted to learn more jazz, and noticed she was grasping the seatbelt in her hands. She didn't have shorts to pick at tonight.

"I hope you like it," she blurted out, pulling repeatedly on the seatbelt strap. "The guy at the music store said it was the best for advanced students. He still uses it himself."

I smiled so wide my jaw hurt. "This is awesome." I set it down safely in the backseat. "But we should go. I don't want to be late and I don't know what the parking situation is."

Halfway into the hourlong drive, too late to turn around, I coughed and said, "Ray, you still go to church, right?"

"Yes, online mostly. Why?"

Another cough. "Well, there was a little issue. The venue wouldn't allow guests under eighteen, so we lied and said you were in the band. You only need to do one song, and James remembered you guys talked about choir and, well, he suggested a Cat Stevens cover, 'Morning Has Broken.' He sings in choir too; you probably remember since he said he told you"—crap, I was rambling—"I learned that piano set years ago. Everyone loves Cat Stevens—*classic*. I, um, printed out the lyrics for you to refresh your memory." How I hoped she couldn't see how sweaty I was. Gross.

"I will kill you," she finally said, deadpan after a drawn-out pause.

"I'm sorry. I knew you were excited, and I didn't want to cancel on you." She huffed, and I said gently, "I downloaded the Cat Stevens version. We can play it a few times. I'm sure, even during online church, they play it occasionally at services."

"Okay, but what if I'm terrible?" She sounded worried.

"Don't worry, James will carry you. He's a great vocalist. The duet was his idea. He's a bass-baritone, and I'm sure you're a mezzo-soprano."

"Did you just speak Mandarin? Because I'm pretty sure it was a foreign language." She huffed again and returned to the seatbelt pulling.

Crap. I didn't want her to be so nervous. Didn't those articles say anxiety caused lupus flares? "What I said was, you'll do great."

"Fine, fine. I know the song, but let's play it."

The second time through the song, I said, "Okay, try singing now?"

And she did. Her voice singing gospel sounded angelic. Haunting. She certainly couldn't be the next The Voice star but her high voice would create an amazing juxtaposition with the bass-baritone of James's.

After at least six runs of the song, she seemed a little more confident, and when we arrived, she smiled over at me. "I got this."

"Damn straight!" I laughed as we got out of the car. She hurried to the back seat to help by carrying my acoustic guitar and then sat and whispered with James about their duet as I went back for the keyboard. Miraculously, or maybe not since James liked black T-shirts, they matched in jeans and black shirts.

It took a little while to set everything up. We decided Ray and James would perform third. Enough time to warm up the crowd, but not too far in they'd doubt she was a band member. We'd start with two electric guitar songs, then I'd do a soft acoustic guitar piece after their duet, and then we'd pick the tempo back up and do our signature jazz sound-off with the keyboard. Our last song would be "The First Cut is the Deepest," another Cat Stevens cover with Ray doing the chorus. We'd tell her during the break. Even Rod Stewart had covered that song, so we felt like we had good taste.

By starting time, my shirt was nearly plastered to my back, and I needed to take some deep breaths. Somehow this was more intimidating than piano concerts. Those were just me, but now I had to depend on others, and I didn't like that. And Ray. I glanced at her exquisite profile. Crap, I didn't want to look like an idiot in front of her. Yet somehow, I knew once my fingers started moving, the music would flow through me and settle my nerves.

The first two songs flew by, and I nodded to Ray as I moved to the keyboard in the corner. When she returned my nod, I started up. Her voice could use a little training, but it was high and sweet paired with James's deep bass-baritone. Gospel might have seemed a strange choice, but she looked kind of angelic with her long, almost white-blond hair and delicate features, and the song hadn't ever fully faded from its billboard stardom.

When they finished to a roaring applause, she blinked as if in surprise and threw me a dazzling smile.

For the rest of the night, she watched from the sidelines, seeming to enjoy it by the smiles and thumbs-up she gave me when I looked her way. When we ended with the full group and "The First Cut is the Deepest," the crowd begged for an encore. We packed up all smiles. Even though it was late, we were all hyped up when the concert ended and gave our business cards to two people in the audience with venues nearby.

The drive home was a slow release. Ray and I both started yawning and growing quieter toward the end.

"You are so talented, it's amazing," Ray said softly before we pulled off the highway. "The piano, the guitar, the electric guitar…"

I felt myself blush, glad it was dark. "I like music. And the piano—I've been playing since I was five. That's twelve years. That song you heard, I have to play it almost every day, hours each day. I should be good. Asian parents, remember? Haven't you heard of the Asian grading scale?"

She laughed before choking out, "What?"

"A is Average, B is Below Average, C is Can't Eat Dinner, D is Don't Come Home, F is Find a New Home," I recited in a flat voice.

"What?" she repeated.

I gulped, wishing she'd just laughed like I'd hoped for. I'd turned onto her street by then and shimmied into a parking spot, so I turned to look at her. "You've never seen those memes?"

I could see her blush even in the dim light. "Charles, we didn't have a lot of Asians at my last school," she said, eyes cast downward.

She shifted in her seat like I'd embarrassed her. I sometimes forgot everywhere wasn't like Ann Arbor or Toronto or the Bay Area, where my cousins lived, with large Asian communities.

"Check this out," I said as I pulled out my phone and googled "Asian grading scale," and about twenty different memes like the one I'd mentioned popped up. She leaned over me, her jasmine scent surrounding me again, making my heart beat faster. She was intoxicating. I could barely think beside her. Well, I could think all right, but it wasn't anything fit for friends.

"It's not really like that, is it?" She sounded shocked, her stunning eyes wide.

I closed my phone and slipped it back into my pocket with a sigh. "I don't know. I've never gotten a B, but when I didn't get into advanced math in fourth grade, my mom made me do an extra hour each night and three on the weekend. She made me retake the test, and I got put in advanced math. I think they'd still love me, but they just…" I struggled for the right way to say it. "They want me to be the best me I can be, as cheesy as that sounds—I'm sure it's in a book or on a coffee mug somewhere."

She laughed, breaking the serious mood. "You're a pretty good you," she whispered, placing a hand on my forearm.

I glanced up at those blue eyes, almost indigo in this light, and swore I saw something there. Now my heart raced at an allegro beat. She moved her hand, and the moment passed.

As she moved to open her door, I felt like an idiot. Her last boyfriend looked nothing like me; girls like her didn't date guys like me.

"I'm going to be pretty busy because my piano competition is coming up in just a week, so I won't be much fun. But I know it's hard to be new," I said quickly, annoyed at myself but unable to resist her. "So if you want to come over and sketch while I practice, don't be a stranger."

"Thanks," she said. "Your piano is actually pretty inspiring, so I might do that."

She got out of the car but leaned back in, clearly not realizing the distracting view of her cleavage I now had. I was doing my best to ignore her breasts hanging out of her top even as heat rushed through me. How could anyone be that beautiful?

"And big thanks for bringing me tonight," she said with a half grin, which helped me focus on her face and not her chest. "I really had fun. And happy birthday again."

"No problem," I said, then decided to use her joke. "Later, gator."

She smiled wider as she waved goodbye. As I watched her to make sure she got into the building, I sighed. I didn't think I'd ever had a crush this bad.

NINE

Ray

"Ray, how are you feeling today?" Dr. Ezra asked.

I glanced down before answering honestly. "I'm tired," I said with a sigh, thankful it was just us, no gaggle of medical students today.

He nodded. "That's one of the most common side effects of lupus. It's normal to be tired. You also have some mild iron deficiency anemia, which can be a side effect of some of your medications, so we're going to start you on an iron pill. Are you taking naps?"

I felt myself blush. For the first time since kindergarten—a decade—I'd been feeling the need to nap in the afternoons. "Yes, sir. Just an hour or less, but it seems to help."

He typed something on the iPad and I cast a quick look at Dad. He gave me a half smile and a small nod. It'd been just over three weeks since I'd decided to stay. I hadn't gone out and directly said it, but I'd been grateful for this time with my dad. We'd bonded in a way that hadn't been possible on our busy trips to Sweden. He'd taken me to three Brown Bags, and if I didn't already think I'd like to be an architect, I was now sure

I did. Or maybe a professor, like Dad. They took their subject and papers so seriously, occasionally breaking into arguments about the legitimacy of their sources. And he'd started teaching me to cook Swedish food. It was fun and made me feel proud of my heritage.

"Are you in any pain today?" Dr. Ezra asked.

"No, sir. Not at the moment." My knees had been swollen a few days ago, but today they were doing better. They'd flared up pretty bad the morning after the concert and I guessed my nerves had caused it, but I hadn't mentioned it to anyone. The Snowblowers were my only friends here, and I didn't want to lose them.

"I'm going to ask you a few questions about how you've been feeling lately. Most doctors use a standardized questionnaire to help us understand how a patient has felt for the last two weeks. You've been through a lot, and sometimes that can make you sad. It's okay to be sad. I want you to answer me honestly. Can you do that for me?"

"Yes, sir."

"Good. For the next few questions, your answer should be: not at all, several days, more than half the days, or nearly every day. I might stop you to clarify." I nodded. "Recently, have you had little interest or pleasure in doing things that you used to do?"

I felt tears well up. "Nearly every day." Dr. Ezra stopped and I noticed both he and my dad were looking at me. I sucked in a deep breath and stared down at my hands. "I used to run six or seven days a week. But I haven't run at all since coming here. I miss it."

His voice was stern but sympathetic. "Running isn't the best exercise for people with lupus, Ray. It is very aggravating to the joints. You're still having an active flare, according to your bloodwork, and inflammation can cause more inflammation. Your joints are pesky and painful, but we don't want organ trouble again. Some patients do get to the point where they can run again, but now isn't the time to try. How about power-walking for now?"

I nodded without looking up and he continued his questions.

"Feeling down, depressed, or hopeless?"

"Yes," I whispered.

"And when you feel that way, does anything help?"

"Drawing helps me relax, and"—I blushed and peeked at my dad—"listening to my friend play the piano. It's so beautiful and reminds me I'm not alone."

"That's great, Ray. It's good to have friends who understand what you're going through. Next question. Feeling tired or having little energy?"

"Nearly every day."

He ended the series of questions with, "How difficult have these problems made it for you to do your work, take care of things at home, or get along with other people?"

"I've been getting along fine with my friend, Charles. He seems to understand, and the same with my best friend from home, Jeffery. But I had to make my dad take me in and that's caused him and my mom a lot of stress and legal fees." I couldn't look at him when I said it. I knew he'd offered. I knew he'd rearranged his life and home for me, but Mom's old words didn't fade easily. I kept wondering when I'd become too much for him and he'd send me back.

Breathing deeply and running my fingers along the exam paper, I continued, "I know my mom was upset about how expensive my hospital stay was. My boyfriend broke up with me because I moved here." I gulped and swallowed again to stop tears I felt were dangerously close to falling.

"Ray, you are showing some clear signs of clinical depression. We are going to start you on that iron pill today, which will give you more energy. I'm going to talk to Dr. Murray about lowering your steroids because sometimes those can make you sad, too. Your X-ray from yesterday looks really good, so I'm going to clear you for light exercise. Start trying to take a walk a day. Being cooped up inside, especially when you're used to running every day, is hard. Moving to a new place is challenging too, but I'm glad you have some new friends here. Did you go to the local support group on Sunday?"

"Yes, sir."

"And what did you think?"

"It was nice to know I'm not alone. Everyone was really friendly." It had been scary to hear everyone's stories, though. I didn't want osteoporosis or to be on dialysis like so many of the women. I hadn't liked hearing lupus was the tenth most common cause of death in women aged fifteen to twenty-four, either.

"Good. I'm glad you went. So, we aren't going to treat you for depression right now, because you have a lot of things going on that might be causing it. We're going to try to reduce those things, but don't feel guilty resting or napping if you need to. We have already prepared the paperwork for your school, and even once the school year starts, we've asked them to allow you to go to the nurse and take a nap, if needed. If you have any trouble talking to them, let us know and we can help take further steps with the school if they aren't accommodating. Okay?"

He waited for me to nod, before getting up to wash and dry his hands.

He continued, "We want to work together with them to help you do the best you can do and stay healthy at the same time. We're going to have you back in two weeks to see if you're feeling any better, but if any time between now and then you want a referral to a psychiatrist or psychologist, Dr. Murray or I can write you one. Sometimes it's good to talk it out." He pulled on a pair of gloves, and said, "Now let's get started on your physical evaluation."

And as we started testing and bending all my joints, I was glad I'd worn leggings. This part always made me feel like one of my little sister's fabric dolls, twisting in someone else's hands.

We left after Dr. Murray confirmed I didn't want a psychologist referral. I told her to ask me again in two weeks.

"You can talk to me anytime you want to," Dad said in Swedish as we wound through the vivid blue hospital corridors. "You know that, right?"

"I do," I said, tucking some hair behind my ear. "I just feel guilty because you're already doing so much for me."

He stopped walking, pulled me to him, and ran a hand through my hair. "Sweetheart, you're my daughter. I'm doing what any dad would do." I nodded against his chest and he slowly released me. "All right, let's take you to Charles's. I *almost* felt guilty not telling your mom I was letting you go out to bars to listen to live music, but if he's making you feel happy, my lips are sealed."

I quirked a grin at him. He'd let me do things—go to a comedy show, hear live music, make an Instagram account—Mom would have never let me do.

"Thanks, Dad."

When he dropped me off, Charles seemed happy to see me, but he had a bit of a frantic energy to him. His hair was a little wild, standing in all directions, and it was kind of a turn-on to see it so mussed.

"Nervous?" I asked him as he led me to the living room, just to fill the silence and avoid saying something like, *You're gorgeous when you play music.*

He stopped and turned around. His obsidian eyes pinned me in place and made me breathless. "Yes, actually. This is my first international competition. I know it's just Toronto, but that's almost worse, because my family is going to be there. You don't know what my family is like, what they expect of me. 'A' is average to them. No, below average. For Caltech, too. Being valedictorian does not guarantee you admission into Caltech. My thirty-six on the ACT won't either. It is a highly competitive school and you know how long, how hard I've been striving to get in there. I need first place. Something to set me apart."

His eyes were impassioned. I stepped forward and lightly touched his forearms. He'd helped me so much recently, and I wanted to give him a little of that comfort back. Excitement coursed through me as I felt his wiry muscles. His skin was so smooth and, unlike Ross or Jeff, his arms weren't very hairy.

I tightened my fingers, realizing I needed to speak and not just awkwardly caress his arms. "You'll be brilliant."

His lopsided grin hovered over me. This close, I had to look up to see his eyes. He must've been at least six-two. Normally he appeared to have almost solid black irises, but now I could see the line between his pupil and his dark, dark brown eyes. I could get lost in that contemplative gaze.

"Thanks, Ray," he said, his dimple popping.

We held each other's eyes for a what felt like a whole minute, until I realized I was distracting him from practicing when he was already nervous. I hastily withdrew my hands. I turned so he couldn't see what I was sure were my red cheeks. I busied myself laying the newspaper I'd brought onto his coffee table before sitting down cross-legged and getting out the rest of my supplies, including my colored pastels. The music hadn't started yet, so I glanced up. Charles was staring intently at me.

I gulped, hoping I hadn't been too obvious in my reaction to his eyes. Oh, Skittles! He was going to tell me he didn't feel that way about me and then I wouldn't have any friends here. I molded my rubber eraser between my fingers. "Charles?"

He shook his head. "I'll be gone for almost a week, but I'll be back before school starts. I was going to say, if you want, I can drive you to school so that, you know, you don't have to take the bus."

I beamed. "Really?" I couldn't keep the excitement and relief out of my voice.

He raked a hand through his hair, disheveling it further, before walking to the piano. "Yeah, I don't mind."

"Thanks, that would be wonderful." I couldn't keep the grin off my face as I gazed at his shoulders. I'd been dreading taking the bus.

Charles began his two-song sequence that I'd grown to love as I started to sketch a copy of a picture of the band. I'd printed it from Charles's birthday concert. It was a perfect thing to sketch because the dark interior and bright stage lights created romantic shadows. It would also be a challenge with the instruments, especially the guitars—hands were never easy.

I'd gotten so into my work I hadn't even noticed the room had fallen silent or Charles had walked up behind me until I heard his intake of breath above me. I turned and met his eyes, suddenly self-conscious. I had to control the urge to hide my sketch.

"That is so cool," he said. Butterfly wings fluttered in my chest and not across my cheeks for once. "Can I send it to the guys?"

"Sure." I moved my hands away, even as I wondered whether it warranted showing to the guys. "I mean, if you think they'd like to see it."

"Ooooh, yea-ah!" he said, and I couldn't resist a grin as his Michigander accent popped out. He snapped some photos with his phone. "This is awesome. We look like rock stars."

Maybe I'd been looking at it too long, but I just saw the flaws: Charles's hand wasn't quite right, and I didn't like the glare on James's glasses.

"It's just missing one thing," he said.

I looked down, unable to figure out what it was, then up at him.

"You."

"What? I'm not in the band."

"You could be. Do you have a free period next year?" When I nodded, he said, "Take choir. James suggested it. Your voice is nice but could use a little training." He motioned to the piano. "I didn't get here overnight. People really liked the duet. James's voice is so nice and deep; yours is high and sweet. Artistically, you complement each other well. We wouldn't want you in all the songs, since that would change the style too much, but we could do a few covers. People love covers. We even talked about writing a song or two for you."

My mouth hung open. "You guys actually want me as a Snowblower?"

He looked down and scuffed his sock, like he was nervous. "Yep."

I jumped up and squealed. I could tell from the look on his face he was startled, but I couldn't help grabbing his forearms and jumping up and down. "I would love to be in your band," I said breathlessly. "I don't need study hall. You got yourself a backup singer."

He beamed down at me and I quickly dropped my hands. "Anyway, I should probably take you home. I need to pack for the trip."

"Sure," I said and hurried to the sink to wash the pastels off my hands before gathering my stuff. But I paused before I put away my sketchbook. "Do you want the band sketch?"

"You'd give it to me?"

I laughed. "Yes, of course! I mean, you've been such a good friend, and you've driven me all over the place." I gently tore it from the book and held it out to him. "Just be careful touching it, because it'll smear. I have a sealant spray I can bring over and apply next time I'm here."

He took it with a look of reverence I didn't think my drawing deserved. Before I turned back to finish tidying up, I burst out laughing.

"What?"

When I could finally talk, I said between snorts, "Your arms are covered in pastels. Sorry, I grabbed you when I got excited. I'm a messy drawer."

"It's okay," he said with his one dimple flashing and went to wash off the rainbow and black fingerprints.

When we got to my place, I leaned over and gave him a big hug. It felt so good to hold him—firm, warm, and safe. His scent, a little like incense and uniquely him, lingered. I didn't want to let go. I enjoyed the heat of his wiry chest too much. Dad gave hugs here and there, but hugging Charles reminded me how nice it felt to be held. Here I didn't have Ross, Jeff, and my sisters hugging me every day.

"Good luck, but you won't need it. You'll do great." I pulled back and opened the door. As an afterthought, I added, "You can call me if you get bored with your family over there. It'll be lonely here without you." Then I jumped out and hollered, "Bye!" before he could answer.

He waved once, an unreadable expression on his face, before backing up the car. Those cicadas in my chest buzzed faster. Charles was brilliant and talented. The only things people ever said about me were I was "a pretty girl," "a sweet girl." He'd never end up with an average, broken girl like me. When Charles dated someone, it'd probably be with the other perfect SAT scorer he'd meet at his international piano competition. Charles was a perfectionist. He would wait, patient and calculated, for someone perfect like him.

It didn't matter if I liked him. He was better as a friend than as nothing. I headed to the door, suddenly a little moody, shuffling my feet. My only friend here would be gone a week. I'd miss him. Jeez Louise, I'd miss him, and I hoped he'd call me.

···
TEN

Charles

The drive to Toronto was long. Tediously long. And full of my parents' questions about when I'd turn in my college applications. Duh, the answer was the first few weeks of school. I'd planned to do early action everywhere. Why not?

As we drove through the bland, green Canadian countryside of south Ontario, I pictured the sharp San Gabriel Mountains framing Pasadena. It wouldn't be flat and humid like it was here. I felt a trickle of sweat roll down my back. Baba was too cheap to turn on the AC, not wanting to get the costlier gas on the Canadian side of the border. Robotics camp, school, competitive piano lessons, Chinese school, and such my parents paid for without question. Everything else, I was on my own. And they were unbelievably frugal.

They'd only purchased the Forester so I could complete all my activities. And the Forester had been a fight. It was a Japanese car, but it was also the best and cheapest used car option that provided great snow safety. They'd relented, and I fixed computers and did the snowblowing to afford my hobbies. I was lucky the street we lived on had many snowbirds who went to Florida for months at a time. Not only was it obvious to leave the driveway unplowed, marking your house as vacant, it was illegal not to plow the sidewalk. They'd been more than happy to pay me to do it while they were gone.

"Baba, please." I finally broke. "I'm getting a headache. Turn on the AC."

"Jia Jia, here," Ma said and turned it on low, rolling up the window. If it was just us, Ma always called me the familiar version of my Chinese name, Jiawei. She was sweating too. Low wasn't much, but at least it was something.

A little while later, we pulled into a familiar restaurant. Da Jo Jo and Da Jo Ma had flown in with Wàipó, my grandma. Their two daughters couldn't come because of school obligations, but Da Jo Jo and Da Jo Ma had wanted to see Ma. Emily had just started her first year of medical school at the University of California, San Francisco, and Jane was going to be a senior at Berkeley studying programing. This summer she had an internship at Google; neither could get away.

I got out and greeted my family, Er Jo Jo and Er Jo Ma, who we were staying with, and their twins, Megan and Marcus. The twins were high school seniors like me.

"Eh, I hate the English translations at this place. I'm always tempted to type them a new menu," Megan complained. "Slippery meat. Ew. No, thanks. That just sounds so gross. It's not even gross."

I laughed. Slippery meat did not sound good. And she was right that dish tasted much better than the name implied.

Wàipó entered with Da Jo Jo and Da Jo Ma, all looking tired. We stood to greet our grandma, who smiled when she saw Marcus and me. "Yun Ye and Yun Yu, how tall you both are."

I looked at Da Jo Jo, her son, whose name she'd called me. He had a pained look on his face.

"Ma, this is Jiawei and Liqiang, your grandsons," Ma told her mother gently. I'd known her Alzheimer's was progressing and she had been losing her English, but I hadn't realized it was this bad. She'd lived with us, helped raised me until I was ten.

Her eyes brightened and she then hugged me, "Jia Jia, you are so handsome now. So tall." She turned to Marcus. "Liqiang, you're getting fat."

Megan snorted but straightened her face to embrace Wàipó.

"Ming Ming, your bangs are so pretty," she greeted Megan warmly, and then we sat down.

As the meal progressed, Wàipó seemed fine, but I heard Da Jo Jo whisper to Ma that she'd been getting worse. After the meal ended, I went with Wàipó and my cousins to their house. My older uncle and aunt and parents went to a hotel nearby. Marcus and Megan sat in the den with Wàipó, but I practiced piano instead for several hours before heading to bed.

I glanced up only once at the bright stage lights and audience before drawing a breath and starting. The Liszt piece flew from my fingers as my hands skated back and forth across the keyboard, twisting and crossing over each other. Then I heard the slip—the wrong key.

It took everything I had to keep going, knowing now there was no way I'd make first. At least I could still place.

I sucked in two deep breaths waiting for the applause to end before switching to my jazz piece, "Sweet Georgia Brown." While it wasn't easy, it wasn't as difficult as the Liszt. As it finished and I stood to bow, a deep, crushing disappointment coiled inside me.

I'd missed one note.

Walking off the stage, I wondered if I could have studied

more. If I should have practiced more and, ungraciously, if I'd allowed my friendship with Ray to distract me from the competition. For so long, I'd wanted Caltech more than anything. Now I wasn't sure everything I'd done had been enough. This was why I just had the band: they understood school was more important than anything.

Hours passed before the judges finally announced the results. My mouth fell open, before I stood. Second place. I'd listened to the competition and knew the songs I'd chosen had been the most difficult. The Liszt was fast and moved across the entire keyboard. Hearing my placement, I was able to breathe again, glad the risk had at least paid off—no one else had dared to play it.

Yet, when we sat down to dinner that night with my family, I was disappointed that after months and months of practice, it still wasn't enough. Da Jo Jo hadn't said anything, but I saw on his and my aunt's faces that they were weighting their daughters' striking successes against my clear failure. Baba had told me to practice more before the next concert. Then he joked that maybe I'd be at Michigan after all. The words stung.

Megan said not to worry, but she'd always been the nicest, least motivated cousin. After dinner, Wàipó went to bed. Megan and Marcus had asked if I wanted to go hang out with them and their friends, but I locked myself in the piano room instead and sat for hours playing—perfecting. I would not be stuck in Ann Arbor another four years. I wanted to go to Los Angeles. Eventually, my fingers cramped, and I headed up to Marcus's room for the night.

I grabbed what I needed to shower and thought about everything I could do to ensure this didn't happen again. I had three messages from Ray and decided to text her in the morning. It was late; even Marcus was already back home and asleep. Part of me wanted to talk to her, though—tell her how disappointed I was in myself. I wanted to confide in her how scary and sad it'd been to have my grandma call me my uncle's name.

Marcus woke me by turning on the overhead lights. "Oh, sorry," he said apologetically. "I forgot you were here." He yawned. "When did you go to bed, anyway?"

"I don't know," I replied around a yawn of my own. I'd been so disappointed in myself; I'd just kept pushing—just one more time.

"Come on, even you can't work all the time. Family first. Dim sum time."

I got dressed, but couldn't stop thinking about how I could fix this for next time. Before I went downstairs, I remembered to text Ray back.

Morning, I placed 2nd.

A few minutes later, my phone buzzed. *Wow! I knew you'd do great.*

My stomach summersaulted. Maybe second place wasn't too bad, but still, I'd expected myself to do better.

Thanks. What are you up to today?

I'm going to a lecture with Dad. Then gtg to school and have a meeting with the teachers about lupus /:

Why?

I dunno. The doctor asked me to. They think I'll miss extra school, maybe. You?

I could imagine hearing her voice and seeing her shrug, and it made me laugh. *I'm spending time with my family, Wàipó is here.*

Wàipó <3 tell her I said hi!

Moisture gathered at the corners of my eyes, but I blinked it away. Wàipó had met Ray so many times when she'd lived with us, but now Ray wouldn't even be able to talk to her. She'd lost her English. Even if she hadn't, my grandmother probably wouldn't remember her.

I will.

I've been practicing some covers. I can't wait to sing with the Snowblowers!!

Her text brought the smile back to my face. At least she wasn't as disappointed in me as I was with myself.

"Charles!" rang out through the house, and I hastily texted back, *gtg. I'll be back Sunday evening. See you Tuesday at 8?*

Back to school (:

The bedroom door flew open again and Marcus strolled in. "Hey, everyone is waiting." He looked at my face and then phone, before asking, "Do you have a girlfriend?"

"What? No," I said, sliding my phone away.

"You just have this ridiculously happy grin on your face that my friends normally have when they're texting their girlfriends."

I hurried down the stairs to our dumpling breakfast. Did I really have a look when I talked to Ray?

···

ELEVEN

Ray

"Nils, wait," the speaker said to my dad as we were leaving the latest Brown Bag. He'd talked about micro-living and the newest complex his architecture firm had helped design, a residential tower in downtown Detroit. Dad had asked many questions, since it also provided a reduced rent option that was right up his economic heart's alley. Dad was a social-economist and providing workers the ability to live safely and affordably downtown? He was interested one-hundred and ten percent.

We stopped and turned. The speaker was a handsome, middle-aged man with silver laced, light brown hair. "Is this one of your graduate students? We're always looking for promising recruits."

Dad put a hand on my shoulder. "This is Ray, my daughter."

"Daughter?" His eyes widened, and I felt myself cringe on Dad's behalf. I mean, sure, Dad looked younger than he was, but it wasn't entirely unthinkable that he could have a daughter my age. Fortunately, he recovered quickly and extended a hand. "Ray, nice to meet you. I'm Larry Davis. I'm a senior partner at Bartley, an architecture and design firm based here and in

Detroit."

I shook his hand. "Nice to meet you, sir, Rayanne Ericson."

"Is that a Southern accent?"

"Yes, sir. I was raised outside Savannah."

His face lit up. "How lovely. My parents have a place on Hilton Head. They're snowbirds now. Are you visiting your dad?"

"Actually, Ray's living with me now," Dad chimed in when I hesitated. "She'll be a junior at Rosalind this year. You have a son about her age, right?"

He smiled and looked at me anew. "Yes, Greg. He'll be a junior at Rosalind, too. I'd love for you two to meet. I'd have to drag him to a Brown Bag, but you looked like you enjoyed it?"

"Yes, sir. I'd like to be an architect."

"Michigan has a wonderful architecture program. And camp. You should consider their three-week architecture camp next summer. They often visit some of our firm's projects."

His phone rang, and he glanced at it. I made a mental note to look up their camp, even though I was sure my savings from waiting tables wouldn't cover the cost.

"I need to take this, but I'll tell Greg to keep an eye out for you. If you don't get in touch, I'll give your dad his number. He wants to study architecture too. I hope to see you around, Ray."

He answered the phone with a wave goodbye. Dad and I stopped at his favorite coffee shop—The Cup, a quirky little place with local artwork all over—for a quick bite before heading to Rosalind Franklin High School for my healthcare meeting.

Surprisingly, the last week of summer had passed faster than I thought it would. I tried all the suggestions Dr. Ezra had mentioned, and the iron did help me feel less tired. Walking wasn't running, but it had been good to get outside and stretch my legs. I'd been doing it early in the mornings, so the sun wouldn't be as bad, and it did make me feel happier. Dad had gone with me most times and pointed out all his interests on the campus—mainly, that was the Economics Department, his faculty office, and The Cup. I'd liked his office in the economics building, and going to the Brown Bags had been fascinating.

Everything here was so different, more urbane than back home. And I loved it. Back home, it'd been all about the beach, the marsh, going fishing, and drinking beer in someone's backyard, not that I ever drank any. Ann Arbor was like downtown Savannah, small enough to walk, and with all the college students, there were so many cafés, coffee shops, and boutique stores.

Dad did everything with me with a smile. We'd been having fun cooking together or going out to eat a variety of food I'd rarely get back home. Dad would eat just about anything, and loved authentic cuisine. Plus, here it was just Dad and me, no spouse or siblings, and I'd never had attention like this in my life. I thought maybe he was honestly as glad to have me there as I was to be with him. He certainly never made me feel like a burden the way Mom had.

He patted my shoulder as we headed into my school healthcare meeting. Dad and my doctors had coordinated this so the school might comprehend lupus and how it might affect my year. I couldn't remember ever having a parent-teacher meeting, and I wore a dress and cardigan like I'd have worn to church. I wanted to make a good first impression.

As the meeting progressed, everyone seemed understanding that I'd miss more school because of doctors' appointments, and might occasionally leave early if I got too tired. Well, everyone except the Spanish teacher. She frowned as she exited, practically rolling her eyes at me.

"Do you think it's too late to switch to Mandarin?" I whispered to Dad.

He glanced at me, then smiled and caught the assistant principal before he left. He was fluent in Mandarin from earning his Ph.D. in economics and was a little obsessed with the Chinese economy. Plus, there were really cool opportunities for architecture students in China.

"Sorry, Mr. Rybinski, but Ray thought she would rather take Mandarin One. Is that possible?"

The assistant principal looked like he might argue for a minute, so I said, "One of my best friends is Chinese, so he can help me if I need tutoring."

He looked down curiously. "Who?"

"Charles Wong."

"Charles? Well, that's great! He's one of our top students. He's a team captain in the Robotics Club and he's in the running for valedictorian. No one's even close to him, but of course we have a whole year, so things could change. Great kid. With him as a friend, I'm sure you'll settle in in no time." He scratched his beard. "You know, there isn't Chinese level one at that time. I'll have to move your schedule around, but I'll try to see if I can get you and Charles into the same lunch section. No promises, but I'll try. I'm sure it's been a rough few weeks for you with getting a new diagnosis and new city. If I can, I will."

The weekend passed in a blur, with Dad hunched over his desk tweaking syllabi and me drawing out my anxiety over starting the new school year. Now here I was on Tuesday morning on the first day of school. The outfit I'd laid out suddenly didn't seem right, but I glanced at the clock and realized I didn't have much time, so I just slipped into the jeans and fitted charcoal crew neck T-shirt I'd laid out. By the time I grabbed my bookbag and purse, I barely made it to the curb before Charles's familiar Forester pulled up.

"Hiya, Charles, the second-place international piano star!" I said as I slipped into the car.

"Second place," he grumbled. "That means more practice before the next one in October."

I thumped him on the shoulder. "Hey, at least I know a fan of your music. I like hearing you practice."

He shook his head, but his grumbling was undone by the grin he couldn't quite keep off his face. It made the butterflies in my chest flutter with approval.

I couldn't control my curiosity. "So when is your lunch?"

"Sixth period, with Knox."

"Really?" I bounced in my seat. "Me too!"

Mr. Rybinski *had* been able to help me out. I asked about Charles's cousins and Wàipó, but he was a little more reserved than normal on the ten-minute drive to school. I was sure he was nervous too. He put more pressure on himself than anyone I'd ever met. I knew his parents were strict, but I also knew the real driving force behind Charles was Charles. He pretended it was them, but they really loved him so much. They might grumble, but they'd love him no matter what, as long as he worked hard and was a good person.

My heart skidded as we walked across the parking lot. What would this new school be like? During the few minutes before classes started, Charles introduced me to a few students and teachers, though I knew I'd never remember everyone's name. I waved in relief to Kevin, who was holding a giant music case. He was a senior, so I knew we likely wouldn't have classes together, but at least he was familiar, even if he'd been the least friendly of the Snowblowers so far.

"What is that?" I asked curiously.

Kevin laughed. "Double bass. I play bass and double bass. Charles is in orchestra too, but he plays piano."

"Wow, your instrument is huge."

"You'd be amazed what I can do with it." He exchanged an amused look with Charles, and I felt my cheeks heat at the innuendo. He added, "Yep, so sorry, gotta run or it'll be impossible to navigate the halls with my *huge* double bass."

Kevin made it down the hall just in time because, less than two minutes later, the bell chimed, and we scampered to our classes.

My nerves continued to hitch up throughout the day as everyone teased me about my accent. I hadn't thought it that strong, especially compared to my friends back home.

But…

My "hi" was wrong.

I was too polite.

No one said y'all.

Heck, everything I said was apparently too country. I was so tired of everyone teasing me, I was starting to feel like a real hick. And everyone here seemed so smart. Maybe it was being so close to the university and that so many students were professors' kids, but intelligence here was the new cool. Back home, I'd been considered decently smart, but here I was feeling run-of-the-mill.

By the time lunch rolled around, I'd had choir, AP Geography, AP Chemistry, world literature, and AP Art. Geography, lit, and art had been great, chemistry was a little intimidating, and choir made me hope I didn't disappoint the Snowblowers.

I walked into the cafeteria, clutching my lunch bag. Knox waved me over. I chuckled, surprised he could see me through the hair dangling in his eyes. He led me to their table as Charles waited for hot lunch. Since he was a senior like Charles, he also wasn't in any of my classes.

"Ray, that drawing," Knox said when we sat down. "Dope."

"Thanks." If I'd known everyone would be talking about it, I would have polished it more before giving it away.

"It's great you're joining the band. You can help me pitch my drum solos," he said with a mischievous grin.

"Sure," I said bumping his shoulder. I liked Knox.

"Knew I could count on you." Knox gave me a fist bump.

My lips turned up, and I started feeling a little better about my day so far. To Knox, I was one of the guys.

Charles headed toward our table, flashing me a dimply grin that lit up his whole face.

As our eyes met, I couldn't control the buzzing of my heart's cicadas, which grew stronger whenever Charles was near. I was excited to talk to him. I suddenly couldn't wait to tell him about my day and hear about his.

Shoot, I realized as I tried to slow my racing heart. I didn't like Charles as a friend—I *liked* him.

TWELVE

Charles

I'd watched Ray duck into Algebra II next door to my AP Calculus, but it had been too crowded for me to get her attention. Lunch had been a rushed affair, and I couldn't wait for the bell to ring to hear about her first day. Maybe I needed to start packing my lunch so I could sit with her the whole time, like Knox had. I was going to be so busy, but I wanted to share a little of my free time with her.

AP Calculus, like most of my classes today, had wasted little time with introductions and most had been digging right in. I was taking six APs and was starting to feel it: AP Physics, AP Government, AP English, AP Chinese, AP Spanish, and AP Calculus. AP Chinese and orchestra were my only reasonably easy classes. The piano I'd studied for years, and I was fluent in Chinese but just needed work on my writing.

In addition to my classes, I'd also be in the competitive Robotics Club, participating in piano competitions, and applying to college. I was overwhelmed already, but if I wanted any chance at getting into Caltech, I needed way above a 4.0. I had to get the highest GPA in my class, and could only do that with a heavy AP load.

I started counting the seconds until the bell rang and was out of my seat, eager to catch Ray as soon as it sounded.

One by one, classmates trickled out of the classroom. I heard her chiming laughter before I saw her, followed by her voice. "That is the worst Southern I've ever heard. I do *not* sound like that."

A deep voice followed: "Uh-huh, sure do."

It was a terrible Southern accent, which I saw belonged to a junior on the football team. I looked up at his broad frame and sandy blond hair and suddenly felt every bit the scrawny, nerdy robotics champion I was. I was just about to walk away and text Ray to meet at the car when she called, "Hi, Charles!" with a eager wave.

"Hi." I hoped I sounded as sure of myself as her new friend. I should have known just as soon as Ray met some more people, everyone would like her. What wasn't to like? She was considerate, amusing, and stunningly pretty. I had no idea why she was so self-conscious. No, that was a lie. I thought maybe years of her mom putting her down made her believe the worse in herself. If she saw herself as I did there would be no stopping her.

He nodded at me. "Hey man, what's up? I think we have a class together."

I looked at him but couldn't remember. I shook my head. "I'm not sure. Maybe AP Government or AP Spanish?"

He laughed. "The look on your face, man. AP Government. Don't look so surprised. Jocks can take an AP too."

I held out my hand, wanting to be the better person, not seeing what I'd said to make him bristle. "I'm Charles."

"Greg Davis." He shook my hand firmly and swiveled to Ray. "I got to run to football. See you tomorrow. I'll work on my impressions. Dad's going to be thrilled we have a class together. He couldn't stop talking about you, and it seems like, for once, everything Dad said was on point." With a wink at her, he hurried down the hallway.

Ray turned to me. "I need to go to my locker. Do you?" I nodded, wondering how she knew that guy's dad. "Want to come with me, then we can go to yours?" I nodded again, so she kept talking. "So how was everything? How were your classes?"

"It'll be a tough year," I said with a sigh.

She stopped and looked at me, her enchanting eyes full of compassion. "Yeah?" she asked, stepping close enough her scent wafted over me. Jasmine. Always Jasmine.

I nodded, unable to speak for a moment with how her gaze seemed to pierce through me, and how she in my personal space blocked out everything else—the bright, hot noisy corridor shifted to her calm, glacial-blue eyes.

I blinked and said, "I'm taking all APs and I'm going to apply early, so these will be the last grades on my transcripts. But schools have been known to kick you out if your grades drop in second semester. Everything counts."

Her delicate fingers touched my arm. "I'm here if you ever want to talk about it."

Her genuineness radiated from her face and the warmth of her hand.

"Thanks, Ray." All I wanted was to sweep her into my arms. But for her, this was just friendship. We held each other's gaze until she turned pink. Oh, crap. I hope she couldn't tell what she did to me. I nodded and stepped back. She moved her hand and opened her locker.

"So, what classes are you taking?" she called with her back to me. When I told her she said, "Jeez Louise, Charles! No wonder you're stressed. And you do the band and piano? *And* robotics?"

"Yep, so Tuesdays and Thursdays, starting week after next, you'll need to take the bus in the afternoons. Then Friday mornings because of orchestra. Sorry."

"Yeah, no problem," she said swiftly as she finished with

her locker and followed me to mine. "Charles?" She said my name so tentatively, I stopped to look at her.

"Ray?"

Her cheeks were still pink. "I decided to take Mandarin. You know, Chinese level one. I don't want to burden you, because wow, you have so much going on, but I was hoping we could talk in Chinese some, so I could practice. But maybe you won't have time."

My heart raced at the excuse to spend more time with her. "I'll make time for you, Ray, but it'll have to be on the weekend."

She smiled. "That'll work! Whenever, you can squeeze me in."

"It's not all bad. The band is my highlight. Even the piano. I like that music is so structured. Organized. It is the best calm."

"You play amazing."

I shrugged and fiddled with my locker, but her words filled me with pride. Then I sighed, realizing I probably needed all my books. I momentarily became absorbed in the task of loading them into my backpack.

"Do you not like Greg?" Her question startled me. I turned to see her chewing her lower lip. "You guys seemed tense. Is there something I should know about him?"

The way she fiddled with her backpack straps, I'd say she was nervous. She always fiddled with something—her shorts, a straw wrapper, the seatbelt strap—when she was anxious. She was anxious a lot.

Jealousy swept over me. Of course she'd like Greg. Greg was on the football team, and what had I even been thinking? Most girls would never give a guy like me a chance. I knew that from last year when I'd asked Lauren, a friendly auburn-haired girl from Spanish class, to Homecoming. She'd been polite, but whispers had come back to me: she couldn't believe *I'd* asked *her*. I'm pretty sure she ended up going with some jock. I'd been so embarrassed, I thought I'd never go down that road again. Sure, I'd like to date, but that had sucked.

I tried to close those thoughts with my locker. It took all I had to shrug. "I don't know him."

She stepped closer and her voice dropped to a whisper. "But I mean, you guys didn't seem like you liked each other."

"I have no idea what you mean." The words felt like ash in my mouth, but somehow, I'd gotten them out. I enjoyed being around her so much. I'd rather have her as a friend than nothing.

"Yeah?"

It was hard to think with her scent enveloping me again. My shirt was starting to cling to my skin. I had nervous habits of my own. She was standing close enough I could feel the heat coming off her. She couldn't be so naïve she didn't realize we both liked her, could she? Her face held confusion, worry, and uncertainty.

"Yeah, I'm sorry I offended him. I was paying attention to the syllabus, not students."

"Okay, cool. I just want to make better friends…"

"Like me?"

She bumped my shoulder. "Duh."

After that, the conversation turned back to school and our classes. It seemed like in no time we were at the car, and then her dad's condo, saying our "see you tomorrows" .

I went right to work when I got home, because the guys were going to come over at seven thirty to practice. I thought about asking Ray to come but decided against it. My crush on her was getting out of control, and I wanted to ask James about it privately. Out of all of us, James had the most experience dating.

Kevin, like me, had never had a girlfriend. He was short, and it was hard on him. Girls might complain about the expectations for them, but I'd seen the impact of height discrimination on Kevin. As a result, Kevin was rarely, if ever, nice to attractive girls. I didn't know if it was a defense mechanism, or he was bitter. Either way, he was a horrible choice for asking dating advice.

Knox's dating life I wasn't sure about. I thought he'd briefly dated some girl from his synagogue. But he was too close to Ray and we all had lunch together. If I asked him, it could make things weird between us. Plus, he had his own girl issues he never talked about. When he'd seen James's little sister today, the most wistful look passed over his face and I wondered why he didn't do anything about it. They even wanted to go to college in the same city, so what was holding him back?

So really James was the only choice for dating advice in my friends circle.

By the time the guys came over, I'd finished all my homework and eaten a quick dinner. We fell into rehearsals after everyone quizzed James on his first day of college. It sounded amazing, and I could not wait, even if James was still living at home to save money.

During one of the breaks, when Kevin and Knox went upstairs to grab drinks, I asked James, "Do you think Ray could ever like me?"

"She likes you," he said.

"But like"—I dropped my voice—"*like*, like me."

He looked at me a moment, shrugged, and went back to flipping through the sheet music. "I don't know why she moved here, but I can tell you've been a good friend to her. I know she likes you." He shook his head. "It's hard to say if she wants to get in your pants or not, but you could ask her."

"I mean," I said, fumbling with my words. "Do you think she'd date a guy like me?"

He stopped his flipping and raised an eyebrow. "Asian?"

I nodded, even though I'd been thinking more nerdy, Asian—the whole thing. I did wonder that too. It'd never seemed to bother Ray before, but that was as friends. The Lauren situation had been a blow to my pride. She hadn't said, but I'd wondered...It was hard not to be self-conscious.

"You're asking me if I think she's racist?"

He shook his head when I shrugged. It sounded horrible to say aloud. To think that of her.

"Man, I don't know. I've thought I was cool with some girls, only to find out they"—he used air quotes—"'don't date Black guys.'" He rolled his eyes. "The world is changing, but there will always be a few who surprise you. Like, who is this? Because, damn. They. Are. Racist. I don't think Ray's like that, but who can say?"

"I meant more I'm, well, who I am."

He leaned back and belly laughed. "Oh, you meant beauty and the geek?"

I shrugged again.

He shook his head. "I'm not as cool as Knox thinks," he mumbled. "I don't know. I can tell you, she looks at you different from the rest of us. Now I don't know if that's because you were there for her when she was going through some personal things, like you mentioned, or it's something else. Like I said, why don't you ask her?"

I swallowed. *Ask her?* I didn't think I could. I didn't want to make her feel awkward if this was one-sided. And likely it was. No, I couldn't do that to her.

"Thanks, James."

"Sure, anytime." He gestured to the guys walking down the stairs. "Should we start back up?"

We played till my ma kicked them out at ten thirty. I felt a lot better after playing and talking to James, but was still confused. Soon I'd probably be absorbed in my studies and wouldn't even have time for her. Yet Ray made me want to find extra time, time I otherwise would have spent tinkering with computers or playing games online.

I didn't think I was brave enough to test her feelings yet, but for now we had plans to study together and she'd agreed to be in our band. She'd be around. Still, I couldn't help thinking about her as I drifted off to sleep, wondering if her lips would taste as good as she smelled and remembering how she'd felt pressed against me when we hugged.

But for now, she had to remain a dream.

THIRTEEN

Ray

My alarm clock blared at me for the start of the second week of school, a loud wailing beside my ear. I reached to turn it off and winced at the pain in my wrist and fingers as I did. In the morning light, I could see they were slightly swollen again. I got up and made a note in the small planner Dr. Murray and Dr. Ezra had asked me to keep. I tried to think of what I'd done this weekend that might have set me off—coffee outside with Dad too long, staying up too late Saturday night studying with Charles, anxiety about the new school—it could be anything. It'd be better if I could go for a run; that'd always helped me before to clear my mind, and become too tired to overthink everything.

But I couldn't run.

Dad had classes later today and was still sleeping, so I slipped in my headphones and played a country mix Jeffery and I liked from Spotify. When "Cruise" by Florida Georgia Line came on, a song Jeffery and I had sung since we practically had training wheels, something tugged inside me and I opened my Instagram my dad had let me set up. I scrolled through some pictures of my old classmates with a wave of nostalgia. Carolyn was all over Ross, and if they weren't dating yet, it wasn't for her lack of trying.

I shut it away. I was glad I wasn't with Ross anymore, but dagnabbit, I'd thought Carolyn was one of my best friends. We'd spoken twice and exchanged a handful of texts in the near two months I'd been here. Jeffery was as loyal as he'd ever been, but besides him, I only traded a few texts with my friend, Ava. Of course, I'd had clipped words with Mom and video-chatted with my little sisters, Gracie Mae and Mary Beth. I knew they missed me. Matthew, my little brother, thought he was too cool to say it, but I had a feeling he might too.

No one else. Was Ross right that I was a "pretty girl?" To me it implied I had nothing else. No substance. I wanted to be liked, like Jefferey liked me, for more than that. But maybe that's all I was. All I had been. I certainly hadn't had tons of friends when I was an awkward middle schooler or freshmen. I'd gotten friends with my curves, and it had never sat right with me. I wasn't going to say no to being better looking than I used to be, but I wanted to be liked for me, as well. But, maybe there was something wrong with me.

I shuffled to grab a coffee because I needed to get ready or I'd be late for school. I frowned taking my first pills of the day; there was certainly *something* wrong with me. I blinked back my tears. I wasn't a kid anymore who could knock on Jeffery's door and say, "Let's bike to the dock," when I was sad.

I'll make new friends, I told myself—even if, so far, the only friends were Charles and the band. Likely, out of guilt, too. Charles probably just felt sorry for me. No one like him had ever wanted to be my friend before.

I tried to make a mental list of who stood out, but in the first week, only Greg Davis had gone out of his way to be friendly. He was interested in architecture, plus he was a junior. Maybe we could hang out some because Charles was too busy for a needy friend. I groaned over how shy I was feeling as I washed my face. But I couldn't ignore the fear that I'd make the same types of friends as back home, friends who hadn't cared I was now sick.

I frowned at my reflection. If you didn't know me, I just had a girlish roundness to my cheeks. If you knew me, you'd know the steroids were making my face bloated. I took my hair down from its bun and ran a brush through it. As I brushed, large chunks came out, nearly filling the brush. I gasped.

I'd never liked how my hair set me apart as a kid, but it was who I was. Hair was one of the pretty things about me—about anyone. While I didn't want to be know for exclusively my looks, I didn't want to lose them entirely. I examined myself carefully in the mirror and didn't notice any bald spots—yet—but I'd read lupus could cause hair loss. Joints hurting, losing hair, and a bloated face: it was an ominous start to Monday morning. I whispered a silent prayer that today was a fluke as I cleaned my brush.

Saying the prayer sent a wave of dread through me. I needed to find a church here—like, weeks ago—but I hadn't been brave enough to go alone. Dad was an atheist, Charles a Buddhist, and Knox Jewish. I could've talked to Kevin or James, since they both went, but I wasn't as comfortable with them. James was older and intimidatingly good-looking, and Kevin didn't seem too keen on me.

A thought for later, I decided when I saw the time on my phone. Rushing to my room, I slipped into a sundress and sweater. I had long legs and normally didn't like wearing dresses to school because they were always shorter on me. I was more likely to get a dress code violation, but it was supposed to be in the high eighties today. I'd been as hot as a popsicle on the Fourth of July in art with my jeans on Friday because the room didn't have AC. I'd laughed when a girl next to me had told me this, thinking it was a joke, but she'd been serious. It'd been pouring rain and humid too. I couldn't have imagined a classroom, anywhere inside, without AC, at least not back home. So, sweater and freezing in some classes, but at least I wouldn't be sweating in Art.

Because I dilly-dallied feeling sorry for myself, I didn't have time for breakfast, so I threw a protein bar in my purse and ran out the door. I'd feel sick from the pill I just took, if I didn't eat it soon. My phone dinged in the elevator, and I raced toward the curb where Charles was already waiting.

"Sorry, sorry," I murmured as I slipped in.

"No worries, I just got here," he said with his usual calmness, drumming a beat on the steering wheel.

We talked about Ms. Cheng, the Mandarin teacher, and how to get an A with her. Before we knew it, we were at school. I steadied my breathing as I got out of the car. My nerves were already flaring up my lupus. I thought again that it'd all be so much better if I could run. I rubbed some warmth into my numb white fingers. Charles always blasted the AC; he was the opposite of me in that regard.

Greg waved at us in the parking lot and got out of an expensive-looking Ford truck. It felt like Ross was walking toward me all over again, except with warm brown eyes instead of ice gray. I pushed that away. Greg was not Ross, and I needed to try to make more friends.

"You ran out of math on Friday," Greg said. "I was going to get your number and see if you wanted to do anything this weekend, being new and all."

I stumbled in surprise but quickly caught myself. "That's awfully chivalrous of you."

He chuckled. "Did you do anything this weekend?"

"Charles and I hung out." I risked a smile at Charles, and my heart raced about as fast as a hummingbird's wings when his dimple flashed back. "We've been friends a long time," I added lamely.

Greg looked at Charles. "Cool. Hey, man."

Charles nodded.

"How's football going?" I asked, trying to be friendly as

he fell in step beside us.

"Great! We're going to dominate this year." He flashed me a grin so cocky I almost stumbled a second time, stunned by how much he looked like Ross's doppelganger.

I wasn't sure I wanted a friend like him, though I reminded myself Greg was not Ross. I should give him a chance. Charles was so busy, I couldn't be taking up all his free time. I wanted to make some of my own friends.

"I'm sure you'll have a good season." Shoot, I wished I had something better to add.

"You guys play any sports?" Football started in the summer, but all the other fall teams would start this week or next.

I think Charles saw the misery in my shoulder slump because he spoke up. "Nah, I'm way too busy, and Ray's likely too busy too. She's taking three APs and doesn't have a free period."

Warmth infused my chest at his defense because, golly gee whiz, it hurt not to be joining cross-country this season. Before I could mouth *thank you* to Charles, because I was not ready to talk about my lupus yet, Greg nudged me. "With legs like yours, I would think you did something." He cocked an eyebrow expectantly.

I cleared my throat, tugging at the hem of my skirt. Ross had always said I had nice legs, but he was my boyfriend. I didn't even know Greg.

"Fuck, that came out wrong. What I was trying to say was, you look like a runner—those muscles came from somewhere," he stammered out.

"I used to do cross-country and track, but I'm not sure about now." I cast another quick glance at Charles, and he gave me a slight smile. "Like Charles said, I might be too busy. And I'll have driving school…"

"Sounds like excuses," he said with a laugh. "All right, Savannah, I'll see you in math."

I looked at Charles. "Charles," I started, but my voice

faded.

He leaned in, almost like he had ESP. "Don't worry, your health is your own business. I'll never mention it unless you ask me to."

"Thanks," I said in a tight voice. It felt too good to have him whispering against my neck.

"Friends, remember?" he said, bumping my shoulder.

I couldn't resist throwing my arm around his waist and giving him a brief squeeze. "Friends," I whispered back and slid my arm away even though I wanted to keep holding him. Snuggling against him made me feel so warm and safe. I missed hugs something fierce; I'd never realized how much I depended on them.

At the start of last period, Greg slipped into the seat beside me and slapped a paper on my desk. It was a parental permission form to do cross-country.

"You're welcome," he said with a smug smile.

I stared at him and blinked. And blinked again.

"I know some people on the team," he said into my awkward silence. "They're all nice. If it's a ride you need, I can give you one after practice. It finishes at the same time as mine."

My hand froze on the flyer and I felt dangerously close to tears as I nodded and folded it into my purse. I forced myself to say, "Thanks, Greg. That was really nice of you to get this for me. I need to talk to my dad."

"No problem, Savannah. I moved here from Chicago when

I was thirteen. I know being new can be tough."

I was saved from responding by class starting. I thought about the flyer like it was burning a hole in my purse as well as my mind. Did I want to risk doing cross-country again?

Yes. Absolutely, yes.

I missed running so bad. It relaxed me like nothing else. But could I run again? I made a painful fist and sighed. Even without running, my joints hurt.

Luckily, I had to concentrate on note-taking. When the final bell of the day rang, I was still wondering what to do about the permission form in my bag. It didn't leave my mind when I saw Charles, shuffled down the hallway responding to him with one-word answers, or opened my locker.

"Hey, what happened?" he said, placing a hand on my bicep.

I nearly shivered at how good it felt as I flashed him the form. "Greg thought he was being nice bringing me this."

The worst was, he really *had* been trying to be nice. Charles frowned. He walked toward the trash can, but I stopped him with a hand on his arm.

"No, wait! I'm thinking about it."

His forehead wrinkled. "But I thought you shouldn't."

I opened my mouth, but I couldn't lie, not to Charles. "But I miss it. I miss running so much, Charles."

He handed back the flyer. "It's not my business. It's yours," he said quietly.

The car ride home was tense with both of us distracted. I knew running was a bad idea, but I loved it. And it'd be awesome to be on a team again.

Dad was there when I got home. When I hesitantly asked him about joining cross-country, he shut me down right away.

"No, Ray."

"But Dad—"

"Ray, I don't want to fight you. I'll tell you what, if you're doing better, you can join track in the spring. If you want to.

Just take it easy this semester. Think about what the doctors said. Please, sweetheart." He said this kindly and patiently, but all day I'd been fighting tears, and now they sprang to my eyes. It wasn't fair.

"I'm going to get fat!" I whined.

My cheeks were already puffy from the steroids and I felt bloated. I used to run about thirty miles a week. Now that I'd stopped, how long would it take until a few pounds started showing up? Greg was right. I had a runner's legs, but I wouldn't anymore if I didn't do any sports. It was bad enough starting a new school, but what if I had to buy new clothes too because I couldn't wear the old ones now that I wasn't working out? Then there'd be no way to afford architecture camp, either.

"Sweetheart, you can do some sit-ups or something, but I'm sorry, not this semester." He looked at me with resolve and I knew his decision was final.

I huffed into my room. It wasn't just cross-country. I knew Dad was right. But what the heck—was everything in my life going to revolve around lupus now? I crunched my fist, feeling pain as I did. I tightened it more, seeking relief in the physical pain over the emotional turbulence inside me.

I paced back and forth, then picked up my phone and texted Charles bitterly. *Dad said no.*

A response dinged back almost immediately. *I'm sorry /:*

I started on my homework. I looked down at my phone a few minutes later and saw another message flashing from Charles: *At the risk of sounding like a creepy stalker, I was bored at my internship a few weeks ago and came across this article about SLE and Iyengar yoga. I looked it up and there's a center 5 minutes from your place. Maybe...*

There was a google link attached. I typed back a quick *thanks* and went to the website. It talked about working with people with medical problems. The owner's email was listed for questions. Taking a deep breath, I shot off an email and turned back to my homework.

Around nine thirty that night, when I was done showering and blow-drying my hair and about ready to crawl into bed, I saw I had an unread email from Lanie at the Iyengar yoga studio. She said she'd love to have me and would be happy to help me do the modifications to make sure I wouldn't hurt myself. She suggested a Saturday morning and Thursday afternoon class. If I was interested, she told me to come in a half hour early with my dad to fill out the paperwork and make sure she understood how to help me not injure myself.

Buzzing with excitement, I hurried to the living room to tell Dad. A wave of guilt coursed through me when I spotted him crammed into a corner since I'd taken his office. I'd been moody and quiet at dinner. It wasn't his fault; he'd done everything to make it better.

"Dad," I said softly.

He paused and looked up.

"I'm sorry for losing my temper earlier."

He walked to the counter and patted the chair beside him. I padded over as he said, "I understand, sweetheart. You loved running and were good at it. I'm not saying to give it up forever. No one is. But just take a semester off."

I nodded, still feeling guilty. "I know. Anyway, I talked to Charles and he read about this type of yoga that's supposed to be good for people with lupus. There's a class nearby. I emailed the teacher and she said she can modify the poses and has had other students with SLE. It's kind of expensive, but I can get a job like I had in Savannah and pay you back if you let me." I slid the phone over to him and showed him the article and then the email.

After scanning it, he said, "I don't want you to work. I want you to focus on getting well this semester. I'm happy to pay for this, Ray."

"Really?" Mom would never just agree to pay for something like that.

"Really. Now, come have a chamomile tea with me and tell

me about your classes."

I turned on the kettle as Dad got out two mugs and teabags. We traded stories about our classes, and for the first time since I woke up, I felt a raw hope in me that maybe, just maybe, everything was going to be okay.

FOURTEEN

Charles

I was a little nervous to see Ray this morning because she'd looked so upset yesterday afternoon about cross-country. Crap, it had just about killed me when she said she loved running with her eyes close to tears.

I didn't blame her. I couldn't imagine just giving up something you loved like that. Like music. I hated to think of not being able to play my instruments anymore. It'd been a rare silent and tense ride from school, too. I could see her fingers were swollen again, but hadn't said anything. I knew she wasn't ready for everyone to know about her lupus, but I didn't think it was anything to be ashamed of or embarrassed about. But it was her decision, not mine.

But apparently, my worries were unfounded. When I pulled up to her dad's condo, she was beaming at me from the curb. She looked like a million dollars in a coral T-shirt dress and jean jacket with the sleeves rolled up. When she slid into the car, she startled me by pulling me into a hug. I momentarily lost the ability to think with her body touching mine, my face pressed into her jasmine-scented neck.

She held tight, sending a jolt of adrenaline through me. "You are the best, Charles," she said before she slowly pulled away.

Did she seem as reluctant to let me go as I felt, or was I imagining things? I put my hands back on the wheel and nervously tapped out a song.

"What was that for?" I asked.

"I'm going to start doing Iyengar yoga twice a week!" As if she couldn't be more adorable, she was practically bouncing with excitement. "Thursday! I'm going to start it Thursday. That was really sweet of you to think of me."

My cheeks warmed at her praise as she rambled all about the class, the studio, and how excited she was.

When we got to school, she was still beaming at me. "The best," she repeated, threading her arm through mine. "You are the best."

I couldn't help wondering again what her lips would taste like. Almost as if she could read my thoughts, she bit her lower lip and tugged my arm, making me realize I'd been salivating over her in the middle of the school parking lot. My cheeks burned, and I looked at the ground and hurried to keep up with her pace, trying to ignore the warmth of our still-linked arms.

As we approached the door, Ray finally dropped my arm, but the butterflies in my stomach didn't disperse.

"What are you two grinning about?" Knox asked with a raised eyebrow.

"Yoga," we said at the same time. We glanced at each other and started laughing—like, deep belly laughing. I didn't know why it was so funny, but her good mood was contagious.

"Right, whatever, weirdos." He shook his head at us, giving us a rare peek at his eyebrows and said. "Anyway, Charles, I'm stuck on this homework question for AP Chinese. Can you help me?"

"You take Mandarin too?" Ray asked.

"Yeah, man," Knox said, pulling out a paper.

"I'm a girl, thank you very much," Ray said, putting her hands on her hips in a way that made us both chuckle.

Knox smiled and winked at me before saying, "*Tā shì piàoliang nǚrén.*"

I wasn't about to disagree with him that Ray was a pretty girl. "Let me see the question." I frowned down at his book and then shot him a disbelieving look. "Knox, why did you get the traditional book? Ms. Cheng said we'd be using the simplified. If you're using this, your pages are going to be all wrong. You need to go to the library and switch textbooks."

"But the traditional characters are prettier," Knox whined.

"You can learn either, and on the exam you can pick either option, but I don't know the page numbers so that I can cross-reference with my book. Go to the library or see Ms. Cheng."

We laughed as he walked away.

"Chinese must be pretty easy for you?" Ray asked.

"I have trouble with some of the writing. The characters are hard. I've only done it with my mom or in Saturday school, which Ms. Cheng also taught, but I decided to take the placement exam last year and I tested in. I didn't want to have a life this year," I joked, half-hearted.

"Yeah, your workload gives me the sweats just thinking about."

I bumped her shoulder. "You have three AP classes. That's pretty impressive."

"Well, one is art."

"Hey, your art is exceptional."

And it was. I hadn't let her know, but I'd hung up her picture of our band in my room and loved looking at it. Her shading was extraordinary, and there was something stirring about the piece—almost movingly somber about the isolated figures in the stage light, yet spine-tinglingly beautiful at the same time. It reminded me of her untouchable beauty combined with her vulnerability.

I leaned in to whisper conspiratorially, "Know what's

the best thing about taking AP classes?" She shook her head, close enough for me to get another whiff of her scent. "They're made thinking about the Southern schedule. We have classes till June, not early May. AP exams are in April, so we get to do fun projects the last month of school. It's still work, but more fun."

She smiled as the bell rang. "I didn't think about that. You're right."

Her smile lingered in my memory the rest of the day, and followed me into Wednesday and Thursday. Ray was becoming my first thought in the morning and last thought at night. Her timid smile, bouncy enthusiasm, and even the melancholy that clouded her eyes when she thought no one was looking—all of it stayed with me long after our short moments together in the car or at lunch.

At lunch Thursday, schedules came up.

"Yo, Charles, did you ever text James back about band practice?" Knox asked as soon as I sat down. "You and Kevin have robotics in the a.m., but are we practicing in the afternoon or on Sunday? I vote for Sunday because Saturday I have a short window."

I sighed. "Well, Sunday is better for us too. Saturday is our long kick-off meeting to break into our divisions. It could be late, and we'll likely be tired."

"Cool," Knox said. "I'll start the group chat. Ray, what about you, any preference on Sunday?"

She flushed red, but Knox's eyes were on his phone. "No, whenever," she said. "You guys know you're my only friends."

Her eyes wouldn't meet mine as she ate. I wanted to make extra plans to see her, but was spread thin. I already had so many assignments piling up, so Friday night and Saturday evening would be all catch-up. I really needed to place first in my next piano competition in late October, which meant I needed to practice more. Despite what people said about me, I wasn't a genius. I studied a lot. Doing well was important to me—more than anything else.

Knox missed it or ignored Ray's comment about us being her only friends. "James said one and he needs to go by five."

"Fine," I said, turning to Ray. "You can come a little early Sunday. We can study and have lunch. I know you like my mom's cooking as much as me."

"Sure, thanks," she said, but she was still picking at her food, not looking up.

"I'd invite you to do something, but everyone is in town for my cousin's bar mitzvah," Knox said. "We have a huge family Shabbat dinner Friday, then the service in the morning. The party's that night. I don't think you'd have fun, because it's all family, but if you're interested…"

"Shabbat?"

"Like a religious dinner for Jewish people—we say some prayers, light some candles, and have some wine. You can come."

"Oh, that'd be nice, but maybe not when it's the whole family. But thanks. Can you invite me when it's fewer people? My own family is intimidating enough."

He laughed. "Yeah, man, I know. We do it every Friday, and you are always invited."

"Knox." I heard the teasing in her voice as she finally looked up. "I'm a girl."

The lunch relaxed after that. All this time, I'd never thought about how Knox rarely made plans with us on Friday night, because I usually studied. He caught me looking and said, "You're invited too."

Maybe it would be fun to go to Knox's sometime for Shabbat dinner. His mom was a good cook and we'd been friends for ages.

Thoughts of anything but school blurred as afternoon classes resumed. Hours later, when the bell finally dismissed us for the day, I waited for Ray. She'd get to try the yoga for the first time today, and she'd told me we needed to get out of the parking lot ahead of traffic so she could talk to the instructor and sign the paperwork.

She walked out of the classroom with Greg.

"So Ray…well, I was wondering," Greg was saying. "That is, if you want to come on Saturday too?"

Ray offered him a shy smile. "I have plans in the morning and Dad's meeting with his graduate students, so I wouldn't have a ride. But thanks."

Greg stepped closer to Ray, invading her space. "I can drive you. I'd prefer to work out in the morning before meeting up with everyone anyway. My dad keeps asking me about you."

"I'm n—"

"There'll be a bunch of us at Luke's. Don't make me beg to be your friend," he said, so low I almost didn't hear.

Her cheeks turned red and she took a step back. "Sure, okay, if you want me to come that bad. I need to go—I have an appointment this afternoon."

Greg put his hand on her arm to stop her. "Wait, let me get your number really quick, so we can work out the details tonight." He got out his phone and looked at her expectantly.

"Sure, Ray, R-A-Y, nine, one, two, fa-ah-i-ve…"

I got distracted by how much more Southern she sounded when she rolled a word into four or five syllables.

"What was that about?" I asked as we went to her locker.

She packed her bag quickly. "Oh, um, Greg just wanted to hang out Saturday," she said with a shrug.

She looked anxious as she picked at her binder, but excited and hopeful at the same time. Suddenly, I was glad I hadn't acted on James's advice, or I'd feel like a real idiot.

FIFTEEN

Ray

I walked into the small yoga studio, just off the main road, with Dad, not really knowing what to expect.

"Can I help you?" a small muscular woman behind a desk asked.

"Hi, um, I'm Ray. I emailed you."

"Yes, welcome. I'm Lanie. Here's the paperwork, and this must be your dad?"

Dad left after we filled out the liability forms, and Lanie showed me where the colorful studio mats were stacked. "Ray, this type of yoga is strict. You must do the poses with the correct alignment—you especially. You'll need two blankets, a strap, and two wooden blocks." She pointed everything out. "Also, you don't do inversions while you are menstruating. We have adjustments possible for those poses though, so don't worry. We have adjustments for everything. Doing the pose isn't important; doing it perfectly is. Doing it wrong inflames the body; doing it right strengthens and soothes. For you this is especially important. If you can't, we adjust. Okay?"

"Okay."

"Dante," Lanie said to a lanky man entering the studio. "Can you help Ray set up her mat while I do check-in?"

He helped me stack the blankets and said Lanie or the other instructors would get super mad if the blankets weren't folded the right way, and to pay attention. He handed me a laminated card labeled "The Invocation to Patanjali" and told me how to sit.

Lanie came in after the class filled and sat cross-legged, like us. "Okay, class, we have a new student today, so I will explain a little more. Is anyone menstruating?"

My cheeks heated as two college-aged girls raised their hands and Lanie nodded.

"Eyes closed. Palms together. All together for the invocation." Lanie began chanting, and the class joined in. It was harmonic. Soothing.

After the invocation, we moved through different poses. Lanie came up to me often, pulling my arm, telling me to straighten my back, or suck in my stomach. It was unlike anything I'd ever done. She led us to the rope wall, and everyone hung suspended, except for the two girls that had their periods. They were on the floor doing something else. I liked the class but dreaded the week I'd come and have to do the poses "more beneficial for menstruating." It seemed embarrassing, but no one else seemed to mind, so maybe it was only in my head. Dante had been right: it was strict, but I liked it a lot more than I thought I would.

I walked home past a few leaves that had turned so soon in the early Northern autumn before even the fall solstice. I was tired but calm in a way I hadn't felt in a while. The night had a perfect breeze and the sun, still so late here, was just starting to set. Iyengar yoga was about as far removed from running as you could get, yet something about it had appealed to me. Before I'd left, Lanie said to drink plenty of water and she'd tell my Saturday teacher about me. And she warned me I'd be sore.

I groaned as I opened the door to Dad's condo Friday afternoon, Granny Young's contact lighting up my phone. I hadn't spoken to her since I'd been here. Granny Young was a more righteous version of my mom, and Mom was intense enough for me.

I couldn't even utter a greeting before, "Rayanne, darling, why haven't you called your Granny Young?" blasted through the line.

"Hi—"

She cut me off. "Too busy to tell me you're living in Michigan now? Hum?"

"I thought Mom told you—"

"What are people gonna say, Miss Rayanne? And your daddy is an atheist. How can you live with him?"

"Granny Young, I was sick, and the healthcare is better here," I rushed to get out.

She drew in a deep breath and I cringed, knowing she was gearing up for a lecture. "Your health is important, pretty girl, but what about your soul, Rayanne? You are living with a *godless* man. Honey, you have to think about your eternal body, not just your physical one. Are you even going to church up there, Rayanne?"

I felt my belly flutter at that hit. I hadn't been yet. "Well—"

"Why, I never, young lady. I knew that man would corrupt your soul. I told your momma, bless her heart…"

I held the phone away from my ear as she screamed about things like "hellfire," "eternal suffering," and "damnation" for several minutes. This was why I hadn't called her. I was pretty sure two people were responsible for my creation, but to my grandparents, there was one person to blame.

After I let her rant for what I felt was long enough, I gently interrupted her. "Granny Young, I'm still watching the sermon videos from back home." I winced at my lie, making a mental note to ask forgiveness later. I hated those videos and Mom's preacher. "I'd love to find some friends at school to go to church with here. Dad is certainly not *keeping me* from going." That was the truth. If I could find a church like Jeff's, I'd be happy as a clam.

She huffed. "I'm going to talk to your momma, sugar plum, and don't think I won't. I don't know why she agreed to let you live with your father. He ruined her life, Rayanne! Your poor momma, bless her heart. One sin and her life changed forever. Luckily, Jesus can forgive us our sins, but you need to keep him in your heart, or else..." She trailed off.

Afraid of another round of hellfire, I said quickly, "I will, Granny Young, I promise. I say my prayers every night."

At least that one wasn't a lie. She was making me nervous. I didn't think I'd let the devil in me, but I also didn't think my dad was damned for eternity just because he didn't believe in God. I didn't think Charles or Knox were either, just because they weren't Christian.

Finally, I got off the phone, and it lit up about fifteen minutes later with Mom's number. I grit my teeth as I prepared for more eternal damnation. When I hung up, after promising to find a church, I heard Dad's phone ring about a minute later.

"Chrissy, no!" he said from the living room. "I don't want our daughter to burn in hell. Who says shit like that? ... Yes, I promise to take her to church, as long as that's what she wants ... No, I will not tell her that! What's wrong with you?"

Finally, it fell silent out there and I peeked out the door. Dad had stood up and was drinking a glass of whiskey. He barely drank, but I knew Mom stressed him out.

"Do you want to go to church?" he asked me.

"Yes," I said.

"Do you honestly want to go? I mean it—not just you don't want your mom yelling at you, because I can handle her." He took another sip, nearly draining the glass. He'd probably need ten more of those before *that* conversation.

"I honestly want to go." I did. Just because I didn't like Granny Young or Mom's church didn't mean I didn't want to stay a Christian.

His face softened. "If you can't find someone to go with next Sunday, I'll take you. I should have thought about it with everything you've been through."

I blinked. "You'd take me?"

"Yes, sweetheart," he said in a tired voice, then took the final sip of whiskey.

I smiled. "In that case, I'll let you pick the restaurant tonight."

He teased me about how gracious I was as we headed out the door.

The next day, yoga seriously kicked my butt, or should I say hamstrings? Apparently, I really did have runners' legs—tight. I stayed extra-long in the shower, groaning over my newfound muscles. When I finally emerged, I winced when I glanced at the clock and the amount of steam in the bathroom. I hoped Dad didn't need a shower.

I debated blow-drying my hair and ultimately settled on a French braid since we were going to the lake and I'd probably get wet soon. Why bother styling it when it'd just get messed up anyway?

Back in my bedroom, I debated what to wear. I hadn't lied to my dad, but I hadn't said I was going to the lake, because I didn't think he'd like that. Heck, *I* didn't like that I was going to the lake, but it had been so embarrassing when Greg had just stared at me. I wanted friends. Greg's parents and Luke's had lake houses next to each other, so it was an opportunity to meet more people. Especially when everyone clearly had plans except me. I didn't want to just blurt out, "I have lupus and should avoid the sun." I also hadn't wanted to just sit around the condo by myself and bother Dad.

I put on my favorite coral bikini—I loved coral—and slipped on a halter dress that hid that I was wearing a swimsuit. I threw in a change of underwear, shorts, the long UVB shirt I'd bought this summer, a ballcap, and a big bottle of sunscreen. My phone dinged with a message from Greg letting me know he was here, so I slipped out of my room and yelled to Dad that I was leaving.

It felt like déjà vu walking toward Greg in his big pickup truck in the muggy parking deck. I hadn't really been impressed with Ross in the end and certainly wasn't looking to replace him, but who was I to turn down friends? Maybe looks would be deceiving. I didn't want to be completely dependent on Charles when he was aiming for one of the most competitive schools in the country and had more than a full schedule already.

Plus, Greg had been really nice, if a little flirty. I would give him a chance. I wasn't looking for Ross 2.0 and if I dated, I wanted to be honest about lupus. I'd like to understand it better myself before I even went down that road. And if I did date someone…my skin heated as I thought about Charles's long fingers sliding over the piano keys and his dimple when he cracked a joke.

If I did date, Greg wouldn't be my first choice.

I forced the biggest smile I could muster and opened the truck door. "Thanks for coming to get me."

Greg looked over at me as I slid into his bench seat. "Wow,

Ray, that's a great dress."

"Thanks," I said again, feeling myself blush as I buckled my seatbelt.

Was this dress too much? I had a boyish figure but decent-sized boobs, because of my narrow frame. With the lower cut of the halter top, they did hang out of this dress much more than my school clothing. Ross had always said they were fantastic, but I figured he'd have said anything to touch them. I used to work out so much, I was generally happy-ish with how I looked. Plus, growing up by the beach and living nearly non-stop in a bikini, then years of running in basically the same thing, made you more comfortable in your skin. But recently the extra bloating and lack of running made me worried happy-ish would be a thing of the past. That was scary; just about the only nice things people ever said about me were she's pretty. Soon, I wouldn't even have that.

So, I *really* didn't want to dwell on my clothing. My looks.

"Anyhoo, you want to do architecture too, right? That's what your dad said at the Brown Bag."

"Oh, yeah. My dad loves it and it'd be awesome to see *my* building, you know?"

"I get it," I said trying not to laugh at how his 'oh, yeah' and 'you know' rolled out. Midwest, Canadian, Michigander whatever this accent was called it was different. "Where are you thinking about applying to college?" I got out without a giggle.

"I'm not sure. Maybe somewhere in New York or Chicago. I want to study in a big city, but of course I'll apply to Michigan too. What about you?"

I fiddled with my seatbelt. "Michigan and Georgia Tech are my top two schools, followed by Georgia. Tech and U of M are top twenty-five in the country for architecture, and Georgia is in the top fifty. Plus, in-state tuition."

"I haven't looked too much into Georgia schools, but I want to get away a little bit. Michigan isn't a top choice for me just for that reason."

"I'd be so happy if I got into Michigan it wouldn't even be funny. I went to some lectures there this summer. It was amazing. Seriously amazing."

He laughed. "Yeah, my dad told me. I got caught drinking, and you were voluntarily going to lectures. I do like it—architecture, that is—and it's a good choice for me because I can intern with my dad's firm, but I want to have fun too. But you really must love it, huh?"

"I love the old buildings and variety of styles. Turning something simple into a more efficient building *and* a work of art is just mad cool," I said. "Savannah is beautiful. And I've visited Stockholm once or twice a year and a few other European cities growing up—Rome, Paris, Amsterdam, and of course our neighbor, Copenhagen. There were always discount tickets available and sometimes we'd go to a city for a few nights before flying home. The old buildings are so intricate. I like the idea of keeping that artistry and complexity alive in the present. I'll probably also apply to KTH Royal Institute of Technology in Stockholm too, since it would be free."

"Wow, really?"

"Yeah, why not? I'm a dual citizen. And that's where my dad did his undergraduate studies. But I don't know. I'm fluent in Swedish, but I don't think my reading and writing are near college level. Plus, maybe it's too far away." I thought about my lupus. My grandparents were there, but I hated to think of depending on them if I got sick. I decided to change the subject. "Will you try to play football in college?"

"Yeah, no. I'm not that good. You have to practice all the time for that," he said with a laugh.

"Yes, you do. My ex is being recruited by some Division I schools, including Georgia."

He took his eyes off the road a second to peek at me. "Are you fucking kidding me, Savannah?"

I shook my head no.

"That's dope as shit. He must have been at it all the time and a fantastic player."

"Eyes on the road, and pretty much."

Ross had practiced all the time. It had been one thing I'd admired about him. Like Charles's dedication to his studies, Ross had been singularly focused on football. His talent wasn't all God-given—I'd seen how many hours he gave and parties and drinks he turned down. I had no doubt he'd get a full ride.

"So there's no way to impress you," he said. "I'm not bilingual, like you, or a Division I athlete."

"Why do you need to impress me?"

He laughed. "I all but had to beg to get you to come to the lake."

I shifted a little uncomfortably. Skittles, I did not want to go to the lake. But I hadn't wanted to seem like I was playing hard to get. "I am a little shy," I said honestly. "It'd be really great to make some more *friends*. Charles is great, but he's so busy. I almost feel guilty asking him to do anything."

"Yeah, that kid is more machine than human. I've never seen anyone study and make grades like him. Even in government, which I can tell is not his thing."

I bristled at the way he spoke about Charles. "Charles is not a machine." He was one of the most considerate people I knew.

"No offense intended. What bands do you like?"

We talked about music and other lighter things until we pulled up to a big lake house that seemed too large to be a second house. It was an architect's dream—huge windows and sleek lines, with a massive deck. Heck, it seemed too big to be a single-family house at all. I was certain our condo could fit in the foyer.

"Come on, Dad wants to say hi before we go next door to Luke's place. My parents have been on my tail since they caught me drinking this summer. You're"—he air-quoted *"sweet as pie"*—and slipped into his truly terrible Southern accent, before continuing, "Three AP classes, taking seven courses and not six. Hopefully if they think I'm dating you, they won't—"

"Wait." I grabbed his forearm, and my eyes flew to his. "We are *not* dating, Greg."

His face turned red, and I felt embarrassed for being rude. "They just think I could use better friends. My dad already likes you, and they've been so strict lately. Haven't you ever had trouble with your parents?" He shook his head, "Never mind, I'm sure you were always a perfect daughter."

"No, my mom and I fought a lot," I said, turning sympathetic. "She grounded me for two weeks when I got a hickey."

"Hellraiser."

"Don't. Your Southern accent is terrible." I couldn't help giggling a little.

He walked around and opened my door, then held out his hand to help me down. "Ready, Ray?"

He led me to the front door and unlocked it. "Mom," he yelled as we entered the house. "Dad, come meet Ray before we go over to Luke's."

Mr. Davis, and a very well-manicured woman with a perfectly styled bob haircut, greeted us as we entered the kitchen. "Hi, Ray. I'm Mrs. Davis. Larry said such nice things about you! It is wonderful to meet you." She shook my hand. "Do you want a pop before you go next door?"

They could make fun of my accent all they wanted, but I never understood how pop became "pah-ap."

"No, ma'am. Thank you, but I don't drink much soda. Could I please have a water, though?"

"Sure. Greg?" She motioned for him to grab it and the rest of us sat down.

I talked to Mr. Davis about some of his projects.

"Ray, if you are interested, maybe you and Greg could come see the micro-living complex sometime," Mr. Davis said as Greg brought me a water bottle.

"Thank you," I said to Greg before turning back to his dad. "That would be amazing! I'd love to see it."

"Yeah, Dad, we'd both like that," Greg said. "We should probably head next door, though. Luke is waiting."

"I'm not a huge fan of Luke," Greg's mom muttered, but no one made a fuss as we walked next door.

"I'm not sure if I owe you or if you just made me look bad," Greg teased.

I was silent and starting to get nervous about meeting so many new people—not to mention, what it would be like to be in the sun. I hoped there'd be an umbrella.

Luke slurred out a greeting, his breath smelling like he'd already been drinking. The others who said hello seemed nice enough. Everyone was just in their swimsuits, so I stripped off my sundress, sprayed some more sun cream, and put on my hat. I didn't want to stand out and thought surely a little while without the long sleeves wouldn't be too bad. Plus, the sun on my skin felt incredible. I'd just keep an eye on my watch. Last time, I'd been in the sun for hours, and now I'd been on my lupus medications for six weeks, so I figured an hour or two of the sun would be fine.

I joined the others as they jumped in and out of the murky-blue water, even though swimming in a pond was weird. We couldn't swim in fresh water back home, because of the gators. Still, it felt good to swim again—I'd always loved being in the ocean, and Mom used to joke I was part fish as a kid.

Most of the group was passing around a bottle of lemonade I knew contained alcohol with how loose-lipped, giggly, and red-cheeked everyone was getting. I declined it. I never drank and didn't want to start now with all the medicine I was on.

I walked over to Greg and whispered in his ear after I saw him take a sip, "If you dare take another, I'll ask your mom to drive me home because you've been drinking."

He must have known I was telling the truth because he got a can of Coke and didn't drink any more of the lemonade mix after that. My life was more important than popularity. I wasn't getting in a car with someone who'd been drinking.

To my annoyance, Greg kept snuggling close to me for his other best friend Sean's pictures, but as soon as he snapped one, he'd let me slip a step away. I didn't want to fight in front of everyone, so I let it go. I preferred more personal space and didn't want him to think this was a date after what he'd let slip in the car.

After we'd been there at least an hour, most of us had taken up chairs in a semicircle on the dock. The sun felt so good on my skin, even though I was debating putting on my long sleeves and hat. I gave it a few more minutes. Just because the sun didn't like me anymore didn't mean *I* hated it.

Luke thundered over and plunked down on the arm of my wooden chair, way too close for my comfort.

"So," he said, loud enough that everyone looked up. "Why did you move up here from Savannah?" He had that booming I-drank-too-much voice.

"My dad's work," I responded, hoping he'd take that to mean he'd gotten a job transfer.

"But isn't he, like, a friend of Greg's dad and been here awhile?"

I nodded, but caught Greg watching the conversation from the water. I sent him a pleading glance, and he swam toward the ladder to climb out.

Luke smiled slyly. "I thought so. Why move to live with your dad?"

"Why not?" I said. I leaned back in the chair. I was seconds away from pushing him out of my way to get up, if it wouldn't make even more of a scene.

"It's weird, that's why." He wobbled on the armrest and I half hoped he'd fall off. When I didn't respond, he leaned in, and you'd bet your bottom he'd been drinking. "My parents are divorced too. And my mom's a divorce lawyer. Dads out-of-state don't just suddenly get custody. Almost never. There's *always* a story."

I had no idea what to say. While my parents didn't get along, custody had never been an issue needing more than the cursory legal paperwork required.

Luke pushed my shoulder hard enough it hurt. "Come on, tell us. Was your mom an addict or something? It has to be interesting. Did an ex get you knocked up?" He winked as a dripping wet Greg bristled, stalking closer like he was about to intervene.

I pushed out of the chair and away from Luke, who was clearly belligerently drunk or a big jerkface. Or both.

He grabbed my wrist, keeping me from leaving. "I don't blame him. Greg didn't exaggerate how hot you are."

Greg's hand thudded on Luke's shoulder. "Luke, man, I think you've had too much."

But Luke swiveled back. "Come on, Ray! Don't leave us hanging. *Tell us.* I know there's some story there."

I tried to calm down, but when I looked at his obnoxious smirk and everyone else staring, I snapped. "I'm a *virgin* and *my mom's not an addict.*" I tugged my hand and he let me go.

My hands shook as I tried to control my emotions. I wanted to puke; this was beyond mortifying. I skirted away as Greg whispered something to Luke, who pushed Greg off him. "I'm telling you, Greg. Dads don't get custody for no reason, especially if they live out-of-state. There is more to the story."

Greg handed me my bag. "Dude, you need to chill out. It's none of our damn business. Ray, you ready to go? I think you've gotten enough sun anyway."

I pulled my bag out of his hand and stalked to the car. I bet that stupid rash was back. This lake adventure had really gone to hell in a handbasket.

"Ray." I heard Greg hurrying behind me and felt his hand on my shoulder. "Ray, I'm sorry. He's a mean drunk. Sorry I couldn't stop him sooner."

I sighed. "Yeah, me too."

Greg opened the door, and I got in after pulling on my shorts and shirt over my bikini. His truck was hot and uncomfortably silent. My fingers were white, and I realized I must be really upset; I wasn't even cold. Someone had just talked crap about me in front of the coolest kids in school.

When I pulled down the mirror, I saw the malar rash was back on my face. My anger turned to something closer to fear as a small tremor shuddered through me. What was going to happen now?

Greg cranked the car but looked at me. "We used to be best friends, but he's really turning into an asshole. He's worse when he drinks."

"Maybe he shouldn't drink."

"You're probably right." He sighed again. "I've told him the same thing. It's hard to watch someone you've been friends with for years become someone you can't stand."

I went silent, not knowing how to respond. If it had been Jeff, my heart would be so hurt.

"Why your parents divorced and why you moved here is your own business."

"My parents...I was a mistake," I said. "They never married." He'd been honest about his friendship with Luke falling apart. It only seemed fair for me to do the same. Especially since his dad likely knew how young mine was.

"Ray—"

"My dad was doing his Ph.D. at the London School of Economics, and my mom was a college sophomore. I used to only see him a few weeks a year. Most of that was flying back and forth to see my grandparents in Sweden. I wanted to get to know my dad. That's why I moved here." It was part of the reason. People would obviously talk anyway.

"Ray, I'm really fucking sorry."

In the silence, the shame of knowing my parents hadn't wanted me filled me as much as the disintegration of Greg's turbulent friendship with Luke. Both made for a tediously long drive back. I looked twice at my face, spotting the malar rash on my cheeks.

"I'm sorry again," Greg said when we got to the condo. "I wish today had been more fun."

I could tell he meant it. "It's fine. I just don't like your friend. You seem nice, Greg. Don't let him pull you down with him."

"Ray—" But whatever else he had to say was cut off by my door closing. I didn't reopen it.

When I walked in the condo, Dad took one look at my face and said, "Where have you been?"

"The lake. And it was terrible. And I'm an idiot."

His mouth opened and closed as I started crying. Pain racked my whole body. I'd never used to cry, but I'd lost count of how many times I'd cried recently. I could feel aching in my knees and couldn't close my hands again. It had hurt to press the elevator button. It had hurt to use the key. It wasn't fair. I was taking so many pills a day. I was nauseous. If I took the medicine, shouldn't I be able to live my life? I didn't want this to be my life. I didn't want *this*.

Dad walked over and wrapped me in his arms. "I don't know how you can be so smart, yet so stupid at the same time."

"I know, Dad," I choked out.

"I love you, sweetheart. We'll get you better, okay?" His voice sounded as pained as I felt. "Your life will be different, but it doesn't mean it's over. But sweetheart, you just can't go in the sun like that anymore."

I just clung to him and tried not to focus on what an idiot I'd been today in so many ways, and how I wished I'd just had the courage to say no in the first place.

SIXTEEN

Charles

I was starving by the time Kevin and our robotics teammate, Dana, grabbed some pizza and snatched up a science table in the back of the room. Today had been pretty awesome so far. We'd watched videos comparing last year's winning teams as a warm-up to our season, but suddenly the Detroit pizza smelled amazing. It was a long opening day and after lunch we'd start our model drawings before we could leave.

Dana and Kevin were both on their phones as we started eating. "Hey, isn't that your girlfriend?" Kevin said, staring down at his phone.

Dana glanced up. "When did you get a girlfriend?"

I blew out some air. Out of everyone, Kevin had warmed up to Ray the least. I didn't know if it was because she was pretty, blond, *and* tall, way taller than him, he assumed she wouldn't give him the time of day, when clearly it was the other way around. Or if those things made him assume she wasn't as smart as he was. He didn't treat Dana that way, but then again, Dana was tiny. Or maybe because she was Korean and went to his church. I wasn't sure. But Kevin had made a few snide comments about Ray before.

"I don't have a girlfriend," I said, trying to keep my voice even.

"Yeah. I think she and Greg might be dating," Dana said, oblivious to the tension.

"What are you guys looking at?" I asked with a heavy sigh.

"Instagram," they said simultaneously.

I debated pulling out my phone, knowing it wouldn't do me any good, but eventually gave in. I'd just gotten to a place last night where I was calm about the whole Greg thing. I didn't have time to date Ray, even if she did like me, which I seriously doubted. Yet suddenly I was burning to see these pictures. Most were posted by Sean, who we all knew from AP Biology freshman year. We weren't really friends, but he'd seemed decent then. They had the hashtags #lazylastdaysofsummer and #lakelife. There were several of Ray and Greg, his arms wrapped around her as they smiled for a picture. They certainly looked like a couple.

My throat was dry, and I had trouble swallowing. They looked right together, their blond heads touching. Crap, maybe I wasn't as okay with it as I'd told myself.

I slipped my phone back into my pocket. I didn't need to see any more. I no longer had an appetite, but forced myself to eat my slice of pizza. I felt Dana's and Kevin's eyes on me, but what was there to say? Clearly the gorgeous, model-looking blond wouldn't be interested in dating me. Her ex-boyfriend looked like Greg, so it made sense her new one would too. She clearly had a type. And why should I even care? We were friends—nothing more. This was better. I needed to focus on school this year.

But if that were true, why had those photos made my stomach burn?

I smiled at Dana, hoping she wouldn't notice my lack of joy, and pulled out our notes. "Okay, we have one hour left here. Can we focus?"

"Did you see the picture of Ray?" Kevin said.

I could see Dana kick him under the table. At least someone had my back. "Ray is my friend. Who she dates is her business. Now, you're on my robotics team and you're distracting us from the project—that's an issue."

"Burrrrn," Dana said with a chuckle. "He told you."

I could tell Kevin didn't want to drop it, but he was as obsessed with winning as the rest of us, and we all buckled down until the session ended.

When I got home, I flopped onto my bed and stared listlessly at the sketch Ray had made of the band. I needed to get back to my massive amounts of homework, but couldn't peel my gaze from the picture, remembering how angelic Ray had looked when she sang. I wished I had a picture of that. After being emo for far, far too long, I pulled out my phone and texted her.

How was the lake? What could I say? Maybe I was a masochist.

Her response was immediate. *Terrible!*

I felt a thrill of excitement at her response, but still sent back, *Social media tells a different story.*

Lies. I got a lupus flare. And Luke is a real jerk-face.

I sat up. Crap, what if she was in the hospital again? A cold sweat broke out on my forehead. *You okay?*

No, I feel like yesterday's guacamole.

I didn't know what that meant. Sometimes I wasn't sure what she said; I didn't know if it was Southernisms or Ray-isms. *But you're not in the hospital or anything, right?* Suddenly my heart was racing, and I wasn't tired anymore.

Groan, no, but lying in bed. Hands look like water balloons. It hurts to type you. Knees feel like grandma. I'm preemptively canceling our plans for tomorrow. I think my bed and I will be having a date instead.

It's OK, but wish I was there.

In my bed?

My body responded hard to that. *I didn't mean in your bed, just there to keep you company.* But oh wow, how I'd love to be in that bed. Crap, now that image was burned in my mind. Concentrating on my work was going to be an issue, but it made me twitchy to leave all my assignments until Sunday.

Oh Charles, you're my only friend. And then immediately, *Here. You're my only friend here.*

Knox is your friend too, I responded, even though her words made me feel eight feet tall.

How? How do you always make me feel better?

I'm lucky 88.

Ha, I hear my bed calling. It says, "sick loser, you should have listened to your body and avoided the sun. Now you will pay."

I laughed as I read her text. *You're weird, Ray.*

She sent me the sleepy emoji. I laughed again, feeling better, which was messed up. I wasn't happy she was sick, but I didn't want to think about her dating Greg, either.

True to her word, Ray didn't come over Sunday. She texted me Sunday night that she was feeling worse and going to the doctor in the morning. Worry gnawed at my gut, but I told myself she was fine. She had really good doctors. The day passed with the usual quick speed, since all my classes demanded nonstop work and left no time for a wandering mind.

I paused for a minute outside AP Calculus when I saw Greg.

"Hey, Charles," he said as he approached me. "Um, I

wanted to ask you in government, but you bolted out of there before I could. How's Ray?" Surprisingly, he looked flustered, picking the edge of his binder. I guess he and Ray had nervous energy in common, among everything else. "She never texted me back when I asked her."

I wanted to roll my eyes, but with a mind to the bell, I said, "Well, maybe you did something. Maybe your friend was a jerk to her." I arched an eyebrow at him, and he staggered back like I'd punched him.

"She told you about that?"

"Look, I have class, but yes. We're friends. But that's not why she's missing school—she's sick."

I turned to go, but he grabbed my arm. "Is this about her face? Her sunburn? On the ride home, she kept looking at it in the mirror."

"She's, um, sensitive to the sun. Like, sun poisoning," I said before walking into calculus.

Before I went home, I stopped by all Ray's classes to pick up her assignments for her. She'd emailed most of her teachers already, but a few had worksheets for me to take her. I swung by my house afterward for my acoustic guitar, then headed over to her place. My place was actually much closer to the school than hers—not that I'd ever tell her I went out of the way to get her in the mornings.

When I showed up at her place, she was in leggings and a ratty T-shirt, her long hair in a messy bun. As disheveled as she looked, she was still adorable. Since she looked like she barely had the energy to continue standing, we sat down at the kitchen table while I went over the assignments with her. Her eyes were dull, like a sad imitation of her usual self.

When I finished, she looked so miserable that I said casually, "I brought my guitar," gently kicking the case.

She cocked her head but didn't reply. She'd told me before that listening to me play helped her relax, but I was suddenly embarrassed about it.

"I can practice some here, if you'd like," I offered.

She brightened just a little, and her eyes sparkled momentarily with their normal blue fire before dimming again. "I'd like that," she said softly. "Let's go in the bedroom."

I followed her, then pulled the guitar out and sat in her desk chair. Ray sat cross-legged on her bed, snuggling her stuffed husky. It warmed something inside me that she slept with it on her bed.

I played what felt to me like it fit the mood: "Run" by Snow Patrol. I wish she'd light up for me. I softly sang the words to her. I hadn't told her, but she was the only person I'd sing to. My voice wasn't like James's, but it just seemed like the right thing to do.

When I sang the last note, we shared a long commiserating look and she wiped away a single tear. Then she patted the bed and I sank into it beside her. She wrapped her arms around me and pressed her face into my chest.

"You see me, Charles," she said, so quietly I almost couldn't hear her. "Even when I'm not sure I want you to see me, you see me." My arms came around her slim frame almost instinctively. Her warm body nestled into mine.

"I see you, Ray," I whispered back, rubbing light circles on her back. She snuggled closer and something inside me pinched. I wished I could take all her pain away. After a few moments, she looked up. "More?"

She nodded and turned her face like she was embarrassed by her red cheeks. She let go, and reluctantly I did too. I picked the guitar back up and played "Let It Be" by the Beatles and then some peppier, contemporary songs. The music helped me, too. It was shit Ray would have this for the rest of her life.

After being lost in the music for several songs, Ray touched my shoulder. "Just *you* calm me down," she said in a low voice. "I'm sure you have assignments—many, many assignments. Just work over here for a little, if you don't mind?"

"Sure," I responded, and her hand slipped away. I missed it.

I pulled out my books on her desk, and she took her assignment and stretched out with a notebook on her bed.

I didn't tell her, but she calmed me down, too. Something about being in her presence made me feel lighter—happier, even when she was so gloomy. Last year I'd been so stressed, and everyone always expected me to be perfect, but it was a lot of work to make top grades, and not everyone liked someone smarter than they were. I didn't think she'd care if I took APs or not; she seemed to just like being around me, just as I liked being around her.

...

SEVENTEEN

Ray

Despite Charles's offer yesterday evening, I'd decided to start taking the bus to school. He wouldn't be able to give me a lift Tuesday and Thursday afternoons anymore, or Friday mornings, so it was time to try to get used to it again. It wasn't like this was something new—I'd ridden the bus my whole life. Well, until Jeff got a car, so most my life.

Charles was striving to be valedictorian on top of everything else; he didn't need me wasting any more of the precious time he had. I felt guilty enough I'd let him stay so long last night, but something about him just relaxed me—reminded me I wasn't alone. I was starting to crave him like I'd never craved anyone in my life. Did he feel it too, or was he just being nice? I wasn't sure, but I didn't want to do anything that'd risk what I had with him. I loved having him as a friend. I *needed* him as a friend.

On the bus, I mentally replayed the lecture Dr. Murray had given me yesterday morning. "Don't you realize how serious this is?" she'd said. "You've already had organ failure once. Next it could be your kidney or something else. This isn't something to take lightly. Your platelets are dangerously low again and I'm sure your complements will be too when I get them back. We need to get your lupus in remission. You are on the highest dose of immune suppressants allowed. Do you want to need chemo or IVIG? If not, you need to take this seriously."

It had been doubly uncomfortable under the eyes of two medical students and a resident. She'd wanted them to see the malar rash in person.

I shifted awkwardly with my face to the window, ignoring the whispers around me. Despite a heavy layer of foundation, it was still pretty obvious I had a rash. I refused to feel sorry for myself—I'd done this to myself, after all.

I got to school right as the bell rang and trudged through my first four classes, dodging even more whispers and questions. "What happened to your face?" people asked again and again.

By the time art arrived, I was exhausted and debating going home to nap. But I loved drawing, so instead I settled for swinging by the nurse for another ibuprofen so my hands wouldn't hurt too badly while holding the pastels.

Becky, the friendly girl who'd been sitting beside me, cast me a worried look when she came in. "Are you feeling okay?"

The snarky response on the tip of my tongue died as I looked into her earnest brown eyes. I shook my head, then tucked some hair behind my ear that had fallen into my face. "I'm really tired, actually. I was debating going home." My dad and doctors had said it would be all right, but I hadn't taken advantage of it yet. You missed so much when you were out sick. I hated it.

She leaned in closer to peek at my fingers, which were clearly swollen. "Ray," she whispered, "do you have lupus?"

I jerked my head up from the drawing I'd started last Thursday. I opened my mouth and closed it.

She nodded and continued in that same soft voice. "I thought so. My aunt ha—um, has it."

"Really?" I didn't think many people knew about it, especially since I hadn't before I was diagnosed.

"Yep." She nodded. "It's more than twice as common in African Americans." Light flashed in her eyes as understanding clicked. "It's why you moved here, isn't it? U of M?" When I nodded, she said, "You should stay out of the sun."

I gave a humorless laugh. "Yeah, I got that memo, thanks. How's your aunt doing?"

Becky frowned. "She's never been very compliant with medical advice or taking her medicine. If you take your medicine and listen to your doctors, hopefully you should do well."

"Okay, um, thanks."

"You don't have kidney issues yet, do you?" Her voice was barely audible, for which I was grateful. I didn't want everyone to know this.

When I shook my head, I saw relief pass through her eyes.

"That's really good. Just listen to your doctors, all right?"

At the concern in her voice, all I could do was nod. Then she asked me about my family and what I thought about Michigan. We were talking more than we had in any other class; we'd usually exchange a brief greeting before slipping our headphones in. This was much better.

After I told her a little about my family, she winked and said, "I think you know my brother."

I squinted, taking in her glasses and quirked, confident grin. "James?" I asked hesitantly. They both wore glasses, and maybe I could see the resemblance—same cheekbones and slender build.

"Yep, he's been encouraging me to become friends with you, but I'm more introverted than he is. He was the one who suspected you had lupus, or at least Raynaud's, but I wasn't sure until today."

I chuckled at that. "Yeah, he can be friendly. He's really cute."

Her expression turned hard. "I don't think he'd date anyone still in high school, FYI."

I felt my cheeks heat. "What? No. I meant he's super-attractive, so it's probably easy for him to be outgoing. I bet he goes on a lot of dates." Although James was a cutie-patootie, for sure, I hadn't seen him like that. Maybe because he was older, or just his personality, but he'd just always given me that wholesome big-brother vibe.

"Less than you'd think." She gave me a sly grin as she mixed her paints. "He's actually kind of a goody-goody and normally only dates girls from our church."

"Where do you guys go?" I asked, growing excited when she named a place down the street from the condo.

"It's cool. They have youth group on Sunday nights, and James and I do choir on Wednesdays." She must have seen how I was looking at her, because she asked, "Do you want to go with me?"

I paused a moment before saying, "I'd really like that. My dad's an atheist, but I'm not. He offered to go with me, but I'd rather go with someone who actually wants to be there."

She chuckled. "Yeah, that makes sense. Gimme your number. I'll text you mine."

We exchanged them before I went back to my project. It was slow work today with my hands flared up. AP Art required a portfolio theme, and I'd wanted to do a theme of juxtapositions. Each image would have a black and white and colored aspect in opposition. Last week I'd created a girl inside in black and white staring out the window to the water in color. Right now I was working on a mermaid swimming toward the surface in color and a boy leaning down to touch the water in black and white. I thought his foreshortened huge hand looked cool.

I was taking AP Drawing and Becky was doing 2D, so she was using paints, while I was using pastels. As usual, Ms. Bellatus made us start cleaning up our messy supplies early, but as I headed out the door to lunch, I felt more energized than I had in a while. It had felt good for my lupus to be less of a secret. Maybe that was why it felt nice with Charles—he knew, so I could let my guard down. Now Becky and James knew, too.

It was kind of a relief.

I asked the guys at lunch if they knew Becky, and Knox flushed red. "What?"

"He super into her," Charles whispered. The cicadas buzzed in me as Charles's breath skimmed my neck. He'd been so sweet yesterday. "She's always been James's little sister, but now she's James's not-so-little sister. He's just too nervous to ask her out."

"Awe, it's like a love story—best friend's little sister. And thanks again for yesterday," I said, feeling my cheeks reddening probably more than the rash.

We locked eyes for a moment before Knox asked about band practice, which made me blush even more.

I caught Charles looking at me twice during lunch, and it made me jittery. We'd been friends for forever and I should have been content with that.

When math rolled around, Greg tried to apologize for Luke again, but I really didn't want to talk about it. It was embarrassing just to remember it. Then Greg asked about my "sun poisoning" that apparently Charles had told him about.

Sun poisoning, yes—that was a good thing to call it. Charles really was brilliant. It made me want to kiss him in gratitude the next time I saw him. Heck, I wanted to kiss him for a whole lot of reasons. My skin heated as I thought about those slow circles on my back or how stunning his eyes had been after he'd played me "Run."

By Friday, my face was finally back to normal, or at least normal enough to be hidden with makeup, and the lingering stiffness in my joints seemed to have temporarily vanished. Unfortunately, I knew it'd return the next time I didn't listen to my body. Although my hamstrings were crying from yoga last night, I felt good—relaxed. I'd never tell my mom, in case she thought it was un-Christian, but the breathing they did at the end of class was really soothing. And the chanting. Maybe there was something to this Iyengar yoga.

Charles had been bugging me all week until I agreed to let him take me to and from school on the days he was free. It was nice; at least a handful of days a week, we had a few minutes for just the two of us. I hoped Charles felt that way too and wasn't just put up to this by his mom, because everyone worried about my health.

On Friday afternoon, I stalled in the car yet again. I was about to meet my dad's girlfriend for the first time.

"So, they've been dating for five years and you've really never met her?" Charles asked.

"Not in person. She lives in Chicago. She's a sociology professor at Northwestern, and they met at a conference. He said she's been respecting our time together because I didn't used to get to see him very often, but now…"

"Now you live here," he finished for me.

"Yep. I've talked to her, though, on video chat. She seems nice…" I trailed off.

I hadn't spoken to my stepdad, Mark, whom I'd lived with for more than a decade, since I moved here. Just like I'd always suspected, I was unwanted baggage that came when he married my mom, who was ten years his junior. It made me nervous to meet Dad's girlfriend in case she felt the same way. Things had been going really well with Dad and me, and I wanted her to like me, too.

"I'd still like to come to band practice Saturday afternoon," I told Charles before getting out of the car.

"Yeah?" he said with a chuckle. "I thought you just—"

"Maybe they want some alone time. They haven't seen each other in more than two months. I just realized that." I blushed. "The apartment is pretty small."

He laughed again. "Right, no problem. I can get you at three, no worries."

I still wasn't ready to get out, my belly flopping strangely as I worried whether she would like me. "What are you up to tonight?" I asked Charles.

"Well, I have this big date"—I felt my stomach drop and then ice over. Of course he did. Charles was nice and smart and cute—"with my calculus and physics books," he finished. "That GPA doesn't happen by itself."

Butterflies replaced the ice as I met his eyes. "Yeah, well, I bet you're just counting down until you can gravitate together."

We shared a smile over my super lame joke. Now I'd been sitting in the car a moment too long and I felt it getting uncomfortable. I was about to bolt when he leaned over and tucked some loose hair behind my ear. His hand lingered on my jaw.

"Don't worry," he whispered. "She's really going to like you."

I looked up and met those dark brown eyes as a jolt ran through me. I wanted to turn my face into his hand. I wanted to press my lips against his and see if he felt it too, this electricity between us. But I was afraid. I couldn't lose this friendship. So I just gazed back into his canny eyes.

"Thanks," I said pulling back, afraid of the emotions I felt. When we'd dated, Ross had made my body burn for him, and Charles was starting too as well. But Charles also called to something buried deeper inside me. Something frightening. When he looked at me, it was like he saw more than Rayanne Ericson. He saw all the shattered pieces of me, like no one, not even Jeffery, ever had.

"You can call me later if you want," Charles said as I put

my hand on the door. The comfort of his words slid over me.

"Thanks, and see you tomorrow."

I slipped out and headed upstairs. I could still feel the heat of his hand on my face and the tingling it had sent through me when he met my gaze. Could he feel it too? Was it worth risking our friendship to find out?

With a deep breath, I opened the door. The aromatic scent of beef stew hit me first. We must have Kalops in the slow cookers, again. Both my dad and his girlfriend turned to me. All five feet of her shot straight up and she hurried over, pulling me right into a firm hug.

When she pulled back, she introduced herself. "Soraya Hashemi. Ray, it's so wonderful to finally meet you! Your dad is so happy you are living with him now."

I fiddled with my backpack straps as I said, "I've heard a lot about you." I cast a quick glance at Dad, wondering what to say, so I blurted out, "Dad says you're Persian?"

Why was that what came out of my mouth? Out of all the things I knew about her, of course I'd have to go say that.

She bopped her head, her gorgeous mahogany hair temporarily covering her face. It was threaded with a little gray at her temples, reminding me she was a few years older than Dad.

"I was born here. My parents left Iran in the seventies for college and never went back." She didn't say it had been for political reasons, but I had learned that from Dad. Her parents had been political refugees and after 1978 couldn't return home. "Look at me blabbing. Why don't you get comfortable and drop your school stuff? I'll be here all weekend to get to know you. I can't wait to hear what you're learning in AP Geography."

As I walked into my room, I heard her say, "Nils, she's even more gorgeous in person! I can't believe how much she looks like you."

I couldn't help the smile that came to my lips. Looking like Dad didn't bother me as much as it once had.

Calmer, I returned to the living room and sat with them on the sofas. "So, what classes are you teaching this semester?" I asked, knowing professors loved their courses more than anything else.

"The intro humdrum and a fun upper level, but my baby grad course is on gender and social media. We are comparing how audiences respond to women on Twitter versus Instagram, and how males versus females respond to those women. We have a heavy discussion on the role of digitally enhanced images, race, and the projection of beauty."

"Wow, that sounds complicated."

"Yes." She nodded vigorously, and her eyes lit up like Dad's when he talked about economics, or Charles's with robotics or music. "A graduate student and I collected research on it for almost two years. He published it as his dissertation."

The discussion continued over my head with Soraya and my dad getting into a complex discussion on gendered economics. It was apparent how passionate they both were and why my parents had been doomed from the beginning. Soraya and Dad aligned, unlike my mom's antiquated views on a woman's ideal economic role—dependent on a man. When they reached a point they disagreed on, Soraya jumped up and practically shouted at my dad, "Your argument is ridiculously flimsy."

The look he gave her back was so heated, I walked to the bathroom, half-afraid they'd start making out.

When I came back, they were holding hands. Then the oven chimed, and Dad stood to take our bread out. He served the Kalops stew that had been in the slow cooker into our mug bowls. I made the salad, while Soraya set the table. It felt very domestic, the three of us. During dinner Soraya asked about my AP Art portfolio.

Reluctantly, I always got nervous when someone wanted to see my work, I showed her some of my pieces when we finished eating. She stared at them more intently than even Ms.

Bellatus and asked me a series of probing questions about why one color over another; why this angle; why the one opposition was the colored one. I felt like she saw my art as no one ever had. She understood.

When I finally yawned, she looked alarmed. "Oh, I could do this all night. I'll see you in the morning," she said, and left my room with a goodnight.

I tried not to think what my mom and Granny Young might say about Dad's unmarried girlfriend spending the weekend here. I didn't know why after five years they weren't married or at the very least, living in the same city. But she seemed like Dad's perfect match.

I hated it when people nosed into my personal life, so I certainly wouldn't butt into theirs.

I'd had an amazing time with Dad and Soraya all weekend, and she'd be driving back to Chicago soon. I didn't know what time she'd be leaving, but I'd be at church for the next few hours. The way she and Dad had been looking at each other, it might not be immediately. I'd given them some privacy when I left to practice with the Snowblowers, but the weekend had flown by. And Soraya had seemed to enjoy my company as much as I'd enjoyed hers. She hadn't made me feel like she was waiting for me to leave once. It was nice. *She* was nice.

As I waited outside the church, I straightened my skirt and a deep voice called my name.

I turned, waving to James and Becky. Standing side by side, their resemblance was undeniable. "Hi! Thanks for inviting me," I said.

Becky and James laughed. "Isn't that the point?" Becky said. "This is church, after all."

"Yes, I guess." I fiddled with my cardigan, hoping it'd be like Jeff's church.

Inside, it was much more elaborate than the church back home, and I immediately liked it. A bouncy, energetic man rushed over, who Becky and James introduced as the preacher. He looked to be around Dad's age.

"Welcome," he said, putting both his hands around mine. "Ray, we are so happy to have you join our family."

"Thank you," I whispered as we found our pew and the service began.

Something warm and homey filled me during the readings, and it turned to pure joy when it came time to sing, especially with James and Becky beside me. The words felt powerful, righteous in a way Mom's church never had. I'd only ever felt this way before at Jeff's church. Becky and James both made me feel like I belonged, as well.

As I left the youth group hours later and strolled back to Dad's in the twilight of the night, the one thing that felt like it had been missing in my life here in Michigan clicked into place. A cold misty rain started up, and the wind had a bite that Savannah rarely did, but I'd never felt happier to be in Michigan than at that moment. I could make it work here—or at least, I was finally hopeful I could.

· · ·
EIGHTEEN

Charles

I laughed at Ray as she bent over, stretching her arms on the back of the basement sofa.

"My hamstrings, Charles, *owww-eee*. Are you sure this yoga is good for me?"

"I'm sure you'll get more flexible." I briefly fantasized about saying something like, *I could give you a massage*, but didn't.

Ray and I were in the same place as weeks before. Sometimes I swear I caught her looking at me as more than a friend, like last Friday, when my hand had lingered on her face too long or when I'd held her last Monday, but then I'd tell myself I imagined things. The more I'd gotten to know her, the more beautiful she'd become. Also, the less I believed she'd ever date someone like me when she hadn't even responded to Greg's flirting.

"Why wouldn't this type of yoga be good for you?" Kevin asked. "Are you special or something?"

Ray ignored his dig and glanced at me and then James.

"I'm ready to start back up," James said breaking the

tension, and we all got back to positions, except Ray. She sat back down with her art supplies. "Let's practice the covers, Ray."

"All right," she said and hopped back up with a grin covering half her face.

We'd written two new songs, one with James and one with James and Ray that we'd practiced at the very beginning of the afternoon, but Ray'd been drawing for a while. Our covers, which we hadn't practiced yet, were "The First Cut is the Deepest," George Ezra's "Shotgun" with Ray in the chorus, and Kid Rock and Cheryl Crow's "Picture." It was fun hearing Ray really crank out her country.

We ran through the first two with no issues, but she missed a word twice in a row when we begun "Picture." Kevin grumbled loudly about starting up a third time while Ray blushed. It was almost six thirty when James's stomach growled.

"Sorry, I was dreaming about shawarma," he said with a laugh.

"Huh?" Ray said.

"Shawarma," James repeated. Ray shook her head. "No, Ray. Tell me you've had Middle Eastern food before?" When she shook her head again, James continued, "Where is this place you are from? Okay then, who's up for a road trip to Dearborn? I think we need to show Miss Ray here what I'm dreaming about."

Murmurs of agreement went around and we loaded into my car to head to the birthplace of Ford and where the "best" Arab food in Michigan was to be found. Not only did forty percent of Dearborn mark "Arab" on the last census report, but it was also home to the country's only Arab American National Museum.

When we got to Dearborn, Ray marveled at all the signs either in Arabic and English or just Arabic. Even though it was a solid hour drive from Ann Arbor, nothing beat Dearborn for this type of food. "Wow, this place is amazing," she said. "All the times I've been to Ann Arbor, I've never been here."

"Ray, get off. You're all bony," Kevin grumbled.

I peeked in the review mirror and saw Ray was half on top of Kevin. "Sorry, but did you see that?" she exclaimed.

Knox chuckled and pulled Ray back to the middle. "We've been here before."

She giggled out, "That tickles," and I wished I could trade places with Knox.

We pulled into the place James had been craving and the hostess seated us. Ray picked out something with a little assistance and everyone but Kevin offered to let her try some of theirs. After thoroughly stuffing our faces and driving back, everyone decided practice was over and crammed onto the basement sofa and chairs to watch *Guardians of the Galaxy* instead. Kevin and James claimed their two usual chairs while Knox, Ray, and I flopped onto the sofa. Knox took one end and Ray took the middle, curling her knees so they slanted toward me.

"Here," I said, moving a pillow so she could lean on it against me. She smiled and curled into a fetal position on her side. My arm hung awkwardly until I found a spot for it on the pillow behind her head. Her warm shoulder settled against my side, and I wished I were brave enough to ask her how she felt about me.

Halfway through the movie, Knox and Kevin went upstairs to make popcorn. I glanced down at the warmth of Ray nestled against me. She'd fallen asleep. Her hair was a riot, obscuring part of her face. Something tugged inside me, and I couldn't resist tucking some of her hair behind her ears and gazing down at her angelic face. Her rash had finally faded, and I was glad. Not because it'd looked bad, but because of what it meant and the way it dulled her personality.

"What's the reason you won't date her? Or at least try?" James said from the chair, startling me into remembering we weren't alone. "I thought about your question, and I don't think being Asian would be an issue for her."

"Because of how she is," I said, not wanting to have to elaborate on the differences between us.

He looked disgusted. "You mean lupus?"

"No!" I said in a firm whisper. "I just don't think, that is… she's my friend."

"Whatever. I thought you were better than that."

"That's not why, and how do you even know about her lupus?"

"Becky. Our aunt had it, remember?"

I shook my head, no. Then did vaguely remember he'd had an aunt who was sick, but she'd died.

"So, if not that, what?" James interrupted my thoughts.

I shrugged. He wouldn't understand. James had lived next door to Knox since forever, but he'd always been miles cooler than us. He was mad fit with huge dimples and a ready smile. I'd seen all the girls, even Ray, stare at him. Beauty and the geek might have seemed like a joke to him, but it seemed insurmountable to me.

"Charles, you don't look at your *friends* like that. You don't brush your friend's hair out of her face. You asked me earlier about her, and I think she likes you too. But don't wait too long. She's nice, funny, and damn cute. If you're afraid because she has lupus, someone else won't be."

His words were true. Anyone would want to date her.

"I said that wasn't the reason," I hissed, and Ray wiggled and murmured in her sleep. In her movement, she snuggled her arm to my thigh, her fingers curling into me. I felt myself stiffen in more ways than one at the pleasure her innocent touch sent through me. I mentally recited math problems until I got myself together.

Just then the guys banged down the stairs, and Ray jerked awake.

"Oh, sorry, did I fall asleep?" Her eyes darted to mine as she chewed on her lower lip and rolled onto her back. My fingers were tangled beneath her silken hair. I nodded and she yawned sleepily before mumbling again, "Sorry."

"No worries." I gently extracted my hand. "I'll take you home." I didn't want to risk her getting sick when she'd just started feeling better. "I've seen this movie a bunch of times."

The ride was quiet, and James's words kept playing in my head.

"Thanks," she said when we got to her place.

"Wait," I said, startling her to turn and look back at me with wide eyes. "Ray, I, um… What I wanted to say was—"

Crap. I couldn't form the words, so instead I just slid forward and pecked her on the lips. I didn't want to be pushy if this was one sided, so I pulled right back.

I risked glancing at her, and she stared at me blankly for what felt like a minute as my stomach somersaulted. Then she grabbed my shoulder and pulled my lips back to hers. This time, instead of an innocent peck, her mouth recaptured mine forcefully. I couldn't help releasing a groan as her tongue sought mine. Her fingers yanked at my shoulders and I unclasped my seatbelt so I could inch closer to her.

My free hand skimmed her face while hers slid around my neck. Our tongues toyed back and forth as passionately as our fingers tangled—gripping, caressing, clutching each other. I didn't know how long we kissed for, but we were both breathless when we drew back, her vibrant eyes meeting mine with a look I couldn't read.

My fingers whispered against her face, unable to resist touching her silken skin. My eyes darted to her swollen lips. I felt my own mouth curve up at the evidence of our kissing with a possessiveness I'd never felt before. My whole body tingled, charged from that kiss. Her smell, her breath, her chest still heaving against mine all overwhelmed me; I couldn't think of anything but her. She was like a drug, and now that I'd tasted her, I wanted her again. One hit would never be enough.

She was the first to break the silence. "I've been hoping

that would happen for a long time," she said.

My grin grew, and I leaned in to brush my lips against hers as I whispered back against her mouth, "Yeah, that makes two of us."

I forced myself to pull back slightly, even when every instinct urged me to get closer and closer. The guys were at my place and we were on a fairly well-lit street. Not the romantic location she deserved. Plus, she was tired; I couldn't be the reason she got sick.

"I should probably let you get back," she said in a faraway voice, but her grip on my shoulder tightened, fighting a battle to create space between us.

"Yes," I said, but I didn't stop stroking her soft skin and hair. It looked like moonbeams in this light. She didn't move away. Instead, she turned into me as if she, too, craved my touch. Her lips parted and her warm breath tickled my skin.

Our lips moved back together like magnets. My hand slipped to her back to urge her closer, her form pressing against me. That electric current charged through me even stronger, setting every nerve ending on fire for her. She sucked my tongue into her mouth and I couldn't resist clutching her more firmly, never wanting this moment to end.

Finally, she pulled back a second time, breathless. Slowly, reluctantly, I retracted my hands, my fingertips languid in their departure from the satin of her cheeks. She gave me a quirked grin as she slid out of the car.

"Goodnight," she said softly, just before the door closed.

As I watched her walk to the condo entrance like I had so many times before, a warmth bloomed in my chest that wasn't just ardor. I'd kissed Ray Ericson—and she'd kissed me back.

NINETEEN

Ray

A loud knock on my door woke me up.

"Good morning, Ray!" My dad stood, beaming, in the doorway. I smothered a yawn, wondering what was going on. "Wake up, sweetheart, I have something planned for you." His excitement was palpable.

"Okay," I said, sitting up with sudden energy. Seeing I was awake, he closed the door. I yelled, "What should I wear?"

"Doesn't matter!"

Gripped with curiosity and still in a great mood from last night's kiss with Charles, I got dressed. Dad's energy was infectious. I bounced into the kitchen, where he handed me a cup of coffee. The black-brown liquid reminded me of Charles's discerning eyes. Charles's—

"Today we are going to the Detroit Institute of Art," Dad said, interrupting my daydreaming with a jolt.

My hold on the cup tightened, and I glanced up in surprise. "The DIA? Really?" Suddenly, I felt ecstatic.

I'd wanted to go there, but with how much traveling to Sweden we used to do, I hadn't been for years. My appreciation for art had certainly evolved since then.

"Uh-huh, just as soon as you have breakfast and take your morning medicine. And then while we are downtown, I'm going to take you shopping."

"Shopping?"

"Dorothy, you aren't in Kansas anymore. *Winter is coming.*"

I gave him a questioning look.

"Tell me you've seen *Game of Thrones*?"

"Are you kidding? Mom would never let me watch it—too graphic. And um, sex," I finished with a blush.

"Fair enough," he relented. "For once, Chrissy might be right. But the weather *is* changing. Now, what you have is all right because it's September and it's been mild. But it'll be October on Tuesday, and it's going to start getting quite cold. Your old jacket barely fit at Christmas. And remember you wore my brown wool sweater the whole time you were here, and Karen lent you some in Stockholm?"

I nodded, thinking about my sleek, cool cousin, Karen. She was three years older and had lent me warm things. They were the coolest clothes I'd ever worn. I always saved up so I could buy a few things in the Södermalm district when I went to Stockholm.

"We need to get you a new winter coat, and one or better two pairs of boots you can wear for the next six months," Dad continued. "Warm ones because of your Raynaud's. And a few sweaters?" He scratched his stubble. "Soraya made me a list and emailed me all the things she expected me to buy you. She titled it *Midwest girl's survival gear*, and said she and I will have words if I don't get everything for you by the next time I see her. Which is next weekend, by the way."

I giggled. "Really?"

"Yeah, happy early birthday! And she said she bought the two of you tickets to Selena Gomez the first week of December. She's playing in Chicago. Coincidentally, I have a conference there, so it's perfect."

"Selena Gomez?" I didn't really listen to her, but a concert had to be fun. I'd never been to a big one before—musicians like her didn't play in Savannah, not that Mom would have let me go.

"I didn't ask, but she seemed excited." He cast me a wry grin. "Sometimes when you love someone, you just say, 'that's great,' and don't question it."

"Okay, well, if she bought the tickets, that's really nice." I meant it, too. "I'll download some of her music. Let me wash my face, and we can go."

"Oh, and bring your new Michigan enhanced ID, because if we have time, we're going to take a walk in Windsor. The view of the city is nice from the Canadian riverfront."

I nodded and hurried to get ready. We arrived at the museum shortly after it opened and spent a few hours there. I sneakily took a picture of the Caravaggio and sent it to Charles when the guard wasn't looking. Thinking about him and our kiss last night brought heat to my cheeks. I hoped it meant as much to him as it had to me.

Shoot, if it didn't, it'd be hard for me not to see him that way. As I recalled it, I felt tingly *all* over. His hands were as dexterous as I'd always imagined. He could rub my back and caress my face and kiss me simultaneously with equal attention. I crossed my arms and sighed. Yep, I was a goner; I wanted more.

Finally, our stomachs pulled us out of the museum and to Dad's favorite Italian restaurant in Corktown. Then we went shopping, wandering the gorgeous Art Deco streets of downtown Detroit, past the buildings I loved so much. I hadn't decided if I wanted to study industrial architecture, like Mr. Davis, or residential, but I loved the intricacy of some of the buildings down here.

Soraya's survival gear list was really extensive. When I protested it was too much—because golly, winter clothing was expensive—Dad blushed and said, "Ray, I used to pay your mother two thousand dollars a month in child support. And it's really cold here. Trust me, when you're waiting in snow and slush for the bus, you'll need this stuff. These boots and sweaters you'll wear till April, maybe May. Please, you have Raynaud's—you need to take care of your feet."

"Two thousand dollars? You didn't." I couldn't believe Mom had been getting that kind of money. She always talked about him like he was a deadbeat dad.

"Ray."

"You did? She didn't tell me."

I stopped in the middle of the sidewalk, completely flabbergasted. Dad guided me to the building's edge as people huffed around us.

I dropped my voice so I wouldn't shout. "That's twenty-four thousand a year." I grabbed his forearms to shake him and see if he was joking, but his jaw was tight, like maybe he regretted his words. In all this time, he'd almost never said a bad word about her. Even I could barely hear my voice as I continued, "She made me work to buy clothes. I've been babysitting since I was twelve and waiting tables for almost two years."

"Ray, please don't hate your mother. It's good to have a strong work ethic. Maybe she didn't want you to be spoiled. I don't understand the way Chrissy thinks—I never have—but I know she loves you. I don't want you to hate your mom; that's not healthy."

Suddenly, I felt suspicious. "Is that why you wanted me to move here?"

Hurt flicked across his face. "No, absolutely not. I wanted what's best for you. Aren't you happy here?" The pain in his eyes made me regret those hastily spoken words.

Just then, my phone vibrated. I thought of Charles and how much I was starting to like my new school. And my friends here seemed genuine, not just ones who suddenly liked me because I grew boobs and dated the star running back. It was weird to think, but I fit in here like I never had back in Savannah. Dad let me be me in a way my mom never had.

"Yes, I'm happier here."

His features softened. "Okay, good, now let's finish so we can walk and then get you to church."

I did enjoy seeing the Detroit skyline from the Canadian riverfront—Dad knew me well. The day had been amazing. No one had ever done something so special for my birthday. Even if it was early, it was one of the best birthdays I'd ever had. But on the drive back, I couldn't help but wonder why Mom had acted like Dad never did anything for me, like he never loved me, like he wished I hadn't been born.

Almost as if reading my thoughts, Dad said, "I've been talking to your mom, and she'd like you to go down and visit this weekend for your birthday. You'd leave Friday. It's been more than two months. Do you think you'll feel up to taking the trip by yourself?"

"Yes, I've done it for years." I wasn't sure I wanted to, but oh goodness, it'd be good to hug Jeff. And my siblings. Even if Mark never made me feel like his daughter, they were my blood. But everyone else, not so much.

"I know, but I don't want you to get too tired." I wondered if he was thinking about the state in which I'd shown up a little over two months ago.

Unaccompanied minors could travel as young as five. I wasn't sure how old I was when I'd started flying by myself, but it felt like my whole life. Some of my first memories had been getting off the plane in Atlanta, Chicago, or New York and hugging Dad before boarding the next one to Sweden. It had been as important to him for me to know my family as it had been for him to see them.

"I'll be fine," I reassured him. He said he'd get me the tickets when I was at church that night. I was so irate with Mom right now—I hoped I could be civil when I saw her. Dad was right, she was my mother, but I did not understand her. Plus, after living with Dad for two months, I'd realized how much more I was like him, or even Soraya, than her.

I didn't know if I'd bring up the child support, but Dad was not the way Mom had always portrayed him. Not at all. And the worst part was, he knew what she'd said about him and hadn't stood up for himself, just because he didn't want me to hate her. I'd always wanted his love and respect, but after getting to know him, that desire had only grown stronger. And even if Michigan wasn't exactly next door to Savannah, it was in the same country, same time zone even. He could've lived in Europe, but he moved for *me*. He could have taught economics and researched anywhere. I hoped when he'd asked me to stay, he hadn't meant for just a semester. I really liked living with him.

I just had a few minutes to change into a new raspberry colored sweater and thick black leggings before it was time to leave for church. I smiled the whole walk past all the cafes, shops, and trees showing off their crimson, mustard, and ochre hues. I beamed even more broadly when I found a seat next to Becky. A sigh escaped me as the service started. Not only did I like their church, but I was relieved I wouldn't have to have that fight again when I went home to see Mom. Choir practice with Becky and James on Wednesday had been fantastic, and both of them had a sharp sense of humor I'd grown to appreciate.

It was late when I walked home, and I was glad I'd finished all my homework Friday night and Saturday morning because I was worn out from the weekend. I yawned, stretching out on my bed for a minute before I worked up the energy to shower and dry my hair before bed.

Just then, Charles texted me, and my heart sped up. *Have fun at the museum today?*

Almost as much fun as last night (:

Almost? Sounds like I need to do better. Is an encore performance in order?

Heat spiked through me as I smiled. *I think an encore is*

definitely needed—the results are inconclusive.

I guess it's a good thing I'll see you tomorrow morning then. I'll have to imagine opportunities for enhancement. Perhaps a kiss to your jaw.

My skin prickled, imagining those lips doing just that. *Perhaps...till tomorrow.*

Until then, goodnight.

I sighed as I got into the shower. I felt something for Charles I hadn't felt for anyone else, even Ross. I felt like he saw me—really saw me, and he liked me anyway. I'd even said as much to him, and it was a little scary. There were parts of me I didn't like, and somehow I felt like those penetrating eyes bore right into them. Despite the hot water, which was an amazing thing I'd be lucky to get this weekend, I felt goosebumps break out across my skin. I really hoped I'd stay here for more than a semester. But even then, Charles would leave next year. Surely he'd get into Caltech, which was so far away.

Stay present, I chided myself. It was one kiss, and he might not even want to date me. He was so busy.

Still, as I washed my hair, I couldn't help but daydream about my kiss tomorrow morning and hope Charles would keep his promise to make it even better than I remembered.

TWENTY

Charles

I drove to get Ray, my fingers tapping "Sweet Georgia Brown" on the steering wheel. We'd kissed. We'd really kissed. I lost the beat with my fingers and had to restart it.

Ray—she eclipsed all other thoughts.

There she was, waiting on the curb in a fitted sweater and skinny jeans. Heat seared through me as my heart thudded an allegro beat. She was stunning. Again, I wondered how she could ever think I was good enough for her. I started the beat on the steering wheel a third time, hoping to soothe my nerves.

"Hi," I whispered as she slid into the car.

She smiled before she leaned over, lips lightly brushing mine. Before she could pull back, I deepened it and slid my hand to cup her delicate face. She moaned back into my mouth before turning her head to place small kisses on my jaw.

"I'm glad we finally kissed," she said into my ear as her breath fanned my neck.

I tilted her jaw so I could pepper it with kisses as I breathed her in. She truly was intoxicating.

"Yeah, me too," I said, scraping my teeth across her earlobe before pulling back.

She feather-kissed my lips once more before buckling up. I put my hand on the gear shift, more for something to do than anything else, and backed us up.

"So, we've kissed. Twice," she said with a hint of humor as I eased us on to the road.

"More than twice. I'm in advanced math. I can count."

"So…" she said after several beats.

"So, I guess that means I'm the luckiest guy in school." I made it sound like a joke, but I wasn't actually joking. I felt like the luckiest guy in the world to have kissed those lips and have felt her body against mine.

Just then the radio played the new Weezer song, "All My Favorite Songs," which we'd just talked about liking. Perfect. The moment couldn't be more perfect.

"Does this change things?" she asked as the car inched closer to school and the song faded to a commercial.

Her words made me start to sweat. I'd never dated before. "Only if you want it to," I managed to say without taking my eyes off the road. "Do you want it to?"

Please, say yes.

She was silent a long moment, and I held my breath as I pulled into the school lot.

"If I did?" Her voice sounded timid.

It surprised me. I didn't risk glancing at her. I tried not to show my own nervousness—gross sweating—and keep my voice calm even as my fingers tightened on the steering wheel.

"I'd be okay with that." *I'd be way more than okay with that*. I wanted to kiss those lips every damn day—more than once a day.

She was quiet as I parked. And then: "Just okay?"

I turned and looked at her. Shit, did she not realize what she did to me? What she'd always done to me.

"Thrilled." I gently threaded our fingers. "Ray, I'm busy. I'm too busy to date a lot of girls, especially if I already found the one I want."

A look of delight overtook her face. "Well," she said. "That's kind of romantic."

She gave me a peck and released my hand to jump out of the car. I took a deep breath and followed her. After a brief hesitation, I reached for her hand once more, now in view of the whole parking lot. Her lips quirked up as she once more let me take it.

The rest of the day, I felt like I was untouchable. I was dating Ray Ericson. I still couldn't believe it.

However, by the next afternoon in Robotics Club, all my thoughts were focused on our robot. Its program wasn't running. No matter how Dana, Kevin, and I tweaked it, it'd stop mid-program. We needed to get this done today because when the real competition rolled out next semester, we'd only be given six weeks to build the entire robot. If I didn't get it geared up, I'd knew it'd distract me all night from my homework.

A touch on my arm startled me.

"Ray," I said in surprise, standing up. "Here." I took her outside the classroom so we wouldn't have to shout over all the noise. "What are you doing here?" I nearly winced at how rough my voice was, but I hated stopping in the middle of a project.

"I had to finish a drawing. I've been doing some extra pieces, and once they're graded, I can sell them," Ray said, tucking some hair behind her ears. "I didn't have any more blue pastels at home, and I thought you'd be able to give me a ride."

She glanced into the loud robotics room. We clearly weren't done yet.

"Of course I can take you, but we finish at six. Just come in and maybe do some homework in the back." I ran my hand nervously through my hair. I really couldn't leave now, and I didn't want to.

"I thought you finished at five. Shoot, don't worry. I can ask Greg. I saw the football team was about to wrap up. It's really loud in there. I'd never get anything done."

She pulled out her phone as I said, "You should have texted me."

She turned her face away from me. "Hey, Greg, are you still here? I need a lift." She fell silent before continuing. "Yes, of course I still want to see your Dad's building, but I'm out of town this weekend—sweet sixteen and all."

Crap, crap, crap. I completely forgot about her birthday. And I wished she'd told me she was going out of town.

Her laughed chimed down the empty hallway. "You know the answer to that. No, I've never been to a Red Wings game. Actually, I've never even been to a hockey game. But let's talk in the car. I'll be right there." She hung up and glanced at me. "I did text you. A few times, actually. It's fine. I have a lot of homework, and I want to stop by The Cup and see if they'd be interested in selling any of my artwork. You know they display pieces there to sell. Art supplies are expensive, and I'm not working right now. Plus, I want to save up to pay for this architecture camp Mr. Davis mentioned. It's not like it's a chore. Drawing and painting—I love it."

"That'd be cool," I said as I pulled out my phone and grimaced. Three texts from her appeared, time-stamped between one thirty and now. "So, Savannah this weekend?"

She nodded. "Dad bought the ticket last night."

I leaned in to whisper, "You'll take care of yourself, right?"

"Yes, Dad," she mocked with a bump of my shoulder.

So far, only Becky, James, and I knew about her health

issues. She'd just missed the one day so far, and it wasn't my place to talk about it.

"Charles, we need you, man," Kevin called from the classroom.

"I should probably go too," Ray said. "Greg's waiting."

It didn't sit right that she'd rather ride with Greg than wait for me to finish. Or that they now had plans to hang out with his family.

"Can I take you out to dinner after yoga Thursday for your birthday?" I asked. I needed to do something—it was sixteen, after all.

Double crap, I needed to go shopping. What did you buy for someone's birthday? Maybe I could ask Knox. I'd never bought a birthday gift in my life and hers was the only one I'd ever received, aside from money. Maybe art stuff—pastels. She needed pastels. Blue pastels.

"I thought you forgot," she said, and my heart dropped with how close that was to the truth.

"Never," I said, hoping she couldn't hear my mounting anxiety. I hated she'd assumed, even correctly, I'd forgotten her birthday. Already, I was a shit boyfriend.

"Sure, I'll call you later."

I glanced around quickly to make sure the hall was deserted and then gave her a quick kiss.

As she walked away, I wondered what I should plan for our first official date and her birthday. I wasn't surprised I hadn't seen her messages—Robotics Club consumed me—but still, it all left a bad taste in my mouth.

By Thursday, Ray's birthday, the weather had turned cold and a dreary rain was falling, but my palms still were sweaty as I waited to pick her up in the damp parking garage. She greeted me with a brief kiss, then we snuggled under an umbrella and I put my arm around her as we strolled down the street to a café she'd said she liked.

As soon as we got to the restaurant, Ray slipped on the wet tiles near the threshold.

"Ope!" the hostess exclaimed. "Dontcha know I just text my boss we need new a mat here."

"It's all right," Ray said, but her cheeks turned fire red. Her hands clinched and her fingers pinched and rolled her tights, just below the hem of her dress.

"It was just wet, Ray. Don't worry."

"I'm not."

"Want a booth or high top?" I asked, letting it go, but I could tell she was nervous. She'd likely have runs in her stockings if she kept it up.

"Booth. They have hooks on the side for our jackets."

"Follow me," the hostess said as she grabbed our menus and led us there.

The rest of dinner was a little awkward with a few moments of halting silence. Despite years of friendship, we were now dating. Things somehow felt different. Or maybe I made it weird. I'd never dated before. But Ray seemed tense too and nearly toppled her water twice.

When we finished eating, we both seemed to breathe out a sigh of relief and things immediately felt more comfortable away from the expectations of a dinner date. When we strolled arm-in-arm down the street, just the two of us, it felt right again.

"Do you want to go in The Cup?" Ray asked, referring to the coffee shop she liked as we passed by it.

"Sure." I let her go in as I closed the umbrella.

With our fingers intertwined, she led me to one of the

walls. "A penny for your thoughts."

I followed her gaze to a series of band drawings on display. One depicted a band from the floor of a concert venue. The crowd and band members silhouetted in pure black, lit from the lights depicted in vibrant shades of red, yellow, and orange. On the sides were smaller pictures of individual musicians in excruciating detail except for their faces: a drummer, a guitarist, and a singing duo that, even faceless, had a strong resemblance to Ray and James. Each piece had a price tag beneath it, along with a dramatic signature.

"Yours?" I asked hesitantly, not wanting to offend if I was incorrect.

"Mine," she replied, meeting my eyes. Her eyes were gorgeous and utterly mesmerizing.

Just then, the owner of Bob's Bar and Bistro, where we'd seen the comedy show this summer, came in. He noticed me and ambled over. "Charles! You guys haven't played in a while. We need to get you back on the books."

"Sure, thank you," I said, not meaning it. Now that I was dating Ray, I felt all of a sudden like I had too much on my plate. "Have you met Ray? She just joined the band."

They shook hands, and he noticed the pictures. "Damn, I like those." He pivoted toward me, asking, "What do you think?"

"I think they're exceptional," I said. Ray squeezed my fingers.

"No, yeah for sure. We were just talking about getting some new art in the bar." He glanced around, then back to me. "I'll text James about getting you guys back."

Ray was giddy with excitement when we exited. "Do you think he'll buy them?"

I laughed. "That'd be awesome, wouldn't it?"

When we got back to my car in the parking structure, before I could even open the door to pull out Ray's present, she asked me in a breathless voice, "Want to come up for a minute?"

I said yes, then grabbed her present and followed her into the dark condo.

"Dad's teaching a graduate class tonight," she explained as she flipped on the lights. She took my hand and led me to their sofa.

I handed her the bag and an unwrapped pad of large drawing sheets. She grinned before opening the bag. As soon as she saw the art supplies, she peppered me with kisses. I kissed her back, just as hungry for her. We soon became tangled in each other, breathless.

A loud throat-clearing jolted us apart, as if we'd been electrocuted. Ray jumped up, completely red-faced. "I thought you had class till nine?"

Professor Ericson raised an eyebrow that seemed to say *clearly* before shucking off his wet raincoat and hanging it on the hooks by the door. "It's nine twenty," he responded with his back to us.

We traded an "oh shit" look as he strode over.

"So," he said as he glanced back and forth. "You guys a thing now?"

Ray turned even redder. "Yes, um, we just started dating," I said.

He rubbed the back of his neck and said, "Lovely, well, I'm going to shower. Ray, we need to leave for the airport at seven tomorrow morning."

I coughed. "I should go too. I need to study." It wasn't a lie. This week, nearly all my thoughts had been focused on Ray, yet I had a few more things I wanted on my application before the first of November early action deadline. First quarter grades and a final piano contest in Lansing in a few weeks would be my last opportunities to make sure everything was perfect.

Ray walked me to the door, and I kissed her cheek. "I'll text you. Happy birthday."

As I headed to my car, I started a mental list of everything I needed to do before my early wake-up for orchestra tomorrow morning. Ouch, it was going to be a long night. Ray was amazing, but this dating thing was more stressful than I imagined.

TWENTY-ONE

Ray

I was still smiling about my date with Charles on my second flight the next day. There had been some bumpy moments at the café as we navigated the shift from friends to boyfriend and girlfriend, but we mellowed out as the evening progressed. Or heated up. Holy guacamole, it had been embarrassing when Dad walked in on us making out on the sofa. He hadn't brought it up again. Gosh, he really was the opposite of Mom.

Charles was just so sweet. He'd bought me a large pack of textured colored pastel paper and a box of thirty-six dry pastels—the brand I liked—and I knew neither of those were cheap. I couldn't believe he'd even noticed what I drew with.

He was smart. So, so stinking smart—he had above a 4.0. Still, I chewed on my lip absentmindedly, wondering if I was distracting him. Ever since I could remember, he'd talked about Caltech and getting out of Ann Arbor, away from his loving but demanding parents. Even though I knew they got along, they were strict.

Shoot, I really liked him. If we kept dating, it would be hard to say goodbye. If he went away—heck, I didn't even know how long Dad wanted me in Ann Arbor. Maybe it was just a semester, and the way I was starting to feel about Charles would crush me when Dad sent me back to Savannah permanently.

Focus on the present, I reminded myself. *Enjoy a good thing while it lasts.*

Once we landed, I texted my mom, Charles vanishing from my mind as I recalled how terrible I'd felt the last time I'd flown compared to today. I wasn't as sore as when I'd started yoga, and I was starting to slowly, so slowly, notice an improvement in my joints since I'd begun practicing. Well, that and two months on immunosuppressants and my other lupus medications. Dr. Murray had said the lupus medicines would take six weeks to really start working, and maybe I finally had a little bit more energy again. The first few weeks before I started probiotics and playing with my diet, my stomach had been a disaster. But overall, Michigan had been good for me. Those last few weeks in Savannah, I'd been tired or in pain almost every day.

It was a little frightening being back here, almost as if Savannah had poisoned me as opposed to my body having attacked itself. It was still strange to think of my body being defective. It wasn't like I had a virus, or a tumor, that maybe one day would go away—that I could fight. I couldn't fight this, couldn't cure or ever get rid of it, just contain and maintain. It was still hard to comprehend that even if I got stable, at any point my body could lose it and attack my skin, joints, even organs again. It wasn't something from the outside invading me—instead, *I* was defective, attacking myself.

I'd attempted to hide my crippling fear. Yoga, church, the band, and drawing helped—they all really helped. And Charles, he helped so much. But my life now held an underlying fear that at any time, any part of me could fail—and there was nothing I could do about it. My coping mechanisms helped push that worry into the farthest, smallest corner of my mind, but it was there. It woke me sweating in the night from countless nightmares I never spoke of. I didn't want to be more of a bother.

I shook my dark thoughts away with my sweater before I headed outside. The heat of the still mid-eighty-degree weather and coastal humidity hit me like a brick as I walked toward my mom's parked car.

She jumped out to give me a hug with genuine warmth. "Happy birthday, sweet pea!"

I tightened my hold on her. My mom. Despite how mad I was at her for many reasons, Dad's words rang in my mind: *I don't want you to hate your mom.* I didn't want to hate her either. One day we may talk, but right now I just let myself sink into her and her overly tart, too strongly perfumed embrace.

We chatted lightly on the drive home and when we walked in the house, Gracie Mae, Mary Beth, and Matthew all ran up and smothered me with hugs. My eyes felt treacherously bright, snuggling the sweet, warm bodies of my siblings. Gracie Mae ran away and scuttled back with my present—a drawing of the two of us. Our heads were dangerously egg-shaped, hugely elongated, but it pinched my heart. Mary Beth then slid the tackiest, itchiest, gold-and-pinkest of handmade beaded bracelets onto my wrist. If that didn't vise-grip my heart, I didn't know what would. I might not want to move back here, but I did love them.

When Mark walked in, I thought my stepdad of thirteen years might hug me, but he just said, "Happy birthday, Rayanne," and nodded.

Bitter disappointment gripped me like ice in my veins. I couldn't help but think of the way Soraya had joyously greeted me—a stranger, but a welcome part of her partner's life—and wonder why Mark had never felt that way about me. I tried to be the perfect daughter—good grades, *yes ma'am*s, *no sir*s, no drinking, no sex—but no matter what, I'd never be his daughter. The realization brought me close to tears.

A loud banging on the front door startled me, and Mom motioned me to get it. Jeffery stood there, looking even bigger than the last time I'd seen him. He wasted no time in picking me up off my feet and twirling me around. He felt and smelled like home—like sweat and the briny marsh. The back of his neck, near where my face was pressed, was pink and smattered with freckles from the perpetual Southern sun.

"I missed you, honey," he said as he lowered me back to my feet.

"Jeff," I said affectionately as I clutched him a second too long. He was my family as much as anyone in this room.

Mom called him inside, and we all ate a quick, early dinner of shrimp and grits with Bisquick biscuits and a whole lot of butter. I thought it was generous Mom had invited Jeffery to join us. She'd even made the saltine toffee cookies I loved, and after dinner, they gave me an Amazon gift card.

"You can buy more books on your Kindle and won't have to carry anything," Mark said.

"Or paper, or whatever," Mom added.

I accepted it with a smile. It was neither the worst nor the best gift I could receive. I thought of Dad's day at the museum and shopping and Charles's art supplies—so personal, so me.

"Thank you," I said, trying to sound sincere, but all I could think about was how much I hoped Dad would let me stay with him longer when I got back.

I ran upstairs and slipped into some shorts before riding with Jeffery to his football game. He fiddled with the music before playing *our* song— "Cruise" by Florida Georgia Line— the one we used to sing on our bikes even before we knew or understood all the words.

"So," Jeffery said as the song ended. "There will be a recruiter there tonight from Valdosta State. Coach asked him to keep an eye on me. If I don't get a football scholarship, I'll go to Armstrong for two years and transfer to the main Southern campus. But wish me luck."

"Jeff, that's awesome!" I was ecstatic for him. Jeff had always been average or below in school, but he was a huge guy and loved playing defense. And he'd always been the best friend a girl could have, so I wanted the best for him. I'd noticed a terribly wrapped something in the back seat I assumed he'd give me at some point. I couldn't resist a curve of my lips. Heart of gold, this one.

"Yeah, I'm excited about it." I'd known him long enough to be able to tell his smile was genuine. "Although sometimes I hate playing with Ross. I keep thinking about our last conversation in this car about how he was pressuring you to have sex, and what a jerk he was when you were sick—"

"It's all right," I said, interrupting. "I don't care. I'm dating someone else now." Saying it aloud made me jittery. It was so new, it was strange to even utter it—like I might curse it.

"That Chinese kid?" Jeff cast me a quick look.

"Charles, yep."

"I'm glad. Ray, you look good. Real good. You still taking all that medicine and everything?"

"Jeff," I said after a moment of hesitation. "I'll have lupus forever."

He nodded. "But you feel good?"

I paused for a moment, not knowing what to say. Jeffery and I still talked pretty regularly, but it was hard to explain lupus to someone. You kind of had to be there and see the good and bad days—the endless blood tests, the fatigue, the swollen joints, the clumps of hair in the drain, and pill bottles—to get it. That was my forever.

"I'm doing better than I was, but some days I'm still not doing very well," I said honestly.

This was Jeff. I didn't think I could be anything but honest with him, even if I faked it around most other people. Except Charles, because Charles always saw right through me.

"I guess that's why I like being with Charles," I continued. "He seems to understand, and he's really busy, too—he wants to be valedictorian. I'm pretty sure he will be."

"Dang, girl! Really? I guess he's Asian. Aren't they smarter than us?"

I laughed because I loved Jeffery but couldn't help setting him straight. "That is called a microaggression. You aren't normally one to stereotype like that. He works hard, you would not believe how hard, but yes, he is also freaky smart. It's not because he's Asian."

"Ray Ray, let me tell you a secret." His voice dropped the way it did just for me. "You're kind of smart, too."

This time when I laughed, it was more than halfhearted. I'd used to think so.

As we pulled into the school parking lot, I suddenly felt gripped by fear. My fingers bit into the edges of my shorts. A home game meant I'd have to see everyone again.

Jeffery's gaze swung to me as if he could sense my withdrawal. "You okay? I have a few minutes. I can run you back…"

I stiffened my spine and put my hand on the door handle. "I can do this."

I was one of the first people there who wasn't a player. I bought a water and texted Charles and Dad simultaneously as I waited for the bleachers to fill and silently cursed the mosquitos I didn't think to spray for. It had been in the thirties in Michigan this morning and it was still in the seventies here. I took a quick selfie of me in my shorts and sent it to Charles with a laughing face. Shorts season was long gone in Michigan.

"Rayanne!"

I tried not to cringe as I turned my head toward the high-pitched voice of someone I used to consider a close friend.

"Hi, Carolyn," I said softly.

"Well, you don't look sick at all! Are you better? Back to Tidemarsh?" She fired off a series of rapid questions as she sat down beside me. Ava gave me a nod and took Carolyn's other side.

"I'm just here for the weekend," I said, trying to keep the distaste out of my voice.

She leaned over to hug me, and I forced myself to hug her

back. "We were all really worried about you, Rayanne."

I stopped myself from snapping back that, for someone who was so concerned, she hadn't communicated very much or wasted any time before flirting with my boyfriend.

Ava spoke up for the first time. "I'm glad you are doing well, Rayanne," she said in a genuine voice. "Jeff has kept me updated. My family and I prayed for you. My abuelita said the rosary every day you were in the hospital. She still says it for you every Wednesday."

"Oh, Ava. Please, tell her *muchas gracias, Senora Garcia.*"

"I'll tell her, and happy birthday."

"Thanks, Ava." I gave her a small smile, but still wasn't really comfortable talking about lupus yet. At least Ava had texted when I hadn't come back. And her abuelita was just as sweet as pie. Our schedules had never meshed well, but Ava was great. "Any news from school?"

"Well…" Carolyn looked like she was debating saying something before blurting out, "Ross and have been seeing each other for a few weeks."

True friend there. I saw Ava shift uncomfortably.

"That's nice. I'm dating someone too."

I didn't feel jealousy, but I did feel annoyance. I didn't know why she had to tell me she was dating my ex-boyfriend, or why she was dating him in the first place. It wasn't like the school was small—it had a thousand students.

"Oh, totally. I saw the pictures of that guy on Instagram—Greg? He's really cute. Looks just like Ross!" She giggled. It was starting to give me a freaking headache.

"Um, no. I'm not dating Greg. We're friends, but no. I'm dating Charles."

Her face went totally blank before morphing to recognition, then astonishment. "The skinny Asian guy? You're dating *him*?"

I felt the hair on the back of my neck rise in irritation. "Yes."

I pulled out my phone and showed her and Ava a picture

of the two of us. Suddenly, I wished I was with Charles instead of having this conversation with Carolyn. Was it really such a surprise I might like someone like him? Or that he might like someone like me?

"Aww," Ava said. "You guys are really cute together. You look happy in these, Rayanne, real happy."

I smiled—I thought so too. Seeing Charles and hearing her words filled my belly with warmth. "It's new. We'll see."

Luckily, the game started, and I wasn't forced to make any more small talk with Carolyn. Now that she'd revealed her true colors, I wasn't sure how much more I could have stomached. Or maybe she'd always been like this and I was too insecure to notice. I should have been better friends with Ava, but both of us had had jobs with opposite schedules, siblings to babysit, and neither of us drove. We *had* tried, but a close friendship just hadn't seemed possible.

Both Ross and Jeffery played well. Despite everything, I was glad for them both, knowing college acceptance hung on these games. Ross and I had months of experiences together and most of them had been good. I wished him well, too.

When Ava went to the bathroom by herself during the third quarter, I whispered to Carolyn, "Hey, just be careful with Ross. He can be a little pushy."

She laughed in my face. "Oh my God, I can't believe it. Some guys on the team joked about you being sick with an STD and Ross told them, 'Shut the hell up, she's a virgin.' And you really are, aren't you? No one believed you dated *him* all those months—Ross Gutterson—and didn't, you know." She paused to laugh again. "That's cute, Rayanne. That's really cute. But baby, *I'm not a virgin.*"

I turned back to the game, unsure how to label the emotions I was feeling. Part of me was embarrassed as hell everyone was talking about my sex life, saying I had an STD, and part of me was grateful Ross had spoken up for me. Some guys might not lie about having had sex, but they wouldn't correct people, either, if they assumed we had. He wasn't always a good boyfriend, but I was glad I hadn't completely misjudged him as a person.

But one emotion was clear: as soon as this game was over, I wanted to get the heck away from Carolyn and hopefully never talk to her again.

As soon as the buzzer ended the game, I waved goodbye, but Carolyn and Ava followed me to the players' exit. I was tired and it was past my bedtime. I'd been trying to be good about following doctor's orders and getting eight to nine hours of sleep, and infrequently ten or twelve, and I wasn't in the mood to be social anymore.

The team busted out of the doors about fifteen minutes later, full of adrenaline and excitement from the win. Dirt, sweat, and joy marked all their faces.

"Rayanne!" Ross yelled above the clamor and made his way toward me. I tried not to grimace in disgust as he pulled me into a hard, wet-sweat-filled stinky hug. "God, girl, you're a sight for sore eyes." I patted him stiffly and tried to slide away. But he pulled me in closer and whispered, "I need to talk to you a minute."

I stepped back. "Don't worry, Ross. There's nothing to say."

He grabbed my hand and tugged me in a way I had no choice but follow if I didn't want to make a scene. "Come on, just gimme a minute."

He pulled me away from the crowd until we were out of earshot of everyone, but he kept his hand on my arm, almost as if worried I'd run away. He sent me a look and I swore I almost saw pain in his eyes.

"I didn't know," he said.

I cocked my head in confusion. "Didn't know what, Ross?"

His cheeks turned pink, and I couldn't recall ever seeing Ross blush before. Seven months we'd dated, and he never blushed. He darted a glance at me and then stared at my tennis shoes.

"The day you left, Jeffery pulled me over to the side before practice. He told me about a conversation you guys had had, and said if I ever touched you in a way you didn't like, if I pressured you to have sex, he'd kick my butt from here to Timbuktu." His hand squeezed my arm almost painfully. "Rayanne, I thought you were playing along. You know—being coy, a tease."

He looked up at me, and I saw real remorse in his blue-gray eyes. "I wasn't."

He wiped his free hand through the sweaty hair plastered to his forehead. "God, I was so ashamed. I couldn't even look him in the eye. I thought about who that made me." His eyes held mine a moment. "Then you got sick and I just…I was too mortified to talk to you. I felt like a creep." He shook me slightly. "I never thought that type of guy could be—would be—me." His expression looked so pained I *almost* felt bad for him.

"No means no, Ross," I said, and he winced at my cliché words.

"I'm sorry. Rayanne—"

"Ross." I put my other hand on his before continuing, "I didn't do anything I didn't want to do. It's not like you assaulted me. It's not like that. But I was uncomfortable, and I would have left you if you kept pushing to have sex. I wasn't ready and had already decided if you'd asked again, I'd leave you. Just listen next time."

He nodded, his Adam's apple bobbing a few times in his throat.

"Sounds like you found someone super willing, so I wouldn't even worry about it."

His face sagged deeper. "I slept with Carolyn. It's true. Several times, and she was more than willing—initiating. I needed to feel like I wasn't—I wasn't—" He met my eyes, unable to say the words. He swallowed visibly. "But no. No, we aren't dating. Not anymore. That girl is way too needy. I needed to focus on football, and she never got me like you did. You were a good girlfriend—you always gave me space and encouraged me to keep up with football and running and make grades that would help me get into college."

Yet again, I almost felt bad for him. "Does she know that? Because she told me you're dating."

He looked to the side, where Carolyn was staring daggers at us. "Oh, hell no. Jesus, no, that's over. Ray, that girl."

I patted his shoulder. "You make your bed, you have to sleep in it. Anyway, I'm really tired. I'm going to find Jeffery and go home."

He released my arm. "I'm sorry," he repeated. "Sorry about how I acted. Sorry that you're sick. I'm sorry."

I just nodded. "We had fun, but don't forget my words."

His face turned completely solemn. "Never, Ray. I swear to God, never."

I reached up and hugged him lightly. He sagged a little, his breath hissing against my ear, and then let me go.

I walked over to where Jeffery and Ava were talking. I looped my arm through his and reached up to give his sweaty, dirt-streaked cheek a kiss. "You're a real pal. You know that?"

He smiled, and we said goodbye to Ava before heading to his beat-up Honda.

"You talked to Ross, honey." It wasn't a question.

I nodded over the hood of the car before slipping in.

"So, what are your plans for the weekend?" he asked. We couldn't stop yawning during the drive.

"Granny and Grandpa Young's for lunch. Then I'm not sure. Church on Sunday, then going back home." I yawned again. "Thinking what I'm thinking?"

"Yes, ma'am. Hopefully, I haven't gotten too big for my bike."

I laughed at that. Since I could remember, Jeff and I used to bike down to the dock and watch the sunset and the fireflies come out. We hadn't done it in a little bit since he could drive now, but it'd be fun.

When he parked, he pulled the clumsily wrapped box out

of the backseat and handed it to me. Inside were a large set of vine charcoals, pressed charcoals, three rubber erasers, and five blender sticks. It was such a me gift.

Before I could even thank him, he said, "It looked like what you used to draw with and the guy at the art store near SCAD said these were the good supplies."

I kissed his cheek again. "This is really nice. I've been drawing a lot more since I can't run. I'm actually selling some pieces too, which is cool. Thanks, big guy."

"Are you taking the driving test tomorrow?"

"No, I'm going to take driver's ed in Michigan. Dad said I couldn't drive there unless I took their driver's ed because it's longer and talks about snow and ice."

"Alrighty then, well, happy birthday and see ya tomorrow."

"Don't let the bed bugs bite!"

"You don't let um bite. And don't scream at the cockroaches," Jeffery yelled back as the door closed. I had not missed those nasty big guys scuttling around. When you opened the garage door at night here, they were everywhere. So freaking nasty. I grimaced as I entered the house and got ready for bed, luckily cockroach sighting free.

My bed felt like heaven when I finally crawled into it. The screened window was open, and croaking of frogs and the repetitive calls of whip-poor-wills haunted the night. Part of it was soothing, like going back in time, yet I missed the shouts of late-night college students on the streets below and the rumbling of the bus stop.

I tossed and turned, missing Michigan as I sent up a silent prayer that Dad would keep me a little longer.

The next day with Mom and Granny Young felt like an inquisition, and they were on the hunt for reasons to crucify dad. I liked my new church and believed in God, yet it was hard to stomach what they were saying, that almost everyone I cared for in Michigan—Dad, Knox, Charles and his family—would go to hell just because they believed something different.

On the drive back, I messaged Jeffery and made plans to head down to the dock to catch up some more. Golly, I needed to get out of the house for a little bit. Catching up with Jeff squeezed my heart something fierce, but as he gave me my last hug of the night and trip, he whispered, "Michigan's good for you, Ray. I miss you, but I'm glad."

Putting away my bike made me miss Jeff too, but not enough to move back to Georgia. Not even for him. I was relieved he understood. The day had been a stressful blend of nostalgia and condemnation. I'd been worried being here might make me want to move back, but it didn't. I wanted to go home to Michigan more than ever.

I was bone-weary, my knees hurting as I brushed my hair that night after my shower.

Dagnabbit! I blinked at the brush, then looked back at the mirror as more hair than usual fell out. I let out a hiss of breath as I inspected my scalp, discovering a small bald spot about the size of a dime. Alopecia—I guessed my lupus wasn't as under control as I believed.

I touched it repeatedly, as if I could magically make it grow, but of course it didn't. I wasn't magic—just defective. I hummed one of the new Snowblowers songs to calm down, glad I was going home tomorrow. Jeff was right: Michigan was good for me.

We'd planned for me to leave straight from church, and I wanted to bury myself right into the pew when the call for prayers included, "For Rayanne Hope Ericson and her struggle with lupus."

It was impossible to walk right out the door after the service following an announcement like that. It was one thing for Senora Garcia to do a rosary for me in the silence of her house, but quite another for half of Whitmarsh Island to be talking about me. That started the fight to the airport, and the fight that ended the trip was spurred by a me telling Mom I wouldn't be home for Christmas. That Dad still planned to take me to visit my grandparents in Sweden for Christmas, like we did every year.

Mom felt like she deserved that holiday since I was now living with Dad. The last ten minutes of the drive were filled with her calling and screaming at Dad before she finally relented as long as I'd be here for Thanksgiving.

With a hug I wasn't enthused about for my mom and a growing eagerness to return to Charles, my dad, and all the things I liked about Michigan, I left Savannah.

···
TWENTY-TWO

Charles

My hand stopped on the hover icon to read the newest publication from Caltech's robotics journal. Yet that eager tempo my heart always thumped while I read this journal hit a dissonant beat. Caltech would be so far from Ray. I'd missed her so much over the weekend. So much, it terrified me.

At least she was coming back today, which made me euphoric. I could almost taste her on my lips, feel her nestled against me, and hear her chiming laughter. Sometimes I could get so caught up in what I was doing I didn't even notice the passing of time, but Ray made me feel alive in a way I never had before. She made my heart speed up and filled me with deep contentment at the same time—a calm. And I'd never wanted anyone like I wanted her. It was like I'd been living in black and white before she moved here and now everything was in color.

I glanced at the calendar above my desk with a sigh. Our family wedding celebration was next weekend and I didn't want to spend two weekends in a row apart. My weekdays were so busy. My second or third cousin—Wàipó's brother's daughter's son, John—had gotten married. It was family, so of course, we'd go. But I didn't want to leave Ray again. I was so stressed by the college application process, I just wanted to lose myself with her: to practice the piano and be able to glance up at her contemplative profile as she drew dangerously captivating scenes. Or kissing her, because I could certainly lose myself that way too.

An idea formed, but I wasn't sure about it yet. Maybe she could go with us. I knew Ray had never been to Niagara Falls and wanted to see it. When I'd described it, her whole face lit up. When she looked like that, I'd swear she was the most beautiful girl in the world. So alive, so joyous. Bracing myself for a no, I stood from the computer chair and paced toward Ma's office.

I pushed the door open. Ma paused, her hand hovering over her grading pile.

"Ma, do you think Ray could come with us to Toronto?" I asked in a rushed breath.

"You want Ray to come to the banquet?"

"Yes, maybe we can take the car that day and see Niagara Falls because she's never seen it." I couldn't get the image of her smile out of my head.

"Actually, Charles, this is a really good idea. Dr. Hashimi was asked to be a speaker at the Innovations in the Social Sciences and Humanities conference at Northwestern next weekend, and Nils was disappointed he couldn't go to support her. But he couldn't leave Ray alone, and we were going to be out of town. I will discuss with her dad tomorrow."

"Um, great," I said, surprised, but now breaking out in a sweat over the thought of actually asking Ray.

Hopefully she'd want to go. It was a lot of driving with my parents. She knew them well, but they could be intimidating, especially Baba. And we hadn't told them we were dating. I just didn't talk to them about those types of things.

I called her that night a few hours after her flight landed. When I heard her sweet Southern "hi," "I missed you" slipped out.

"I missed you too. I missed Michigan." She paused. "I wish I was there with you now. I'd show you just how much."

My breath hitched. "Oh yeah?" I said, and it came out hoarser than I intended.

She giggled. "I could think of a few ways."

My insides warmed at her words and flirting. "Um, Ray, we have a family event in Toronto this weekend."

"Noooo, another weekend apart. It's okay, but you'll have to make it up to me. I like mango fro-yo."

I laughed. "Actually, I asked my parents if you could come. Mom said she'd talk to your dad. Would you want to come? We could see Niagara Falls."

"Niagara Falls? You really think my dad would let me go?" I heard the excitement in her voice. "He caught us kissing. He knows we're dating."

"Maybe? You'd sleep in my cousin Megan's room. You'd like her. She's a senior. There'd be four adults there."

"Oh my gosh, that'd be so cool!" The staccato beat of my heart exploded to a crescendo at her words. "Shoot, is that the time? Charles, I have to go to church—well, youth group. Let's talk tomorrow."

We said goodbye, hope running through me at the idea of a whole weekend with her. With a sigh, I turned back to my mound of schoolwork that never seemed to end.

The week between the trip flew by, especially after her dad agreed, with us both trying to get as far ahead with our studies as possible. Things between us were going well, but even though it was clear we were dating, every day after math class Greg still flirted blatantly with Ray in front of me. Ray always tried to make a point of holding my hand or giving me a quick peck on the cheek if no teachers were around, but still, Greg was annoying. And the thing that really got under my skin was I could tell despite his flirting that Ray enjoyed his company. They both wanted to study architecture, after all. And they were both juniors. I just wished he'd take the hint that they were just friends.

Finally, Friday afternoon rolled around and, armed with our bags and a notarized letter stating Ray had parental permission to enter Canada, we loaded into the car bound to Toronto.

The over-four-hour drive had a few tense moments, with Baba saying incredibly awkward things. Sometimes I honestly wondered if they talked *at all* in his lab. However, for the most part, my parents were nice, if a little overeager, to help Ray with her Chinese and ask about her classes. Eventually, they fell into a conversation about what they were doing tomorrow too rapid and advanced for Ray to follow. I discreetly threaded our fingers together under the coats in the middle seat. I rubbed my thumb back and forth over her satiny skin. She blew me a quick kiss before turning back to the window.

I hoped she was looking forward to tomorrow, our almost-whole day together, as much as I was. Between the band and our schedules, we had too little time for just the two of us.

At almost eight thirty, we pulled into the restaurant where we were meeting my cousins. I heard Ray suck in a deep breath after my parents exited the car.

I leaned in and whispered, "They will like you," before placing a quick kiss under her ear and slipping out of the car.

My cousins, Er Jo Jo and Er Jo Ma, sprang up when they saw us and exchanged hugs. Ray hung back, but Ma introduced her to everyone as a family friend. She shook hands with the adults first and then the twins, Megan and Marcus. We asked if they wanted to go with us to Niagara tomorrow, but they politely declined.

After dinner, I helped get Ray set up in Megan's room and made sure she was okay before saying goodnight. She and Megan were talking up a storm when I escaped.

I paused on the landing, hearing Er Jo Jo and Ma talking. "Ma will come live with us. I'll work less," Ma said.

"Da Jo Jo says she can't be left alone. You need to hire someone when you aren't there. It'll be expensive," Er Jo Jo said in a hushed whisper.

"We'll have to make it work. We can't ask Charles not to go to Caltech. He's wanted to go forever, and we always said we'd pay for it. We make too much for him to get aid. Maybe we could refinance the house, but the economy isn't so good for housing right now. It's okay, xiǎo dìdì, we'll make it work. I'm the oldest. Ma is my responsibility."

My heart hammered in my chest. Was Wàipó that sick? Tuition and board at Caltech cost $75,000 a year; Michigan's in-state tuition was less than $15,000. I might even qualify for a scholarship there. Suddenly, I wanted to hear back from them more urgently than I ever had.

I slid back to Marcus's room silently, not wanting Ma to know I'd heard.

"Charles," Marcus whispered. "Is Ray your girlfriend?"

"Yes," I mumbled as I got ready to shower. I needed to think.

"No offense," he said with a laugh, "but that is not what I pictured your girlfriend looking like."

"I'm going to shower. I don't need the light," was all I said back.

Just like Kevin *still* thought Ray was too pretty to be smart or have any personality, Marcus thought she was too pretty for me. I was quickly realizing Ray was judged on her stunning looks, and not in a good way, too often.

My shower didn't do anything to ease my anxiety about next year. Even when I crept back into Marcus's room, I found

I couldn't sleep, not right away. Eventually, I pulled out my phone and, with crushing disappointment in my chest, looked up the robotics program at U of M. It was still top five in the country.

I tossed and turned, glad I had months to make a decision. How could I choose something that would hurt my family? But also, how could I give up my dream?

The morning was busy with everyone going their own ways and confirming what time we needed to meet back at Er Jo Jo's for the banquet before we hit the road. I was glad we had a busy day lined up. I didn't want to think about the conversation I'd heard last night. I'd asked Megan to discreetly give me a change of Ray's clothes because I'd bought us tickets to take the boat under the Falls and I knew sometimes, despite the gear, you got wet. Er Jo Ma reminded us three times to dress warmly, because Niagara would be colder, before we headed out the door.

After sitting in way too much Toronto traffic and passing ten-dozen wineries around Lake Ontario, we finally arrived. The look of delight on Ray's face at her first glimpse of the Falls might be forever seared into my brain. Fingers threaded, we walked along the pathway high above the water. Holding her hand made me feel like I could forget the conversation I'd overheard. Like it was just Ray and me. I couldn't resist stopping and kissing her when we got to a turn in the walkway without many people. She simultaneously burned and soothed me. She still seemed like a dream. Like I might wake up and none of it would be real. Like my dull, colorless life would be all I had.

"Come on," I said as I led her down to the boat area at our designated time.

Her eyes sparkled like sapphires in the afternoon sun. "You didn't."

"I did," I said, flashing her a grin.

She squealed and threw her arms around my neck. "Thank you, thank you, thank you!"

We were still smiling as we boarded, hand in hand. Like I'd been told, despite our best efforts, we were generously soaked. The northern autumn breeze was cuttingly crisp. I drew Ray against me and she snuggled into my arms as if it was the only place in the world she belonged.

Our lips couldn't seem to resist each other. Then I was drowning in her kisses and stroking her chilled, wind-brushed cheeks as her loose hairs tangled around us as intertwined as we were. Her mouth was hot and demanding, but given we were in public, we eventually broke away but kept each other's gaze.

Maybe I still felt a bit lost, but being with Ray also made something warm and home-like spread through my chest. I couldn't resist tucking her drenched, slightly knotted hair behind her ears and slipping her protectively back against my chest. I turned us toward the retreating Fall with a sigh on my lips. If there was a heaven, it must feel something like this.

...

TWENTY-THREE

Ray

As we climbed the ramp back toward the carpark, I tried to mask a yawn as I nestled deeper into my coat, but Charles caught it.

"Tired?" he asked quietly, concern flicking across his face.

He saw me.

I was.

We hadn't gone to bed until late last night—Megan talked more than Gracie Mae, and we'd been up early to make this drive so we could be back before the banquet tonight. I tried to hide my exhaustion with a smile. The Falls had been devastatingly beautiful, the day magical. Charles had made today so special, and I didn't want him to think I was bored.

"A little bit. Maybe we can grab a coffee before driving back."

"Sure," he said stepping forward and pulling me against his side and heat. "I had Megan get me a change of clothes for you too. Why don't we change and go back? If you're tired, you can nap on the way back to Er Jo Jo's."

I snuggled in as a blast of frigid wind whipped down the river, making me shiver. We both picked up our pace.

"No, I'd feel bad if you had to drive and I just slept," I said. We looked at each other a moment and I turned my face into his shoulder. "Okay, maybe a little nap."

He just squeezed my shoulder, making something close to love flutter through me. Charles really tried to understand what it was like for me. In dealing with my lupus, he had been thoughtful and kind, more than I'd ever hoped for in a friend or boyfriend. He and Dad were more patient with me than I was with myself. I nuzzled my face against his shoulder again, feeling grateful—feeling loved.

When we got in the car, changed and dry, I put my head down for a minute and woke to the stop-and-go of traffic. I smothered a yawn as I stretched and muttered, "How much longer?"

Charles jolted a little. I must have surprised him. "It's only an hour-and-a half drive, but with this traffic, I think we have at least another thirty minutes."

I nodded, even if he wasn't looking at me. He seemed worried, and I hoped he wasn't thinking he'd given up some school project for me.

I yawned again. "I'm still confused about what we're going to. Is it a wedding? A reception? A dinner?"

He chuckled, his face softening. "John and Mei already had a wedding, but we have a huge family. My wàipó was the second youngest of seven, so these are my mom's cousin's children. But we do this banquet just to celebrate, eat, and get together as the entire family. And so they get the red envelopes—money is typically given to help them start their family. It's tradition. And a whole *lot* of food."

"If it's just family, I don't have to go. I could just do some homework or read at the house."

He didn't risk taking his eyes off the road but simply patted my leg. "It's fine. Don't you want to see Wàipó?"

"I do."

"Good. Plus, I want you there. She isn't—" he stammered.

"She's, um, Wàipó hasn't been doing well. She lost her English and she called me and Marcus my uncle's name last time." His voice was brittle in a way I'd rarely heard from him.

I put my hand on his thigh. I didn't have words. I was an accident, so my grandparents were younger than his parents. His mom had been in her forties when she'd had Charles, so Wàipó was somewhere in her seventies. It seemed early for Alzheimer's, but it was as old as my great grandparents. It was still hard to believe; she'd always been so vibrant.

He took one hand off the wheel and threaded our fingers. "It'd mean a lot if you were there. She's almost like a mom. You know how she lived with us for a long time when I was little. It's hard to see her so fragile. I can't imagine…" His voice broke, but I could guess what he would have said.

I kissed his shoulder before straightening in the seat. "I'll be there. Charles, you've done so much for me. I'm glad I can do something, too."

"Thanks, Ray." He squeezed my fingers, and we rode in silence, our fingers intertwined until he needed two hands to get off the highway.

I was glad to support Charles, but I was still nervous later when I hopped into the shower and lathered my wind-tossed hair with extra conditioner before I rushed to get ready. Charles's family had always been nice, but I'd always felt so ordinary next to him.

I fussed over my dress. Dad had helped me pick out a conservative but form-fitting Ferrari-red sleeveless one. I'd thought it might have been a little too bold. Yet Dad had assured me I wouldn't be the only one in red, and it was a polite and respectful color to wear. When I strode into the hall, Charles was already dressed in a suit, his tie the exact shade of my dress. My breath caught at the sight of him all dressed up. He looked good—really good. The way he gazed at me said he felt the same.

"Wow," he said. "That dress is something else. You

look…" I stared up into his eyes, hoping it wasn't too much. "You look gorgeous."

We shared a brief smile that pinched my heart. Then he glanced down the hall and pulled me close for a quick, scorching kiss.

I touched his chiseled cheekbones and whispered, "I'm here," before I turned to Megan's room to grab my shoes. A few minutes later, we were piling into two cars, with Marcus driving us and the adults in the other.

"Charles, I can't believe your parents let you bring your girlfriend for the whole weekend," Megan said from the passenger seat. "My mom never would have agreed."

Charles chuckled. "I'm not sure she's realized we're dating."

Megan turned around, eyes widening. "Really?"

We both nodded. "Ray *is* an old family friend," Charles said. "And she did really want to see Niagara. And her dad did have an obligation this weekend."

"Okay, but does she not see the way you look at each other? I'm kind of jelly. You two are cute together. You shouldn't keep it a secret."

"It's not a secret," Charles protested, threading his fingers through mine. "Mom just hasn't caught on yet. And it's not a cancerous cell, so Baba would never notice."

"Am I going to be the only non-family member?" I asked, suddenly horrified.

Three *maybe*s filled the car, and my stomach felt like it might revolt. Charles squeezed my fingers again, rubbing his thumb over the back of my hand. It was nice, but I felt almost like vomiting from anxiety. No way I could back out after Charles had asked me so emotionally to come.

But the nerves didn't dissipate as we moved inside the beautiful banquet hall. Crimson—vibrant red roses, garnet chair and table covers, and scarlet paper decorations—filled the enormous space. There were also beautiful golden adornments, like the double happiness symbol, spread throughout. It was truly a humongous gathering, unlike anything I'd ever seen. Not only was I likely the only non-family member, I was clearly the only non-Asian too, and certainly the only blond. Charles and his family were all fairly tall, but still, with my near white-blond hair and high-heel-boosted height, I stood out. Or at least I thought I did. Dad hadn't led me astray with my clothing, though. Many people were in shades of red, and most of the decorations were, too.

Then Charles's grandmother arrived. I'd never forgotten her. She'd lived with Charles for years and he was right: you could see her age. The reality that I wasn't able to talk to her and she'd have no idea who I was hurt something fierce. I breathed out a sigh of relief when she called Charles his Chinese name and spoke to him for a long time. Charles's shoulders relaxed too.

When we walked away and found our seats, he had an expression on his face I couldn't read. He found my hand under the table and held it for several minutes, rubbing his thumb over my knuckles, before finally letting go when the food came. When he did, he mouthed, *thank you.*

After dinner, everyone mingled, yet most conversations around me were in Mandarin way to fluent and fast for me to follow. I swiveled my head as I heard Charles's mom say my name, followed by the words "friend from school." That much I understood. I was introduced to several older cousins, including a programmer at Google, a corporate lawyer, and an interventional radiologist, and felt smaller and smaller by the moment. His cousins had attended some of the world's most prestigious schools: Princeton, Stanford, Berkeley. Everyone asked about Charles's piano or robotics competitions.

I wondered as I stared at his striking, suited profile how I compared to everyone in the room. I'd never felt more aware of the fact that I wouldn't be top of my class or in the running for an academic scholarship. I'd never felt more average than I did here with his exceptional family.

Despite everyone being welcoming and polite, I was relieved when the banquet ended and I could go back to Megan's room. I was beyond ready to lie down—not only emotionally, but I was sure my heels had given me a blister. I was so tall I rarely wore them, and they brought me eye-to-eye with Charles.

"Ray, are you okay?" Megan asked softly as we climbed into bed. "You just got really quiet at the end of the night."

"Oh, I'm fine. It's just…is all your family like that?"

She turned in her twin bed to give me a curious look. "Like what?"

"So—accomplished."

She laughed. "Pretty much. Tiger moms all around. They call me the unambitious one." Her voice dropped, "It gets a little stressful. I made a B-plus last year in trig and my mom grounded me for a month and took my phone away *and* made me study math, even though it was summer!" She sighed loudly. "I don't like math. And this summer, when Charles got second place in that contest, he was so upset he wouldn't go out with Marcus. He just sat in the piano room, practicing and perfecting. But I think that's just Charles, not my aunt and uncle."

She leaned up on her elbow and flashed me a grin. "I guess that's why it's nice to see Charles with you. He can be so obsessive. He is usually working all the time—so driven. Sometimes he barely even talks to us and just goes to study in Marcus's room after a few grunts. He's even more focused than the rest of us. I've seen him smile more on this trip than maybe, I don't know, a few years. He seems happy for the first time since we were kids."

"Really?" I asked, butterflies going wild in my stomach.

I was beginning to think I loved Charles, but I didn't know if that was a good thing or not. We didn't have much time before he left for college, and I'd never go to school out in California. I was going to a state or Swedish school with reduced tuition. I didn't need decades of crippling student debt.

She nodded before rolling onto her back and closing her eyes. "You guys complement each other well. Night, Ray. And don't worry, Charles is the most decisive and single-minded person I know. He wouldn't be with you if he didn't think you were worthy."

"Thanks. Goodnight."

I knew her words were meant to reassure me, but I wasn't sure if they did or not. Suddenly, I was worried I was distracting Charles, preventing him from reaching his full potential. This trip had made it more than clear that maybe I wasn't good enough for him.

TWENTY-FOUR

Charles

The next morning on the drive home, Ray was quiet and withdrawn. I wasn't sure if she was worn out or if something was bothering her. I'd been relieved when she relented and napped on the drive back yesterday. I couldn't help but remember how small and fragile she'd looked, lying in the hospital bed this summer, tubes and cords hanging off her. Or the sad, tired eyes she'd had after going to the lake.

I knew she was doing better, but the worst of what that had happened to her could return at any time if she didn't take care of herself. Her body had literally attacked itself for no reason, which scared me. Her health wasn't a precise mathematic formula or program I could control—it was a messy science experiment of trials, errors, and pills.

I cast her another glance and she gave me a small smile, so I attempted to push my worry away. Maybe she was tired. *I* was tired. And as soon as we got back, I had to study for everything I'd put off for this family weekend and for the opportunity for Ray to come with us. And I couldn't stop replaying Er Jo Jo and Ma's conversation or remembering how good it had felt to be around Wàipó. Going to college so far away suddenly didn't have as much allure as it always had. But Caltech was my dream. I'd been killing myself to get there, losing sleep and giving up so many fun opportunities. I'd worked for it my whole life. If I got in, could I really decline such an incredible school? I didn't know.

When we got home, my parents dropped off Ray, so we didn't get a chance to say the kind of goodbye I would have liked. Maybe that was a good thing, because suddenly I was grumpy, anxious to get back to all my schoolwork. Normally I would have mostly ignored my cousins to study on Saturday, but we hadn't even had an hour for that with the party and all the driving.

I had more work than I'd anticipated, and it was after one when I finished everything. I grimaced as I got into bed, knowing some of it was hastily done.

The week was a blur, and I felt more and more behind as the days progressed. Each night I was up past midnight, and was still barely keeping my head above water. James was excited because we'd been invited to play Bob's Bar and Bistro after not playing for a few weeks. As much as I didn't want to do anything this weekend, the look on the guys' faces wouldn't let me say no.

I caught Ray Thursday afternoon as she was exiting math class. She'd been taking the bus because she'd said I looked stressed, and I appreciated it, because I was. I'd eaten lunch in the library too, so I'd barely seen her—I was just so behind, I'd skipped lunch all week. Keeping myself singularly focused on school was easier than thinking about my parents refinancing their house, or about Wàipó.

"Hey," I said, running a quick caress up her arm.

I couldn't believe how much I'd missed her, how addictive she was. It felt like if I drew her into my arms and held her, some of my problems might melt away.

She smiled back, strengthening the urge to pull her to me.

"So, Friday night we got asked to play at Bob's. You're going to sing, right?"

"Sure!" she said. "James and I have been practicing some extra duets at church. Are we going to practice before?"

"Yes, but not until tomorrow afternoon. I'm swamped."

I saw sympathy in her eyes, but before she could respond, Greg butted in. "Wait, you guys are in a band? And playing somewhere?"

We both swiveled to see him, and Ray nodded as I said, "Yep, at Bob's Bar and Bistro."

"Dude, that's cool! I love that place. Their cheese dip, you know? When are you playing?"

Ray shuffled her feet and tucked her hair behind her ears as she waited for me to respond. I really wasn't interested in Greg coming, but since I couldn't say that, I just said, "Friday at eight."

"Right, see you guys tomorrow night, then." He laughed. "Well, after class."

He waved and headed down the hall. He and Ray had become friends, but I still got the feeling he'd rather have something besides friendship from her—that he was waiting for Ray to realize she belonged with someone like him, not me. Something slimy slithered around inside me as I thought about next year, when I wouldn't be here to stand in their way.

"I better run to the bus too," Ray said.

I watched her a moment as she hurried down the hall. I frowned. Was she *limping*? Maybe she waws still sore from yoga. She whined about being sore a lot, but I knew from the way her eyes lit up when she talked about yoga, she loved it.

I was up till one again trying to get everything done, and even when I fell asleep, I didn't sleep well. I kept waking up and thinking about the physics test we'd taken Tuesday. It had been harder than I thought, and we were getting it back tomorrow.

When the alarm blared in the morning and I groggily turned it off, I wondered if I had slept at all. My classes blurred together until suddenly, Mrs. Bhatt was passing back our test after a stern lecture. She'd expected better from us, and the highest grade was an A-minus.

I twirled my pen, waiting for my paper. When she dropped it facedown and I saw a B on it, my stomach flopped. This was the last quarter grade that would be on my college applications. And it was physics. I stared at it and blinked, hoping I could change the grade by reopening my eyes. *Nope.*

Sweat gathered at my back. This was bad. Really bad. I hated that my first thought was that if I hadn't asked Ray to Toronto, I could have studied last Saturday instead of wasting the whole day with her. When she waved at me at lunch and started talking all hyped up about our concert, I couldn't keep up with her enthusiasm.

She must have noticed because she said, "Hey, what's wrong?"

She rubbed my arm, but I didn't feel like being comforted. "I need to study a lot this weekend," I snapped as I shook off her arm, feeling the stress and lack of sleep. "I promised to do the concert, but I won't have time to see you at all. I really need to study."

I regretted my harsh words the moment I said them. Ray's eyes got big and overly bright. "I left something in art," she said. "I'll see you after eighth period."

"*Dude*," Knox said after she rushed away. "That was pretty rude."

"I need to study, Knox." Yes, it had been a little rude, but him pointing it out didn't make me feel any better. But I was exhausted and I needed to catch up this weekend. I liked Ray more than I thought I could like someone. I might love her. But I didn't want even her distracting me from school.

Or maybe I did. Then I wouldn't get into Caltech and it wouldn't be my choice anymore.

"Whatever, man," Knox said, and turned silently back to his food.

I didn't even know what I wanted anymore. I sighed as I pushed around the food on my plate. I stared at the door where Ray had gone, wishing I could take back my words.

I got a text from her before the end of lunch. *Hey, I know you're really busy. You guys start practice without me—I'll take the bus. I'm going to get changed and drop off my school stuff and Dad can drop me off at 5:30. Save you the time of stopping by my place. PS I have plans this weekend too.*

I shouldn't have been so surly with her.

Later, I waited for her outside math class. She wasn't there, but Greg was.

"Ray left already," he said. "Didn't she tell you about her *doctor's appointment?*" He smirked as he said it, and we both knew that was BS.

"Right, I forgot. She doesn't have service there."

He looked at me like he knew we were both liars. "I can't wait to see you guys play tonight."

I hunched my shoulders as I shuffled to my locker, my stomach twisted in knots. I'd snapped at her. I was the one who'd offered to take her to Toronto; she hadn't demanded my time. She'd been there for me when I was upset about Wàipó.

The guys looked at me questioningly when Ray didn't come right after school and I muttered some excuses. Five thirty came, then five forty-five, with no word from Ray. James arched an eyebrow at me, and Knox mumbled under his breath.

Finally, at five to six, Ray flew down the stairs, looking like the sexiest thing I'd ever seen in a short black dress she'd never worn in front of me before and black boots. I still didn't understand how someone so skinny had curves like she did, but she looked fantastic in that dress. Both Knox and Kevin's breath hitched.

"Sorry, sorry," Ray said. "I fell asleep. My dad woke me up when it was time to leave."

"No worries." I walked up to her and dropped my voice. "Um, about earlier—"

She cut me off with a quick kiss. "It's fine, you're busy. I'm busy this weekend too. Let's practice, okay?"

I really wanted to apologize. *Later*, I told myself.

We ran through a mock performance and then it was time to go. I couldn't lie—I was distracted by how Ray looked and couldn't help feeling things weren't okay, despite what she'd said.

When we stepped inside Bob's, Greg was there with Sean. The knots in my belly tightened, especially when he gave her a lingering, handsy hug.

TWENTY-FIVE

Ray

I pulled away from Greg as quickly as I could, feeling Charles's eyes on me as I walked toward where they were setting up. Greg and I were friends, but I'd seen how self-conscious Charles was about him specifically. And Greg had a super flirtatious personality. How Charles could feel that way was beyond me. I couldn't forget the room full of his family and all their accomplishments. People just said I was pretty, but I wanted to be known for something I'd done. But, no matter how hard I worked, I wasn't going to be valedictorian. I wasn't getting in to Princeton or Caltech. If I did really well this year, I could *maybe* get into Georgia Tech or Michigan.

I glanced at Charles and tried to control the hurt. He'd barked at me earlier and it'd made me cry. Not just the words, but because I felt he should be with someone more like him—someone who lifted him up, not me with all my health problems and lack of friends. I demanded too much of his time—I dragged him down.

As if to add to my insecurities, I heard someone giggle and turned to see Dana and another girl from the robotics team talking and flirting with Kevin and Charles. That was the type of girl Charles should date. Kevin gave me an unfriendly smirk, hefting his bass guitar again and walking toward what would be our stage. I briefly made eye contact with the girls and tried to give a friendly smile before I walked up to James and flipped through our sheet music.

"Little Ray of sunshine," he said throwing his heavy arm around me. "Doing well tonight?"

I winced. That blister was a real pain the rear.

"I'm a little tired, but hopefully it's nothing."

"Ray?" There was worry in his voice and he dropped his arm and looked at me. I couldn't forget his aunt had lupus. He knew how serious it was.

"It's nothing," I said more firmly than I felt, but I refused to meet his eyes. The truth was I could barely rouse myself from my nap earlier.

I flashed him a grin. I'd wanted to cancel, but if Charles could make it tonight when he was stressed, I could too. It was one of the reasons I'd worn this outfit. Maybe it wasn't the most self-respecting thing I could have done, but Jeffery and Ross had always told me I was *darn sexy* in this dress and I wanted Charles to think so, too. Also, my feet and ankles were a little red, and no one would be able to tell with these boots.

The sets flew by and, despite how tired I'd been earlier, it was loads of fun. I loved watching the guys play. They all enjoyed music so much, it was pure pleasure to watch their faces get lost in the sounds and rhythms. I didn't love music the way they did, but their happiness was contagious, and I liked being part of it. It was why I'd drawn so many pictures of them—this look on their faces was how I felt when I drew. This look was displayed on the far wall above the bar. I smiled every time I peeked up and spotted my art.

During a break, I flopped down into a nearby chair. My foot was killing me where I'd gotten a blister last weekend. It had been getting redder all week and I hoped it wasn't infected.

I'd been using some antibiotic cream, but didn't know what else to do.

Greg came over and sat next to me, close enough that his thigh brushed mine. Charles was near enough that I could see him stiffen out of the corner of my eye.

"So, Ray," Greg said smoothly. "Can we get you at eleven tomorrow? We'll grab a quick lunch and tour the building before the game."

I cast a hesitant look at Charles. I hadn't mentioned my plans with Greg, but I didn't have anything to be guilty about—we were friends. "Eleven is good."

Greg caught the look and the delayed response, and turned to Charles. "Do you and Ray have plans tomorrow, Charles? Need her back by a certain time?"

Charles's jaw tightened. "No, I need to study all weekend."

"Perfect!" Greg turned back to me. "You'll love hockey. You're a Michigander now, and it is a requirement you like the Red Wings. What other sport do you get to sing the American *and* Canadian national anthems before every game?"

I laughed. "Ohhh, yea-ah," I joked with a heavy Michigander accent. "But actually, I'm more excited to see the micro-living, but thanks for inviting me to the game, too. I'm sure the tickets weren't cheap."

Greg was pretty nice, and I was so curious about his dad's project. It wasn't like this would be a date; we'd be with his parents. Still, Charles didn't look thrilled.

"Of course! And my dad has a season pass. He just traded a friend so we'd get four seats instead of three."

The guys motioned break was over so I hopped up, trying to hide a wince as my foot hit the ground.

By the time we finished and packed up, I was smothering yawns. I couldn't wait to shower, but when I made it home, I cringed at how much worse my foot looked when I stripped off my socks. My entire foot looked swollen and a hard, painful scab had formed over the blister. I decided to cancel yoga tomorrow and just sleep in. I debated texting Greg to say I couldn't go, but it was just a little blister. Hopefully with some sleep, it'd be fine.

Throbbing pain radiated from my foot to leg as the alarm clock wailed me awake. I flinched as I moved and knew I should cancel. I thought about what I would say to Greg, who still didn't know I had lupus. We'd been coordinating this for weeks. It'd be fine. I'd just be sitting at the game most of the day anyway, right? It should be no different than staying at home, and it was Saturday—not like I could talk to my doctor about my foot. I'd stay at home and rest tomorrow, and if it was worse, I could go to the doctor on Monday. How bad could a little skin infection be?

Mind made up, I got up and limped around to dress. I felt dizzy and warm and figured Dad must have had the heat on too high. Before I knew it, Greg texted me they were here. I attempted to hurry down despite my throbbing leg.

I strained not to grimace as I walked to the car, which seemed excruciatingly far as my foot pulsed with pain.

They'd been late and traffic was bad, so we decided we'd eat at the game. The ride with Greg's parents was interesting; his mom was an industrial interior designer and they all loved buildings as much as I did. Yet it was surprisingly hard to focus, and I felt slightly feverish and clammy. I was starting to feel loopy.

When it came time for the building tour, I was barely controlling my winces. Greg noticed and asked what was up.

"My foot really hurts," I admitted.

He slowed down and was nice about it, but it was still torture. In fact, it was so agonizing that, by the time we made it to the Red Wings Arena, I was nauseous. I was afraid the pain might literally make me sick. They offered to buy me a hot dog since we'd skipped lunch, but I knew if I ate, I'd throw up.

When I started shivering in the stadium, Greg laughed. "Oh, Savannah, it isn't even cold," he said. "I hope you can survive the winter."

I did too. We weren't even into the first quarter when I was sweating and shivering, feeling more than a little woozy.

Mrs. Davis looked over at me and said, "Ray, are you okay? I think maybe you have a fever."

"I don't feel good." A tremor racked my body and my teeth chattered. Sweat was dripping down my face.

"Greg, I think we should go," his mom said kindly.

Greg glanced at me, and whatever he saw made him nod and stand up. When I got up, I felt myself sway.

"Whoa, you okay?" Greg said, grabbing my arm.

"Thanks, um—" I didn't know what to say. I felt wobbly on my feet and cried out when my other foot hit the ground.

"You're really hot," he said, looking worried. "You definitely have a fever."

His dad got up on my other side and together they helped me walk up the stadium stairs. I whimpered as each touch jolted excruciating pain through my left leg. They stopped moving.

"What is it?" Greg's grip on my arm tightened, thankfully holding me up.

"My foot," I bit out, feeling embarrassed as tears rolled down my cheeks. It hurt so bad. Oh sweet peas, it hurt.

"Let me see." His dad kneeled down and whistled as he lifted off my boot and sock.

My foot was now a puffy, solid red that red ran up my leg and disappeared into my tight jeans.

"Greg," his dad said softly, and Greg picked me up.

"What happened to your foot?" Greg said, carrying me up the stairs like I weighed nothing.

"I got a blister."

"That's a lot more than a blister," he said solemnly. "That's an infection. A bad one. God, how could you even walk?"

Despite the pain, a wry chuckle escaped me. "In case you didn't notice, I can't."

He laughed and I tightened my grip on his shoulder.

Finally, we made it to the car. I lolled against the door as they drove us home, sweat dripping off my body. I'd been begun shaking in full-body trembles.

"Ray, you seem really sick," Greg's mom said from the passenger seat. "I think we should take you to the hospital."

We were almost to Ann Arbor, so we decided to go to the University Hospital. Dad hadn't answered his phone.

"Ray, it's going to be all right," his mom cooed.

"I don't know," I moaned. "I have lupus. It's an autoimmune disease. It, um, well, it attacked my organs this summer. Please, Jesus, don't let it be my organs again." My teeth started chattering again.

"We're almost to the hospital, Ray. Anything else we should know?"

"I take immune suppressants. I think the doctor mentioned I could get bad infections, but I just thought my foot would get better. I've never felt like this before." I grabbed Greg's forearm at a stoplight. "Please, don't tell anyone at school. I didn't want everyone here saying they're praying for me, too." It was a nice sentiment, but it made me feel like I was about to die.

"Hey, don't worry. It's okay." But his expression held concern as he got out of the car.

Dad called right before we got to the ER and said he was on his way. Greg carried me in and luckily, the waiting room was nearly empty. The admission lady heard my symptoms and lupus and ushered us right back to a room.

"Greg, I'm fine now. You can go. Thanks for everything.

Just remember, only Charles and Becky know," I said, hoping he'd leave. I didn't want an audience for this.

"We can stay until your dad arrives. Do you want me to call Charles?"

"No, please just go. This is embarrassing enough," I said, wiping more sweat from my forehead. "I'll call him later."

A nurse shooed him out of the ER bay. "We need to get her in a gown."

"You'll be fine, Ray," Greg said as he left.

I almost giggled, feeling hysterical. "He's saying that more to himself than to me," I whispered to the nurse.

"No, he's right. Let's get you changed," the nurse said in a gentle voice. I was so unsteady on my feet, she had to hold my arm.

"Her blood pressure is really low," someone said, but I could feel myself starting to fade.

Almost immediately, they cut open my blister. It was disgusting what came out, and they took samples of my foot infection while they took my temperature. One-hundred-five. My blood pressure was considered dangerously low, and after several attempts, they started an IV. In a rush, they started me on antibiotics and took me to a room on the floor. It must have happened in a hurry because I beat my dad there.

He burst in a few minutes later and hugged me tightly. "Sorry, Dad," I said guiltily. "I didn't think it was that bad. I'm sorr—"

"Shhhh, it's okay. I know you would have told me if you thought you needed to go to the doctor. It's okay," he repeated. "I'm here now."

"Please don't tell Dr. Wong and Charles," I whispered into his chest.

"Why not?"

"He's really stressed with school. His Caltech application is due soon. I don't want him to worry about me." I burst into tears and shook him slightly. "Please, Dad. Promise me."

"Fine, I promise," he said, but I could tell he was reluctant.

He moved to sit beside me to hold my hand. I sagged against the bed, too tired to hold my head up. The nurse came in and said I'd be staying overnight and that the rheumatology and infectious disease team would be by when they could. I tried to smile bravely at my dad, but the pain was agony, and I was scared.

TWENTY-SIX

Charles

It was Wednesday and I hadn't spoken to Ray since Friday night. She'd sent me a few brief texts, first on Saturday saying the game had been fun, but she was tired and going to take it easy. She didn't send any Sunday, and I was buried under my books and prepping for the piano competition on Saturday in Lansing, so I hadn't tried to, either. This was how I needed to be totally focused, like last year. Yet it left me feeling empty and curious what she was doing.

When Monday morning arrived, I'd asked if she needed a ride, but she didn't respond to my multiple messages until after first period.

Something came up and I'll be in Savannah a few days. Don't worry if I don't respond right away. Hope school's going well.

This was what I had asked for—time to study—and now I regretted it. After not seeing her for a few days, I realized not how much vivacity she'd brought to my life and how lonely it was without her smile and infectious laugh. I thought about next year without her, Wàipó and my parents' finances weighing on my mind. I wanted to talk to her about everything. I missed her. I knew if I held her, I could make it through the next few weeks.

Mrs. Bhatt had even given us an extra credit opportunity because so many students had failed the test. I'd been able to raise my 86 to a 96 with the extra points, so it certainly shouldn't hurt me in the long run, or on my quarterly grades. But none of it meant much without Ray and as corny as it sounded, my world was a little dimmer without her around. Now I knew she wouldn't make my piano competition anymore, and disappointment dragged me through the week even as I got ahead on my schoolwork.

The competition came and went. Ma cheered loudly and told me I did well, but she was pensive on the drive back. Even though I'd taken first place, I swore she kept looking at me like she was deeply disappointed in me. She started and stopped several sentences without finishing them—something was distracting her.

Crap, I hoped she wouldn't ask me not to go to Caltech.

Finally, she asked, "Did you and Ray break up?"

I looked at her, too stupefied to respond. I hadn't even realized she knew we were dating. "No, we're still dating. She had something come up and went down to Savannah. That's why she couldn't come."

"Did she?" She sounded bewildered and fell silent for a moment. "Have you talked to her?"

I felt myself flush with embarrassment. Where was she going? "We've been texting."

"You should call her." Her voice was as stern as was when we talked about school. "She's a nice girl, and if she has something going on, maybe she'd like to talk to you instead of just texting." She glanced at me a second before turning back to the road, a look of sharp disapproval in her eyes that filled me with shame.

I wasn't sure why Ray hadn't texted me more, or why we hadn't talked on the phone. We'd video chatted when she'd gone down before. I'd been so absorbed in my work, I hadn't considered it, but it was uncharacteristic of her. Suddenly I panicked, wondering if she'd moved back and simply not told me, or if she was sick again, then told myself I was being silly.

Ray wouldn't lie to me.

But I wasn't sure. She knew how important school was to me and unexpectedly, I wasn't so sure she wouldn't lie, not if she thought she was helping me.

I called her as soon as I got home, and she answered the phone with a weak voice. She asked about my competition, and I told her I'd gotten first place. After a few minutes, I heard some voices in the background.

"I'll be here a little bit longer, but I'll let you know as soon as I'm back," Ray said softly.

"Ray, why did you go down there?"

"I need to go. It's been really nice talking to you, and I'm glad you did well. I thought about you all day, Charles. You don't know how much I wished I could have been there." Her voice cracked, and I wondered if she was crying. "I'll call you when I can."

But she didn't call me back Saturday or Sunday, and barely even responded to my messages. Now that I had the first-place piano score in, I submitted all my applications, but Ma kept casting me strange looks all weekend. It was a relief when Monday came and I could finally escape the house.

The day passed with its usual swiftness, but I longed for Ray at lunch. I missed her jokes and sweet smiles. I stared joylessly at my mystery meat. Even Knox was silent, both of us apparently missing Ray.

I was surprised when Greg grabbed my attention after eighth period by yelling, "Wait, Charles!"

We hadn't spoken since the concert. He dropped his voice so no one in the emptying hallway would overhear. "I have some makeup work for Ray."

I looked at him in surprise. Of course Ray should have

work if she was out, but I wasn't sure how I'd get it to her in Savannah. Well, I guess we had a scanner.

He continued so quietly I had to strain to hear. "How is she?"

The concern in his eyes alarmed me. "She's fine." As soon as I said it, I wasn't sure she was.

His face softened with relief. "Good." He stepped even closer and dropped his voice to the faintest whisper. "She texted me she was doing better after everything, but I don't know." He shook his head. "I was so worried about her. It was like something out of a movie—she started sweating and she looked so pale. Jesus, her leg looked terrible, and the way the ER took her right back…I didn't know about the lupus, but I looked it up. It makes so much sense now. God, it all makes so much sense, like why she got so upset about her sunburn. Why she didn't do cross-country. I wanted to visit her, but she said she was too sick. When is she getting released from the hospital? Do you know?"

His words were like a knife to the gut. I stumbled back a step, ears ringing. *Ray's in the hospital.* He stopped and stared at me as I felt my insides twist.

Disbelief and then anger flickered on his face. "You didn't know she was in the hospital, did you? She's *your* fucking girlfriend."

"I will find out why she didn't tell me." I grabbed the papers. "I'm going to see her."

I raced down the hall and drove home as quickly as I could and burst into Ma's office. With a nagging suspicion she knew already, I confronted her.

"Did you know Ray was in the hospital?" She nodded and I demanded, "Why didn't you tell me?"

I felt tears roll down my cheeks, but I wasn't embarrassed. All this time, she was here and sick. She'd lied to me. I imagined the fragile girl I'd seen this summer. It tore me up to think of her like that. But it was more painful I hadn't been there for her—

that she'd lied to me for whatever reason.

"She asked her dad not to tell us. She knew the competition was important for your Caltech application. Eventually, he had to communicate with me because he needed help covering his classes, but he made me swear not to tell you. Ray wanted you to focus on school." Then she asked in an even tone, "Is Ray more important than school?"

I staggered back. "What? I'd have wanted to know. I can see her and still do fine in school."

She hugged me. "I hoped you'd say that. Ray wasn't sure what you would choose, or if you'd be angry if you picked her and your application suffered, so she said nothing. Charles, your dad and I want you to do well, but you push yourself as much as we do. That's fine. You enjoy succeeding, but you aren't a robot. People matter, too."

I pulled back, my stomach pinching horribly with guilt. The disappointment on Ma's face this weekend made sense now. She thought I'd ignored Ray in the hospital.

"I want to see her. I wanted to know. You shouldn't have kept this from me."

"She's still at the hospital. Fifth floor, room 337B. Do you want me to go with you?"

I shook my head, still angry she and Ray had lied to me. I started to walk out the door, but then on second thought, I went and grabbed my guitar. Ray always said it relaxed her to hear me play music; she liked the piano best, but that wasn't as portable.

My heart pounded as I marched down the hall toward Ray's room, my feet loud on the linoleum floors. When I got to her door, I stopped. Ray had chosen to lie rather than let me know she was sick. It was shame I felt most strongly because I'd let her believe school was so important that I couldn't let her bother me. She was so selfless, she'd rather lie alone in a hospital bed than let my grades suffer.

With some hesitation, I walked inside. Ray's mouth

dropped open. "Charles," she said wistfully.

"Ray." I stepped forward.

Her dad's gaze darted back and forth between us. When Ray nodded, he cleared his throat and said, "I'm going to the cafeteria for a tea." With that and a harsh look at me, he left.

I took his seat and lightly put my guitar down. Ray was pale, her cheeks gaunt, and she had dark circles under her eyes. I could see several bruises on her pale inner elbow and wrist closest to me. Her other one was bright red. Cautiously, I reached a hand toward hers, letting it linger at the edge of the bed, just a centimeter from hers. She closed the distance and touched mine gently. That was all the encouragement I needed to hold her hand. My eyes watered. What had happened to her?

I looked up into her eyes, unsure what to say, or if I should say anything. She bit her lips, which looked painfully dry and had bloody cracks.

"I guess you know I lied to you," she said.

"I know why you did it." I squeezed her hand. "Next time, don't. I was frustrated I was getting behind, but people I care about are more important than perfect grades. Ray, I care about you." I felt my head droop, and tears gathered behind my eyes again. "I would have been here. I would have wanted to be here. You don't know how much I care about you. How much guilt I feel not having been here for you."

And I did. I deserved her dad's and my mom's irritation for not figuring out Ray was sick. She might have lied, but if I'd tried harder to talk to her, it would have been obvious.

She squeezed my hand back. "I wanted you to do well. I thought about your whole family and didn't want to be a sinker around your neck. It was a scary few days." She drew in a deep breath. "It's bad enough I have to deal with this without dragging everyone else down with me."

I met her gaze, brushing my tears away with my free hand. "Will you tell me what happened?"

She nodded weakly. "I got a blister at the banquet. And

I was run-down and tired. I stayed on my feet too long and the immunosuppressants, and everything else…well, I got an infection. I thought it'd go away, but it got worse. We played that show and it was bad. But I thought, it's just a blister. It was worse Saturday, and I got a high fever. I'd felt so sick I didn't eat anything, and my blood pressure dropped. I was brought here Saturday from the game and started on antibiotics. They kept me because my blood pressure and platelets were so low and my fever was so high. Plus, the immunosuppressants."

She paused and caught her breath before continuing. "The second night here, late Sunday night or Monday morning, I started itching really bad. My skin and whole body hurt. It got hard to breathe, and I woke up in the middle of the night, gasping for air. I was covered head to toe with a rash—with continuous hives almost half-an-inch high. My whole face and ears were swollen, and I was all pink." She flicked her head toward her opposite wrist, and I saw pink running up her arm, too. "It hasn't quite gone, but after three days, my facial swelling and most of the hives went away. They said it was good they caught it immediately. It's why my lips are split."

Her lip had almost started bleeding just from talking this much.

"They stopped the antibiotic and started me on steroids and antihistamines. They needed to start me on a new antibiotic, an IV one this time, because the infection had spread to my thigh and the test finally came back as hospital-acquired MRSA—basically, a bad drug-resistant infection. They were worried about a bloodstream infection. They wanted to keep me here while they monitored the new antibiotics, and also because the infection was so bad. They kept giving me fluids." She exhaled, looking exhausted.

"Ray, I wish you'd told me. I would have dropped everything to be here." It hurt I'd made her feel she couldn't depend on me. I felt more disappointed in myself than I'd ever been. Tears threatened to fall again.

She nodded. "I should get to go home tomorrow. I switched to an oral antibiotic two days ago in addition to the IV medicine. I'm getting better, but because of the steroids I need to take for the allergic reaction, I'll need to take antibiotics a full three weeks. My platelets are low but not dangerously so anymore. If that goes well, then I can come back to school on Thursday. The rash comes and goes. Dad wants me to take it easy and get caught up. I'm really tired."

I wanted to crush her against me. Instead, I squeezed her hand again. "I want you to promise me you'll tell me next time."

Her eyes were glistening, but she nodded.

"I brought the guitar." I motioned to it. "I could play a few songs, even though my voice isn't as sweet as yours or as mellow as James's."

"Okay." She gave me a hesitant smile, then grabbed some Vaseline for her lips.

I bent and picked up the guitar. "Speaking of James, how about a little James Taylor?" I played "You've got a Friend" and sang softly to her. I saw her dad lean into the room, smile, then walk back out.

"Call me next time, Ray," I held her eyes and said, quoting the song.

She sniffled and nodded. I thought about it just a second and followed it with Cat Stevens's "Hard Headed Woman," mumbling, "Sounds like someone we know."

She gave me a watery smile as it finished. I moved straight into "Run" by Snow Patrol. We both loved that song. I kept my eyes shut, fighting back tears as I thought about how much she lit up my life. After I strummed the last note, I set the guitar down a moment.

"Ray." I squeezed her hand.

"Charles," she whispered, reaching up to brush away a stray tear.

I played as many other songs as I could think of before her nurse came in with her dad. I stopped mid-song and put away my guitar, knowing she needed to rest. She looked sleepier and more peaceful now.

I kissed her on her forehead and said, "I'll see you tomorrow."

With those big blue eyes, she looked like an angel again. "Will you bring the keyboard? I want to hear 'Let it Be' again, but I love it on the piano best."

"Of course." My heart pinched as I nodded to her dad and left. It was so hard to leave her lying there looking so damn fragile. I promised myself I'd do better next time.

TWENTY-SEVEN

Ray

It had been more than two weeks since I was released from the ten-day hospital visit, and I had just three days left of antibiotics. Last week, I'd been able to restart yoga and church. Becky and James had made me feel so welcome there. My teachers, for the most part, were understanding. I'd missed the most in Chinese, so it was lucky my boyfriend and Knox could help me catch up.

October had gone, and with its departure came wind colder than I remembered, along with endless gray skies. It couldn't be the truth, because it was always this cold—colder—when I visited my grandparents. But they'd always bundle me up in spare jackets, and I'd never stood waiting to catch the bus stomping my frozen toes.

Back home, they were likely still running the AC, and would be for another few weeks unless they got a cold snap. Here, I was freezing even bundled into multiple layers—wool sweaters and socks, boots, and the big, waterproof down jacket Dad bought for me. I'd almost forgotten what my skin felt like, but I couldn't because my wrists still itched and turned bright red whenever I showered.

I'd needed mittens, not gloves. We'd learned after Friday morning I'd, when I'd taken the bus. After just a few minutes waiting for it, my fingers had turned painfully white and stayed that way long after I got into the heated bus. After school, Dad had walked with me downtown and bought mittens so poofy everyone but Charles made fun of me for. They were extravagant for people without Raynaud's. Most people could dog-sled across Greenland in these mittens. Charles told me I looked like a cute boxer in them. He understood. *He saw me*, even if it frightened me how much he saw me.

Every night for the past week, he'd called me at exactly nine. It was a little compulsive—exactly nine, not a minute later—but I thought it was endearing. Some nights we'd talked, and others he'd just played for me while I drew. It was like he wanted to make sure I knew he was there. Sometimes at lunch, I caught him staring at me like I might slip away. I wanted to tell him I was right here, but I was scared too. I didn't know what my body would do. My body didn't know what it would do. So I'd given him feather kisses instead of saying anything. I poured my emotions into my drawing and belted them out in church between James and Becky.

I was taking more pills than ever. The steroids had changed my easily coverable, dime-shaped bald spot to quarter-shaped. It took a little more styling in the morning, and I'd had to change my part to fully conceal it. My cheeks were chubbier from the steroids, too. Charles still looked at me like I was his favorite treat, so I was trying not to let it get me down. Some days, that was easier than others.

Today, he was bent studiously over his guitar. I sighed at his concentrated frown over the newest piece giving him trouble. He was right—he wasn't perfect, but he worked damn hard to get as close as he could.

We were practicing in his basement again. Charles had handled me like a delicate flower since I'd been released, and while it was sweet, I wished he wouldn't. I was still a girl inside and wanted more of his affection than he'd been giving me in his chaste kisses and brief hugs.

"What are you working on?" I asked so I had an excuse to lean closer to his sheet notes.

I felt his body tighten, then quiver slightly where we touched, and was glad he was as aware of me as I was of him. I looked down at those beautiful skilled hands and my core tightened with how badly I wanted them on me.

Before he could answer my question, I whispered just for him, "I want to tell them."

He looked at me, confused. I flicked my head toward the others, and he whispered in my ear in a way that left me trembling: "About lupus?"

I stepped back and nodded, suddenly needing more space. I'd been craving more than he'd been giving me as I recovered, and I needed to remove myself from the distraction of his body.

I walked to the center of the room. Kevin was muttering over his bass guitar, and Knox was twirling his sticks in the air. It had felt good to have Becky, then James, then Greg know about lupus. It felt good not hiding what I was coming to realize was a part of me, just like having blue eyes. It was a piece of me now, and it felt wrong to keep it a secret from my friends.

"I want to tell you guys why I've been sick," I blurted out.

James's lips turned up into a warm and welcome grin before he nodded reassuringly at me. I glanced at Charles and my heart beat faster. *I love him*, I thought, not for the first time as I gazed into his calm, comforting obsidian eyes. They held so much encouragement, bolstering my confidence.

I took a breath to steady myself. "I have lupus. It's a chronic, lifelong autoimmune disease, but don't worry. It's not contagious."

Knox was silent. I wasn't sure why I'd felt so self-conscious about it before, but it felt good to say it. It wasn't something to be embarrassed about.

James pulled me into his brotherly, engulfing hug. "I'm

proud of you for finally speaking up, Ray."

I squeezed him and stepped back.

"Are you going to die?" asked Kevin quietly.

We all looked at him. I almost wondered if I'd misheard him.

Kevin turned tomato red and began rambling. "You know, James's aunt who had lupus died. It's not like I want you to die. I was just—I thought it was one of the most common causes of deaths in girls your age. I don't know—are you?"

I looked at Charles first, but he wouldn't meet my eyes. I turned back to James, hurt filling me, but before I could speak, James did. "She wasn't compliant with her medication or doctors. She wasn't like you, Ray. She had kidney failure, but because she wasn't compliant, she wasn't on the transplant list. She stopped taking all her medicine and left the hospital against medical advice. She died two days later."

I swallowed.

"That won't be you," James insisted. "Because you listen to the doctors. You take your pills. You don't have any kidney issues. It's the fifth cause of death in Latinx and African American women aged fifteen to twenty-four, but only tenth for all women that same age. For whatever reason, you should do better. Mom, Becky, and I read a ton about after her sister died. You'll be sick a lot. I'm sorry—it sucks, but," he glared at Kevin, "she shouldn't die any younger than the rest of us if she's compliant with her medications. And it looks like she's responded well to them. Not everyone does. Aunt Ama never responded well to the medicine, so she didn't take it."

I felt numb. Suddenly, Charles was crushing me against him. His wiry frame and strong arms surrounded me, and I felt grounded—safe. I squeezed him and nuzzled his chest that seemed to always smell like the incense his mom liked to burn, and something uniquely *him*.

"Come on, let's get out of here," he whispered in my ear, still holding me tucked against him. "All right, practice is over for today." He took my hand and led me outside to the car.

"Where are we going?"

"Cider mill."

"What?"

"We are going to a cider mill." He glanced at the clock on the dashboard. "We have just enough time. You need cheering up, and I need a donut." He turned up, "All My Favorite Songs," which just started on the radio.

After several minutes of driving that took us to the highway, I asked, "Did you know the whole time, about James's aunt?"

"No. I remember James going to a funeral, but a few years ago but I didn't pay attention, except she'd died. It was really sad. I didn't know what lupus was when you were diagnosed. I eventually put two and two together a few weeks in. But like James said, his aunt isn't you."

"Becky never told me."

He sighed and turned down the radio so we weren't shouting over it. "She probably didn't see the need to, Ray. You are going to have this forever, and that really stinks, but no one has said your life has to be shorter. Bumpier, but not shorter. You said your lupus been doing well since you started the medications. Yes, your last hospitalization was because of your drugs, but not lupus. Your lupus *is* much better. That's what's important. Those drugs are crap, but you just need to be more careful on them. They *are* working."

We fell silent as his hand slid into mine. What he said made sense, but it was still scary. Finally, we arrived at the cider mill. It was cute, with a little water wheel. Charles was excited for me to taste the apple cider, so I didn't tell him I thought it was way too sweet.

It was cold as we walked around outside, but he nestled me under his arm and we found ourselves alone and kissing like we hadn't in weeks. His hard body pressed against me and I pulled him closer. Our hands tangled in each other's hair and gripped each other's backs as we closed the breath of space between us.

He seemed as thirsty for me as I was for him when our tongues met. How I'd missed the feeling of him.

Finally, we broke apart, breathing hard and staring at each other. "I've missed you," I said, like I hadn't seen him every day for two weeks.

"Me too," he said as he leaned forward to kiss me again.

We hadn't been very physical lately. Almost like he was afraid I would break. But now we were both hungry for each other. I could feel it in his jeans as he pressed against me, and I wanted more. Suddenly, I wanted so much more from him. I wrapped my arms around him, greedy for what he'd been denying me.

A loud throat-clearing reminded us we were at a no-longer-deserted side of a public building. We broke apart, laughing, and made it back to the car, hand in hand.

Charles stopped at a diner on the way back to Ann Arbor, where we shared some pretzels and cheese sauce, him a burger, and me my usual grilled cheese, before getting back on the road.

"So," he said as we approached my highway exit. "Want to swing by my place for a little while? We can watch a movie."

I leaned over and kissed his neck. My whole body tingled from nerves and the awareness of him. "Or other stuff."

He couldn't keep the excitement out of his voice as he repeated, "Or other stuff."

I felt myself flushing and kissed his neck again before I slid back over to my side of the car.

We both laughed as we ran down into his basement. He

fiddled with the music a minute as I twitched nervously on the sofa before he came back over. His eyes were black and mysterious in this light, but still so expressive and beautiful. No one had ever looked at me the way he did, not just with desire, but like I was something to be cherished.

His hand came down gently and cupped my jaw, then his lips were on mine and my tongue in his mouth. I tugged him, grabbing his shirt, and he almost tumbled on top of me. He tried to pull away, probably to see if he had crushed me, but I wrapped my legs around him and didn't let him escape.

I needed this. I'd been hospitalized twice this year, and wanted to feel something that reminded me I was still beautiful and alive. I let my hand slip under his shirt and felt his tight warm back muscles under my hand. He shivered under my touch, twined his hand in my hair. I moaned into his mouth and whimpered when he pulled back.

"Can I take off your shirt?" he whispered, like it would break the spell to say it any louder.

I tugged it off and pulled at his. I wanted to feel his heat against my skin. He didn't start kissing me again like I thought he would. Instead, his gaze traveled along me in my turquoise bra. Heat stirred along my skin and traveled all the way to my core. The way he looked at me made me eager for more. For him and his touch.

Finally, he said, "You are stunning."

"Please," I whispered, not really sure what I was begging for, but my body was demanding something from him. "Don't stop kissing me—touching me."

He leaned back in. His lips trailed along my neck and chin with kisses and nips, as his hands wandered. Fire burned through me, almost scalding me with desire. I wiggled under him, wanting more still. He seemed to realize the same thing, because he lifted off and found my gaze. His hand hovered over the waistband of my jeans. "Do you want more?"

I held his eyes for a minute, then nodded.

His hand stopped again at my jeans button. "Sure?"

"Yes, but not, you know, sex?"

He kissed me and chuckled. "Yeah, I think there would be more conversation before sex." He nibbled the side of my neck. "I've never done this before, but…I could touch you. I can try to make you feel good."

His normally self-assured voice sounded hesitant, so I whispered back, "Please."

He had no reason for nerves. His agile, dexterous fingers took me to a place I'd only imagine possible. After, as I opened my eyes to stare into his molten ones, my breath still coming in pants, he told me tenderly, "You are the most beautiful thing I've ever seen."

I reached up and touched his face. "I think so too."

Before I could consider returning the favor, my phone rang loudly, and I saw it was Dad, who rarely called me. I briefly considered letting it go to voicemail but answered instead. "Hej hej, Pappa," I said, still slightly breathless.

"Ray, there is a winter storm warning. The freezing rain and snow have started. I just wanted to let you know, I'm driving to get you right now. I don't want you in the car with a teen driver."

"Okay." Despite my best efforts, I could still hear how deep and loud my breaths were.

"Are you at Charles's?"

I looked down at my flushed, shirtless form. "Yes."

"Can I speak to him?"

"Sure." I switched to English and said to Charles, "My dad wants to speak to you."

I hastily dressed and couldn't hear what my dad said, but it was short, and Charles had suddenly turned into a tomato. He said simply, "Yes, sir."

I stood up, trying to right myself and fix my hair. Charles handed me the phone and kissed me softly. He wrapped himself around me and breathed me in deeply before leading us upstairs.

I was grateful he seemed as affected by what had transpired as I did.

My dad's car was there within minutes, and we gave each other one last quick kiss before I left.

When I slipped into the car, Dad was silent a moment, humming to an oldie on the radio. When we got onto the road, which was filling with a coat of ice, he said, "I'm going to make an appointment for you to see the women's doctor next week."

I opened and closed my mouth. I thought about protesting, feeling embarrassed…but maybe it was a good idea. I wasn't ready for sex yet, but was inching closer to that point. I liked Charles in a way I'd never felt about Ross. I trusted him. I could also ask the doctor the questions I'd never been able to talk to Mom about. And my rheumatologist had suggested it, too, because my medication caused birth defects. They recommended two forms of birth control if you were sexually active.

"Okay," I said. I looked out the window, bracing for more, for chastisement, but when it didn't come after the entire song finished, relief filled me.

I watched the white snow and ice fall with a joy I hadn't felt in a long time. Charles made me feel like something pure and beautiful. I wanted to share a part of myself with him I'd never shared with anyone else. Dad saw that and didn't judge or lecture me for it. He just wanted me to be safe.

"Thank you," I said.

I thought he didn't hear me, but he subtly nodded and continued humming along to the radio.

...
TWENTY-EIGHT
Charles

I waved at Ray from across the auditorium. She looked so damn cute in her ski cap and matching sweater the color of her eyes. She blew me a kiss, and I couldn't control my grin. All week, last weekend had been at the forefront of my mind. We hadn't had time together like that again, but I really hoped we would again soon. I was craving more than just our hurried kisses in the car.

My gaze fell to her poster that had our robotics team name on it. I laughed at the image of our robot driving over the other team's. We didn't actually fight, but it was cute she'd made a poster. She gave me a thumbs-up and I laughed harder, realizing she'd done it on purpose to relax me.

Becky sat on her side and Knox one down. Those two were snickering about something too, their heads together. It was hard to say whose curly hair was wilder. They'd just started dating—finally. Knox was worse than I was. James seemed a little grim about it, but I'd never seen Knox happier. Both hoped to go to college in Atlanta next year.

"Charles, can you stop ogling your girlfriend for five

minutes here?" Kevin demanded.

I turned to face him. "Do you need something?" I asked, trying to keep my voice flat. I was still pissed about what he'd said to Ray last weekend, about dying. Have a filter.

Dana handed us the competition sheets, and we sized up the teams we'd be playing against. It wasn't a true tournament for advancement, but this was the last time we'd compete with other schools before the district qualifier and should help us hone our skills.

Hours seemed to pass in minutes as we watched the robots advance or crash. The mechanical captains rushed to collect and fix the robots' pieces. Whenever I glanced up, which was often, Ray would blow me a kiss or give me a thumbs-up. I still couldn't believe the stunning girl staring at me was my girlfriend. I knew when most people looked at her, they saw her physical beauty—how could they not? But she was also so brave and gentle. I'd never met anyone else I could talk to and feel like I wouldn't be judged. For so long, I'd been pushing to stay on top of my grades, my piano, everything—but Ray helped me relax and let go. When I held her in my arms, I felt a comfort I hadn't known was possible. She always told me, "*You see me, Charles*," but I thought she saw *me*, too. She was one of the only people who seemed to see me under my grades and books. I was falling in love with her.

No. I'd fallen in love with her. I just hadn't told her yet.

It wasn't long before we competed again, and our teammates congratulated us on having a top-scoring robot. We were all smiles as we walked back to Mrs. Bhatt's room.

I glanced down at my phone when we arrived. There was an email from the University of Michigan. My heart sped up as I opened it.

Congratulations, Charles Jiawei Wong,
You have been accepted early action to the University of Michigan.

I saved it in my college folder and put away my phone

with a grin.

Kevin saw my face. "What is it?"

"I just got accepted to Michigan," I told him, relief pouring through me.

"Must be nice getting in to your backup program," he said with a laugh.

"Well, it might not be a backup anymore." I hadn't decided, but part of me hoped I didn't get in to Caltech. I hadn't stopped thinking about Wàipó and my parents' finances. And then there was Ray, the girl who'd stolen my heart.

"Caltech? You have a shot at getting in! You have a 4.25."

"Maybe I won't get in." If I did, I'd have to make the hardest decision of my life. "Plus, it's far away." I shrugged, not wanting to talk more about it.

"That's stupid, Charles! Don't throw away Caltech for some chick with long legs and big boobs. Yes, she's really hot, but you and Ray probably won't even stay together."

"Kevin," I gritted out.

I knew he was only trying to be helpful, like a good friend would. Throughout elementary and middle school, I'd complained about Chinese school while he' complained about Korean school. We'd been friends for more than a decade. But I hated how he acted around Ray. Since I'd started dating her, Kevin had been harder on her at band practice. Like just because she was pretty, she couldn't also be a decent person. He'd taken his own insecurities over him being short and her tall and blond out on Ray, too often, even when she'd never been anything but nice to him.

"What? The truth hurts."

I shot him an exasperated look. "Ray is more than that, Kevin. But this isn't about her. It might be too expensive—the school and living in LA. My parents are professors. They do well, but I don't know, man. Maybe I'd rather not make them pay out-of-state tuition. They'd never let me take out loans unless they really couldn't afford it."

Ray bounced into the room just then, all smiles. But Kevin, facing me, didn't see her.

"Is it because she's sick?" he said loudly. "Don't throw your whole life away just because you feel sorry for her."

Behind him, Ray's face drained of color. She'd clearly heard Kevin, along with half the room.

"Stop," I told Kevin. "We can talk later, in private." I nodded over his shoulder. "Hi, Ray."

"You'll regret it if you don't go," Kevin said, still ignoring her.

His words hit home. I hoped for what felt like the millionth time that I wouldn't get into Caltech. Otherwise, I dreaded being forced to make that decision.

"Looks aren't everything," Kevin continued. I saw Ray stiffen as he rounded on her, finally acknowledging she was there. "You are so selfish. If you really cared about Charles, you wouldn't be with him. He has half as much time to do his work, because of you. And now you're pressuring him to stay in Michigan? His dream has *always* been Caltech."

Ray flinched like Kevin had struck her. I knew that was her biggest fear: that she was dragging me down, and I'd eventually resent her for it. She'd told me it was the reason she'd kept her last hospitalization from me.

"I'd didn't ask him to stay. I don't know what you're talking about." Her eyes meet mine filled with confusion.

I tightened my fist as I spun toward him. "Kevin, shut up. Let me worry about myself. You need to stop with Ray. My parents would have to refinance their house to send me to Caltech, since Wàipó needs to come live with us. We have to pay for her medical care, okay? I wanted to discuss this *in private*. I just told you that. This has nothing to do with Ray."

I turned to her. "Ray." I hugged her, then led her out to the empty hallway.

Ray started to talk, but I stopped her with a kiss that left us both clinging to each other. I fanned her face with my hands as I pulled away, fingers caressing her cheeks. "I'm sorry about what Kevin said. So sorry. He's just being protective of me, but still it's not right."

She nodded, head still in my hands.

"I don't know what I'm going to do, but you are special to me. So special. I want to be with you like I've never wanted another person. And it's not just your looks."

She pulled my lips back to hers, as if her body could speak to my soul better than her words. As if neither of us knew what else to do. Too aware we shouldn't be making out in the hallway, I sighed, stepped away, and led her outside.

When we made it back to my place, we exchanged a look before heading to my bedroom. As soon as the door closed, we tore at each other's clothes, and Ray seemed especially eager to return the favor I'd given her last Saturday. After she completely shattered me, I held her, running my hands along the satiny skin of her arms and bare back. Just this was so amazing, I couldn't imagine how earthshaking actually having sex would be. She fit perfectly against me. When I held her warm body, it seemed like everything would be all right in the world.

"What are you going to do?" Her breath fanned against my neck as she spoke.

"I don't know. I didn't lie to Kevin; Michigan is still an amazing school. It's Wàipó..." My voice trailed off.

"Just please don't make your decision based on me. Dad hasn't even told me how long I can stay here. Maybe your life was better before I moved here. Easier," she whispered, nuzzling against me.

Her baseless words made my arms tighten around her. My life had been sterile and lifeless before her. Just imagining it contrasted with our current position made me caress her skin more fervently.

"Ray." It was all I could say. For so long, it had seemed like my life was on a straight path, but lately there had been so many curves in the road.

Her lips found mine again, and I was eager to show her exactly what she meant to me with my body, if not with my stumbling words.

Later with her checks flushed, her sated eyes fluttered open to meet mine with a small smile curving her lips. I nestled her closer to me, realizing just how much I loved the girl in my arms. I wanted to be with her more than I'd ever wanted anything in my life. Before her, I'd been alive, but too nervous and working too hard to really be living. I'd been pressured to always be the best at everything, to the point of closing myself off from life. Ray had brought me to the light. And I knew she liked me, Charles Wong, nothing more, nothing less. I didn't want to think or talk about the future; I just wanted to hold her now.

...

TWENTY-NINE

Ray

I stared out the airplane window as the marshy ground approached, trying to decide how it felt to back in Savannah for Thanksgiving. It was late this year, November 28th. I'd been in Michigan four and a half months. And now I was back here again.

I missed Charles already. I wouldn't confess this to Jeffery, who'd be picking me up in a few minutes, but Charles had become my best friend. Between his calming presence, yoga, church with Becky, and my art, I felt I was managing my lupus well. Selling my pictures had been so cool, especially because they hung somewhere we all liked to go. And if I kept it up, I could pay for the architecture camp this summer at U of M, which might help me get accepted there. Michigan was not my backup school; it was my top choice.

I was trying to manage it all. Yet, no matter what logic told me, it still seemed easier to imagine Savannah poisoning me than my own T-cells attacking my body. I'd improved so much since I left. I kept taking my pills, but I'd dropped my immunosuppressants from four a day to three, and was finally off steroids again.

Six pills a day. Every day.

But it was better than eight.

I was trying to be better about listening to my body. Sure, I'd had the really bad infection and allergic reaction, which were side effects of my medications. But at least it wasn't a lupus issue—organ failure. Dr. Murray had finally said my complement markers she used to measure my lupus were starting to normalize for the first time since I'd started seeing her. They still showed "active" lupus, but they weren't as abnormal. My joints weren't swelling and arthritic as frequently. I'd have to manage this disease, whether I had an active flare or it went dormant, with pills for the rest of my life.

Overall, living with Dad had been amazing, even if he still hadn't talked to me about how long I could stay. I had even started looking forward to Soraya's visits because she made sure we always did something special. And she'd brought me an expensive Caravaggio book, when I was feeling depressed during my second weekend in the hospital. Everyone knew how anything art related—whether supplies or anthologies, filled with detailed high resolution color images—cost.

But while Michigan had been good for me, I was still worried I wasn't good for the people I loved in Michigan. Charles had endless potential. No matter what he'd said on Saturday and how tenderly he'd held me, or how safe I'd felt snuggled against him, I couldn't stand to be part of a decision that kept him from his dream of Caltech.

I pushed the thoughts away as the plane arrived at the gate, and threw my heavy winter coat over my arm. The airport was packed the Wednesday before Thanksgiving, everyone hurrying to get home or to visit loved ones. After people-dodging in the salt-tinged, humid air, I made it to Jeffery's car.

He jumped out and gave me a huge hug before getting us settled into the evening traffic and rapid-fire questioning.

"How's everything?" I asked, glad to be talking in person

instead of texting.

"Classes are fine."

"Okay, big guy. What else? You never told me if you heard back from that recruiter."

"Yeah, they talked to me," he said with a shrug.

"Yeah," I said with a light punch to his shoulder. "And?"

"I don't know. I'm pretty good, but not great. I don't think I'll get a scholarship. It wasn't a yes or no. But I heard from Armstrong. I got in."

"Yeah!"

He was grinning, so I hoped he was happy.

"Well, that's good," I continued. "I bet your mom would be thrilled you'll be in Savannah."

"Maybe too close, but we'll see. I don't have your grades. Never did."

"Hey, you'll save a ton going there. Plus, your parents aren't strict."

"Yes, my eternal Ray of optimism. Anyway, tell me about your boyfriend and everything else happening up there in the frigid north."

"Charles is good," I said, unable to keep the smile off my face. "Oh, and I sold some of my artwork! Thanks again for the drawing supplies."

He reached over and tousled my hair. "Yeah, no problem, Ray Ray."

We chatted comfortably or sang along to country music on the radio, windows down and my hair going wild in the wind and coastal humidity, until we hit the bridge to Whitmarsh Island.

Then Jeffery said, "Well, I wanted to mention, too, that Ava and I started dating."

"Ava Garcia-Lopez?"

"Yep, that one."

"Oh, Jeff! She's as cute as a button. And so nice! When did this happen?"

"Don't know. I think right after your last visit?" He was blushing as we pulled up to my place.

"That's more than a month ago! I'm only letting it slide because it was new and I was sick. But I will get details. So don't think because you told me when we hit the driveway, I won't. We're going biking before I go home?"

"Yes, ma'am," he said, pulling me in for a side hug.

"All right then, bye, Jeff." I got my stuff out the backseat.

He waved out the open window and pulled away. Already breaking a sweat in the warm, damp air, I lugged my stuff up the front stairs.

Gracie Mae started crying when I opened the door. "Rayanne, I missed you," she said, and it just about broke my heart. I needed to be better about calling her on video chat.

"Sweet girl," I said, crushing her to me. "I missed you too."

Mary Beth came crashing into us and we landed on the ground in a giggling tangle of hugs and tickles.

"Did you eat lunch, Rayanne?" Mom asked, walking into the foyer.

"No, ma'am." I stood to embrace her. It had been a rush to get to the new terminal for the Savannah flight and I hadn't had time. It was almost four in the afternoon now.

Mark came in with Matthew and surprised me with a big hug. "We've missed you around here, Rayanne. You were a good role model to your sisters." I felt my face heat at his unexpected praise.

"Come on, girls, let's get Rayanne something to eat." Mom led us into the kitchen.

I held my arms out for Matthew, who crushed me against his growing, twelve-year-old body.

"I missed you," he said with a crackling voice that told me my little brother wasn't going to be little forever.

I squeezed him tighter and said, "I've missed y'all too."

And I had. Michigan had been good to me, but I'd lived my whole life with the people in this house.

Mom surprised me again by pulling my favorite tomato pie out of the oven. "I thought you might be hungry." She motioned me to sit and made me a small salad as she waited for the dish to cool. "We were really worried about you when you got that infection. Is everything better now?"

I nodded. I still couldn't believe a tiny scar was all that was left of it. "My wrists still get hives when I shower, but it's less frequent." The doctors had said I'd be on antihistamines a few months more.

She eyed my cheeks, which looked okay but were a little puffier than they ever were when I lived here, thanks to the steroids I'd just finished. I still felt like a chipmunk some days. It took everything I had not to scratch my rapidly re-growing bald spot—it itched all the time—under her scrutiny. I was skinnier than when I lived here, after being hospitalized twice in five months. Yoga, and most of my friends being guys who ate all the time, had helped me gain some muscle and weight back, but I was aware I wasn't the girl I was six months ago. I wasn't her in so many ways.

I must have passed her test, because she nodded and finally said, "We miss you here. I just want you to know that. We haven't forgotten about you." She put my plate down. "Now, let's pray. Girls, Matthew, hold hands." We took hands and bowed our heads like we did before every meal in this house, and Mom led us in prayer. "Our Jesus Christ, our savior, thank you for this food for the nourishment of our bodies. Thank you for bringing Rayanne home safely and deliver us from evil. In Jesus's name, we pray; amen."

"Amen," we echoed. The food tasted like home. She gave my siblings some cookies as I ate, and their happy voices rang through the kitchen.

When we ran around, fighting over four of us needing one bathroom to get dressed in our Sunday finest on Thanksgiving before going to my grandparents' house, it felt like I'd never left. Granny Young was on her best behavior, too, especially after I told her all about my church, choir, and youth group in Michigan.

After lunch, I stepped outside into the South Georgia sun. It could be cold on Thanksgiving, but this year was a warmer one. The seventy-degree day felt almost like summer. I knew I couldn't get too much sun anymore, but I hadn't turned into a vampire since getting diagnosed with lupus. I still missed the feeling of the sun on my skin, so I'd stay out at least for a few minutes.

I pulled out my phone and video-called Charles. When his face popped up, it made my heart hurt with how much he'd come to mean to me. "Are you wearing a sleeveless dress?"

I smiled. "Uh-huh. Jealous?"

"Yes. It's supposed to snow tomorrow."

"I'll be back freezing with you soon enough, don't worry. Until then, happy Thanksgiving! Tell me one thing you're thankful for."

He smiled, and then his face turned serious. "Ray, the thing I'm most thankful for is you moving to Michigan. It's quiet and lonely without you here."

"Are you saying I talk too much?"

He lifted an eyebrow. "You? Never."

I giggled. I couldn't help it. He made me feel a certain way—giddy. We talked for a few minutes. Then he sighed, looking tired. He was worried about his grandmother and his parents' finance. It was a lot to deal with.

"I miss you, Charles. I just saw you, and I miss you," I admitted.

"I miss you too, Ray. But go back to your Thanksgiving and family. You'll be here soon but won't see them for a while. Will you call me before you go to sleep?"

"Sure," I said as he waved and hung up.

I tried to soak up the sun for a few more minutes before I went back inside for dessert. Nothing in the world felt like the sun warming your skin, I realized with a twinge in my chest. But I was alive. I was doing well. *Find joy in what you can, not can do*, I told myself. With a sigh, I went back inside for dessert and more bonding.

We didn't stay at my grandma's too much longer, just long enough for me to help hand-wash the fine china and silver, which was good, since I was nearly in a food coma. I napped on the drive home in the back of our minivan. When we were almost back, the shrieks of my siblings fighting over the iPad woke me up, and I messaged Jeffery.

I changed into some cut-offs and a baggy sweatshirt before I headed down to the dock on my bike. When I got there, I strode out to the edge of the pier and sat enjoying the last rays of sun with my legs dangling over the edge. I missed the sun. No matter what it did to me, it was the sun. I leaned back and soaked in a few late afternoon rays as the tangy scent of the marsh hit my nose. *Home.* I heard as much as felt Jeffery's lumbering frame on the creaky wood as he sat beside me with a thud.

After a minute, I whispered, "I miss this and you."

"But you ain't coming back." His voice was low.

I opened my eyes and turned to him. "Everything's been moving while I've been away. I didn't even know you had a girlfriend."

"That's life, Ray Ray. It keeps rolling along, ebbing with the tides. Isn't there a poem or somethin' about how life is change?"

I loved that quote and couldn't control my grin. "Heraclitus, 'The only constant in life is change.' No, I don't think I'm coming back, even though I miss you. I miss you so much, Jeff."

He looked at me with those familiar umber eyes locked with mine in time and understanding. "I miss you too." He shrugged and peered down into the marsh, dropping my gaze. He continued softer and more reluctantly, "I miss you somethin' terrible. But I'm glad you left." He glanced back up and said more firmly, "You're my best friend. I love you, Rayanne—as a friend. I'd give up anything to make you well." He chuckled, shaking his head. "You might have a bald spot, but you're alive and kick'n. You never complained much, but I knew you weren't right. At least, you weren't right your last few months here. Michigan is good for you. You don't belong here. You belong there." His brow furrowed, making him look more somber.

"Jeff—"

He squeezed me into him, engulfing me in his massive frame, smelling like sweat and brine—and Jeff.

"Shut that cute mouth. Don't. You'll always be my girl. I know I'll always be your fellah. Your Jeff. Bonnie and Clyde, member? Even if you're a prissy Yank now going all Heraclitus on me."

I bumped his shoulder and pulled away. "I do love you and miss you."

He ruffled my hair with his big hand. "I know you do."

We turned to watch the ocean and the marsh. The tide was out, exposing the reeds as herons and egrets hunted for the last crab or fish of the day before flying to roost. Eventually the birds all flew home, and the last rays of the day drifted down and colored the sky a brilliant red and purple before indigo faded into black. The Big Dipper and the North Star shone low on the horizon.

We faded into silence, like the day, and I thought about how much I liked Michigan and would ask Dad to finish high school there when I got back. But this would always be home, and it was comforting in its own way.

I didn't want to end the evening. This time, I understood Dad's comments about Mom. She hadn't always done right by me, and certainly not by him, but she'd still been a kid when she had me. Dad was right: I didn't want to hate my mom either.

We sat there till the no-see-ums had us both scratching too bad to enjoy the evening a second longer, and in unison, we peeked at each other, chuckled, and stood.

"Can we ride a little more?" I asked.

"We sure can," Jeffery responded, and we rode our bikes through the quiet streets with Spanish moss hanging eerily from the big oaks lit by the glow of street lamps. We pedaled from one end of the island to another until we were both sweating and laughing and feeling like kids again.

I missed this and Jeff, but not enough to move back. Not even for him. I was glad he understood, and was moving on just fine without me living nearby. Still, I was determined to enjoy this short trip. If things went well with my discussion with Dad, I didn't know when I'd be back.

Like magic, my rash reappeared on my wrist as I showered that night, and I hesitated a moment before calling Charles. That selfish part of me wanted to pray and hope he didn't get into Caltech, but I pushed it away as I reached for the phone, bright smile ready for a video-chat. *I loved him.* If he wanted Caltech, which I knew he had his whole life, I'd be a pickle to stand in his way. That wasn't love, even though the thought hurt like H-E-double-hockey-sticks.

···
THIRTY

Charles

I was flipping through Michigan's robotics engineering pages on my phone and sipping a pop in the back of the McDonald's, waiting for the text that Ray's flight had landed.

Would the University of Michigan be so bad?

I'd convinced her and her dad to let me get her, and was trying to pass the time now. But my swirling thoughts made it hard to concentrate.

My phone's ding had me rushing to go to the bathroom and back outside to pull the car around to the arrivals. I turned up the heat to seventy-eight but didn't blast it as the car warmed up. Ray'd be cold. Probably because her only body fat right now was in her boobs. She'd always been thin, like her dad, but after her hospitalization, you could see her ribs under her collarbone. I could feel her sharp hip bones when we kissed. Everyone was trying to help her gain some weight back so she'd be a little healthier, but until she did, she was always freezing.

The terminal was packed, and between my inching forward and her deplaning, we arrived at the curb at the same time. I jumped out and briefly hugged her as we settled the bags into the car and hurried to get in before the honking started.

I risked a quick glance at her. I needed to just bite the bullet and talk. "Ray, I, um—I got into Caltech."

She was silent for a moment, and I thought she didn't hear me. Then she said with false cheer, "Charles! Happy Thanksgiving, indeed. You're going, aren't you?"

"I don't know. We are going to move Wàipó here over winter break." My heart seemed to skip a beat with how much I just... "I don't know," I repeated.

"Charles, your parents have saved up their whole lives to send you there. I'm sure they can handle both."

"Maybe," I said, but I wasn't sure. I'd heard the worry in Ma's voice, and I'd looked up how much home healthcare options were. They'd hired a contractor, too. He was fixing the downstairs bathroom so it was more handicap accessible. None of that was cheap.

She went silent again. "I want what's best for you. You'll hate me if you don't go to Caltech because of me."

"Ray—"

"You have worked hard your whole life. I don't want a few months with me to blow it for you."

Her words cut into me. I felt like I couldn't get enough air into my lungs at the thought of not only losing her as my girlfriend, but her being gone—out of my life. I thought of my cold, sterile life before she'd invaded it. It was like one of her drawings for art class, where everything was shades of gray except for one section of color. I'd felt lifeless until she moved here.

I pulled off the highway at the next exit and into the first gas station I saw. Then I turned to look at her and said, "I love you. No matter what happens, I want you to know that."

This wasn't how I'd imagined saying it, but I'd known since I kissed her at Niagara Falls. I surely had recognized it when I saw her in the hospital.

The look she gave me crushed my heart. "I love you too,

Charles. That's why I'm going to say this. You have to pick Caltech."

"Don't…" I didn't have words. Instead, I pulled her to me. I was grateful she didn't resist and seemed to need to touch me as much as I needed to touch her. The kiss we shared was slow, sensual, her tears dripping onto my hands as I held her face and my tears dripping onto hers.

Finally, I rested my forehead against hers and whispered, "I just need time to think." Her hand cupped my jaw, and I held her firm. "Michigan is a good choice, though. I promise. Ray, it's hard, and I don't know what to do. But maybe I want to live here with Wàipó a few more years, too. If I'm so far away, she might forget me. I don't want my parents to refinance their house. And no, I don't want to leave you either."

I pulled back and was lost in the ocean of her eyes. She tugged me to her, and I got lost in her lips and touch. I'd never wanted anything like I wanted her. But I'd wanted Caltech my whole life.

What was the right thing for my family?

My stomach suddenly felt icier than the road outside.

Ray pulled back. "I love you. And because I do, I want you to go."

"I don't know anything anymore. But when I do, you'll be the first to know," I said, losing myself in her eyes.

Her phone started dinging. I gave her one more kiss, then pulled us back onto the road. We kept our fingers threaded, but my heart was heavy.

THIRTY-ONE

Ray

The next weekend, as we pulled into Soraya's complex in Chicago, I drew in a breath and blurted out, "Can I finish high school with you?"

Dad blinked. "What did you say?"

I looked down at the mittens I was trying to put on. "We haven't talked about how long I was staying with you. I thought about it over Thanksgiving break. I want to keep living with you." Even if Charles left in the fall.

"Sweetheart," he said softly. "I thought you knew I wanted you to finish high school here. And if you get into U of M, of course you can stay with me. I didn't think I needed to say it. While your health is stable, you still have to follow-up with your doctors. Your bloodwork shows the lupus is still active. Plus, I like having you live with me. I thought that was obvious."

"You've done so much for me. Thank you." I looked up to meet his gaze, his gold-flecked blue eyes so much like mine. "I haven't said it enough, but thank you."

He pulled me into a hug. "I didn't think I had to tell you, but I will. I want you to live with me. Everything I've done since you got here, I'd do again." We looked at each other for a long time. "Come on. It'll be freezing in here in a second, and I'm starving. Let's not keep Soraya waiting."

I nodded, and we headed up to her place. It was late for us to eat dinner, but only eight here with the time change. Soraya barreled into me first, giving me her trademark tight, enthusiastic squeeze. I hugged her back. She'd been up to see Dad several times since we'd met, and I'd come to enjoy her company. She'd even come to see me in the hospital both weekends I was there.

She gave my dad a quick kiss and forced us out of our coats and to the table, where she had a *ton* of food out. "I know you guys are likely starving with it being so late."

"I'm famished," Dad said.

"Right, well let me tell Ray what it all is." She started pointing to the various dishes. "Fattoush Salad, I remember you said you enjoyed that in Dearborn. The Persian version is even better," she teased. "Kashke bademjan," she indicated to a purplish dip, "with fresh store bought pita, so much better than what I bake." She winked at that. "Saffron rice, mint leaves, walnuts, and feta, all the givens. And three kabobs, chicken, lamb, and beef."

"Wow, it looks amazing. I hope you didn't go to too much trouble," I told her. It really was so much food.

"No, I actually love it. Maybe I'm turning into my *mamani*, grandma, that is. I'm part of the Persian community here in Chicago, as are my parents, but I normally just have time to go to events a few times a year, like Persian New Year. So, I make things here and there. But to cook and eat it all together, how it's best?"

She paused and shook her head, and healthy mane of hair, to her rhetoric questions dramatically.

"Not everyday. So thank you guys. Plus, most taste fine the next few days. Now enjoy, that's the best thanks."

We dug in and spices and tantalizing flavors exploded in

my mouth.

"Ummm, Soraya," Dad moaned. "We are making time to buy those spices you are always hunting for in the pantry for next time you visit."

She laughed.

"It's seriously amazing. Thank you," I agreed with Dad.

"I'm enjoying it, too." Soraya's eyes sparkled as she asked, "So, have you figured out why I got the Selena Gomez tickets yet?"

I froze, fork halfway to my mouth, and shook my head no. I'd listened to more of her songs, but I hadn't heard anything that might indicate why she'd gotten them. I was still excited—it would be my first big concert.

Disappointment flashed across her face. "She has lupus, too. And look at everything she can do and is doing. I thought you'd want to see her."

"Really?"

She nodded. "You should watch her *Today Show* interview where she talks about her kidney transplant. She's like you, Ray—what a brave young lady. Neither of you let that disease get you down, even though I know it must be hard some days."

I felt my cheeks heat. Most days, I didn't feel brave. Most days, I just tried to survive without everyone knowing I was different.

"Thank you."

"Of course! When I heard the concert was the same weekend as your dad's talk tomorrow, well—it just seemed too perfect. Tomorrow we get the whole day together. Do you want to go to the Chicago Art Institute in the morning? We can shop at Nordstrom on Michigan Avenue afterward. Make it a fun girls' day?"

"It sounds wonderful." Her enthusiasm was contagious, and even Dad was smiling.

The next morning, Dad was already gone when I went into the kitchen and ate toast and a pear with Soraya. We bundled up in a million and ten layers to take the train from her condo between downtown and Northwestern. We arrived at the Art Institute just after it opened, glad to get out of the icy December breeze coming off the lake. After checking our coats, loaded with winter accessories, we wandered for hours.

It was one of the best museums I'd ever been to. A few times, I couldn't resist standing in awe in front of a piece until Soraya probed me with deep, intellectual questions about it. I would never tell Dad, but she was even better to have at a museum than he was. She promised when it warmed up to have us down for the architecture tour. I told her all about my savings and plan to attend the architecture camp this summer.

When we finished, we layered back up and braced for the wind to take some pictures in front of the Bean before wandering into a nearby Christmas market and getting hot coffees to warm our frozen hands. I texted some of the pictures to Charles.

He sent back, *Looks fun! Staying warm? I've been working on a surprise for you. When do you get back tomorrow?*

Maybe six or seven? Dad has the conference in the morning, then we're leaving.

Can you have him drop you off?

Okay. My hands are frozen. gtg.

I put my phone away and slid my hands back into my warm mittens, wiggling my frozen white fingers and stomping my numb toes. Thinking about Charles leaving felt like a punch to the gut. I couldn't imagine it. Luckily, I didn't have long to as Soraya led us into Eataly, a huge Italian grocery store with restaurants tucked into it.

After lunch, we went back to the condo for a little bit, and I took a quick nap so I'd be awake for the concert. I was trying to be better about listing to my body after the second hospitalization. It wasn't always easy. Sometimes I just wanted to push myself, like an ordinary sixteen-year-old could, but I wasn't ordinary. If I didn't listen to my body—slow down, take my pills, avoid the sun, protect my joints—my body became inflamed. I just didn't have a choice.

I was sad to leave Chicago the next afternoon. The concert had been so much fun, and Soraya had bopped around like a teenager herself. In the middle of it, she'd pulled me close and said, "I'm glad you moved here, Ray. I've been with Nils five years, and I've never seen him this happy."

I just squeezed her firmly and said, "Thanks."

Dad and I filled the car ride back with happy chatter. He was so passionate about his conference it made me smile, despite not really absorbing most of what he was saying. He probably felt the same way about my description of the museum, walk along Michigan Avenue, and concert. I didn't start getting nervous until we got close to Charles's house.

Suddenly I felt sick. I wanted Charles. I wanted him with my whole being. I loved him. If he went to California, it would be hard. I'd try to make it work if that was what he wanted. When you loved someone, you didn't hold them back. But shoot, it hurt to think of him leaving—sour Skittles, it hurt.

Charles opened the door when I arrived, and we stared

at each other in silence a moment before he waved me in, his fingers twitching in a silent beat in a way I knew meant he was nervous.

"Come downstairs. That's where the surprise is." His house was silent. "They're at a fundraiser and won't be home for a few hours," he said as if reading my thoughts.

I sat down when we got to the basement, and he paced back and forth. "I worked on this with the guys all week so we could record it this morning. Ray, I wrote this song. I speak best with music."

He started the recording, and the piano came on as he handed me the sheet of music.

Slow piano intro:

(James)
It's hard to think
Because when I do
All I think
Is I'm stuck on you.

Where to go?
I don't know.
Should I stay?
Or go far away.
(drums solo)

But my hand's on the door,
And I can't take anymore.
I think I have to stay.
We'll have to find a way.

It's not just you,
But it's my family too.

They are my glue,
So I guess I'm going Blue.

I should have told you before,
But you have my heart.
Let me hold you once more
Because I can't depart.

So let's continue to try
Because with you I can fly
Because with you I'm better.
I can't promise you forever,
But baby we'll try.
So, baby let's try.

Slow piano fade…

Charles sat beside me and took my hand. I looked up as the last note sounded. "I'm going to Michigan," he said.

"You really mean it?" I whispered.

"Yes, Ray," he said as he leaned forward to kiss me. "I already sent in my acceptance. Their robotics program is ranked almost equally high, and I'd regret it my whole life if I didn't stay to help my family when Wàipó and my parents have done everything for me. I wouldn't be able to look myself in the mirror if I came home and Wàipó had forgotten me. Or if my parents were in debt. Plus, there's also this gorgeous, amazing, sexy, sweet girl in Ann Arbor I'd miss a whole lot."

I smiled and couldn't resist running my fingers through his hair. "I love you. I love you more than I thought it was possible to love someone, but promise you didn't do this for me, did you?"

He chuckled. "I love you too. I'm glad I'll get to be with you longer, but like I said, Caltech or Michigan, that has to do with my family. You're the bonus. An amazing bonus, but yes, the bonus. Don't worry."

I kissed him tenderly and deeply. Slowly, we peeled our clothes off until we were both in our underwear. I feather-kissed him, then pulled back. "I decided something too." I looked down, bit my lip, then looked back up. "I want to have sex."

His eyes widened. "Like, right now?"

I nodded. I'd already been to the gynecologist and gotten an IUD. I hadn't told him, because I still felt like it was private, but I didn't have many birth control options between my medical conditions and medications I already took. It had been awkward and painful, but it was safer for me and would last for years. I couldn't risk getting pregnant, especially with the medicines I was on. Maybe it was a sin, but I loved Charles and he loved me, so I was sure a loving God would understand. Just like I was sure God would understand about Charles and Knox's families not being Christians. Even if Charles had said he was leaving for Caltech, I wanted this.

He must have wanted an actual verbal response, so I sucked in a breath and looked up into those smoldering brown eyes. "I want my first time to be with someone I love. I hear the lyrics—we're in high school. It might not last forever, but the first time, for the first time, I want love."

He and I weren't stupid, and knew first love wasn't always last love. We knew we were young, and things didn't always last, no matter how much we loved each other now.

A look of understanding passed over his face, and he grinned before kissing me with a feather-light touch. "I love you too. But you're sure? Like, sure, sure? This isn't just because I'm staying, right?"

I nodded and pulled his hand back to me. "I've never wanted anything more than I want you in this moment."

He stood and brushed his hair out of his face, then fumbled in his jeans until he pulled out two condoms. "Your dad told me to buy these that night of the ice storm," he said, blushing and not meeting my eyes. "Just in case. He warned with your medications, there couldn't be any mistakes." He set them nearby and glanced back up.

I pulled him back to me. "I want this," I reaffirmed, and boy, did I.

Our fingers and mouths re-found each other, heating my skin fervently. I hadn't lied—I wanted this, body and soul. And Charles was amazing, sweet, and so patient.

As we lay together afterward, holding each other like we'd never let each other go, I couldn't resist teasing him. "Do you think we could do better next time?"

Charles laughed and kissed me. "Baby, we'll try."

And we did, and like everything else, Charles endeavored to work hard and learn. He was right, he wasn't perfect, but with practice, he got pretty close.

Charles

I couldn't resist chuckling as I looked over at Ray, drawing away on the coffee table. I would swear she always got as much charcoal on herself as she did on the paper. She currently had a streak across her cheek and the tip of her nose I had no intention of telling her about.

She heard me laughing and looked up. "It's on my face again, isn't it?" she asked, smearing it worse.

I went and got some wet tissues from the half bath down here. Then I patted the sofa, and she sat beside me as I gently dabbed her face.

"Ekkkk, that's cold!"

She twisted away, and we were both laughing. Before she leaned forward again grumpily, I attempted to cheer her with a kiss.

I didn't think it was possible to love someone this much. We'd grown even closer, body and soul, this last year. I still occasionally thought about Caltech, but Michigan was amazing. I'd never regretted my decision. They'd even given me a full scholarship in April after an extensive interview process.

The robotics labs were world class, and so was Wàipó's nui rou mien. And Wàipó seemed to do better living with us and actually started remembering Ray. Michigan had been the right choice—I had zero doubts.

And being with Ray really was the sweetest bonus in the world. While I'd like to say it'd been perfect being together for the past year, it wasn't. Sometimes I'd gotten busy, especially during the six-week robotics building when we'd literally barely seen each other. But she'd embraced it and had gotten busy entering this huge art competition with Becky. She'd done well in it too, no surprise there. And unfortunately, Ray had been sick—like the severe flu that had her hospitalized last March and made her miss two weeks of school. She was still on immunosuppressants, but her organs hadn't been attacked again in more than a year, and her blood work had been steady—not quite normal, but steady. So she stayed on those pills, even if their effects could be harsh.

She tried to hide the sad look in her eyes when our friends went to the lake or the cross-country flyers went up, but she couldn't hide from me. Just like I couldn't hide from her. Nor could she hide her occasional wincing when the arthritis flared up. But mostly she was cheerful and handled it with a quiet grace. She'd been more respectful to her body, and her lupus had been much less reactive to her as a result of that. That and the heavy dose of medication she took. She seemed happy most of the time and didn't let it get her down. It was life, and between health, long-term happiness, and temporary satisfaction, there were compromises we all had to make.

I leaned forward and kissed her because even after more than a year, I still couldn't resist those coral lips. We more than made it work—we made each other happier. We forced each other to chase our dreams. She never held me back, only encouraged my hard work. She really was my "Hard Headed Woman," and she made me the best and happiest me I could be. She still saw me, and I saw her.

But the last few weeks had been the hardest of any of our time together as Ray's college acceptance letters rolled in, but not the one we wanted most—Michigan. I'd do long-distance for her; hell, I'd do anything for this girl. She was everything to me. But I'd miss her if she went down south for the next few years. Or worse, to Sweden, where she'd also applied.

I'd seen her touching her alopecia spot, that had recently flared up. She was nervous, too, and I hated what that did to her body.

"I'm doing the playlist for a little bit," Ray said when I released her. But when she opened her phone, her hands trembled. A few big fat tears rolled down her face.

"Hey," I said, pulling her onto my lap and wiping them away. "What is it?"

"I got in." She sucked in a deep breath. "I didn't think my grades were good enough, but maybe the art contest and the architecture camp helped. Michigan, Charles. I got in to Michigan."

Ray and I stared at each other, and then I broke out in a grin to match hers.

"I love you," I whispered against her lips, my arms tightening around her.

We knew we were young, and the future could change. We understood one day we might grow apart, but the kiss we shared said we were both glad we could continue to together. A love like this was worth holding onto.

The End

Thank YOU, reader! If you enjoyed please consider writing a review on Amazon, Goodreads, or Bookbub; it is MUCH appreciated!!!!

Get the latest news, read her note on her diseases, and find other books by Liz here:
www.lizhsubooks.com

...

ACKNOWLEDGMENTS

For my parents, who always believed in me. To my best friends, you are my support system through thick and thin. To my in-law family, *wo ai nimen*. Thank you for accepting and inspiring me. And above all to my husband, Eugene, the most wonderful and special person in my life, who gives me strength and CALM every day. While you can do anything alone, friends, family, and love are what make life living and fighting for.

Big thank you to my writing village, GDRWA. You inspired and embraced me. You told me I could do it. You made me laugh, provided amazing learning opportunities, gave me tools, and have been my cheerleaders throughout! Also, shout out to both the Troy Library and Oakland County Writers' groups. Sarah LoCascio, you helped me get my first place, Young Adult, in the OCCRWA's Orange Rose Contest for this book with your encouragement, tears, and critiques. So many thanks.

To the editor—Rachel Lynn Solomon it was a great pleasure to have you edit this work. I always appreciate your insight and love your positivity. Thank you. C.K. Brooke you caught those pesky last faults, which were many, and smoothed the edges. Thanks a million.

It is estimated there are 24+ million Americans with an autoimmune disease. Lupus is the #10 killer in all women 15-24. I wanted our voices to be heard. I hope it inspires you to remember the end is yet unwritten and the sun will always come up tomorrow (that means us lupies get out the sunscreen). We all have the ability to become the hero in our own stories.

NOTE: The https://screening.mhanational.org/screening-tools/ depression was used in Chapter 9.

...

ABOUT THE AUTHOR

Liz has a deep love of traveling, the people of the world and their dynamic histories, and reading and writing. She holds a B.A. from John Cabot University, Rome, in addition to a M.A.T. and M.A. in World History from Georgia State University. Her first two romances feature characters with lupus, a chronic autoimmune disease. Lupus has had a significant impact on her on a personal level since before her diagnosis in 2009. From Atlanta, she now lives in Metro-Detroit with her Chinese-American husband, daughter, and adorable Pomeranian.

Made in the USA
Columbia, SC
06 March 2021

33987996R00154